D0699118

FESTIVAL IN FIRE SEASON

FESTIVAL IN FIRE SEASON

ELLYN BACHE

August House Publishers, Inc.
LITTLE ROCK

© 1992 by Ellyn Bache
All rights reserved. This book, or parts thereof,
may not be reproduced in any form without permission.
Published by August House, Inc.,
P.O. Box 3223, Little Rock, Arkansas, 72203,
501-372-5450.

Printed in the United States of America
10 9 8 7 6 5 4 3 2 1

LIBRARY OF CONGRESS
CATALOGING-IN-PUBLICATION DATA

Bache, Ellyn
Festival in fire season : a novel / by Ellyn Bache — 1st ed.
p.   cm.
ISBN 0-87483-189-X (alk. paper) : hb $19.95
I. Title.
PS3563.A845F47   1992
813'.54—dc20   91-38542

First Edition, 1992

Executive: Liz Parkhurst
Project editor: Judith Faust
Editorial assistant: Ed Gray
Cover design: Kitty Harvill, Harvill-Ross Studios
Typography: Lettergraphics/Little Rock

This book is printed on archival-quality paper which meets
the guidelines for performance and durability of the
Committee on Production Guidelines for Book Longevity
of the Council on Library Resources.

This is a work of fiction. Names, characters, and incidents are the
product of the author's imagination. Any resemblance
to actual events or persons, living or dead,
is entirely coincidental.

AUGUST HOUSE, INC.   PUBLISHERS   LITTLE ROCK

Acknowledgments

I'm indebted to many people for assistance with this book, but especially to three North Carolina firefighters who helped me at every stage of the writing—Ernie Bryant of the Hampstead Volunteer Fire Department, John Forestell of the Wilmington Fire Department, and Jerry Vuoso of the Myrtle Grove Fire Department. Early on, John Forestell walked me step-by-step through Jordan's first fire scenes, telling me what Jordan might do in a given situation and what he wouldn't. Jerry Vuoso lent me stacks of training tapes that taught me more about modern firefighting than anything I'd read in books. Ernie Bryant pieced together for me the history of the Holly Ridge fires of 1986, which devastated many acres of Pender County, North Carolina, and on which the forest fires in this novel are loosely based. Later, all three men spent many hours reading the fire sections and checking them for accuracy. Without their help, I couldn't have gotten very far, and I'm deeply grateful for their generous response to a stranger making additional demands on their time and expertise.

While I'm at it, I'd like to mention that I, not they, invented the weather conditions in the novel—conditions that didn't exist in North Carolina in 1988 and 1989—or even, quite, in 1986 during the fires.

I also want to thank the many people who helped me with the various drafts of this book, especially those who read it in the early stages—Kathleen Ford Bonnie (who read the manuscript *twice*), Kent Boseman, Ruth Moose, Michael Moye, Peggy Parris, Beth Perry, Patricia Ruark, Nancy Tilly; my husband, Terry Bache; my agent, Jonathan Dolger; my publisher, Liz Parkhurst; and my editor, Judith Faust. ◆

• *PROLOGUE* •
1967–68

My first taste of fire and of the Festival area school system came close together—not after I'd become an administrator, but as a high school freshman, the year after the schools were integrated, the year I was stalked by humiliation.

I snapped my locker shut at lunchtime and turned, coming eye-to-chest with a blue T-shirt that smelled sweet with detergent, sour with menace. In the dim light, the guy's skin was tar, his hair black wool, his muscles glistening. I was short for fourteen; he was enormous. Except for the two of us, the hall was deserted.

"Gimme a quarter, man," he said.

"I don't have a quarter."

"You got lunch money, don't you?"

"No."

He moved closer, cut off my escape with his bulk. "What's your name, boy?" *Boy.*

"Jordan."

"Next time, bring a quarter, Jordan." He whispered this, bending down, crooning into my ear. A dark hand over my nose, my head turning, slamming into the locker. A metallic jab to the cheekbone, and my eye began to swell. He was gone before I looked up. I left the grounds and walked home.

The house should have been empty. My mother was a nurse at the hospital, and my brother was in junior high. My father was supposed to be at work, but he was sitting in the living room with a receptionist from his office. We'd moved to Festival over the summer. From what I could tell from my parents' late-night arguments, we came largely to curb his infidelities. But I had never, until now, actually seen him with another woman. He was calm, as if it were natural for her to be there. I might have been more offended if he hadn't seemed to forget the receptionist and to focus, entirely and sympathetically, on my eye.

"Got a shiner," he announced, standing, testing the swelling with his thumb. He peered at my eyeball. "I'll get you some ice."

As he disappeared into the kitchen, the receptionist rose from the couch and moved toward the front door.

My father returned. He held a dishtowel filled with ice. "What happened?"

"I got sucker-punched by a black kid."

"I'm not surprised." He nodded and applied the ice to my eye. "I knew it might be a little rough over there." He examined the position of the ice pack, rearranged it, lifted my fingers so I could hold it. "Keep it on till you can't stand it anymore." He leaned to my ear much as the black guy had, conspiratorial. "Probably shouldn't mention this to your mother." He gestured toward the eye and toward the receptionist. He winked. "There are some things you don't tell the women."

I didn't understand completely, but when my mother asked about the eye, I said I'd gotten hit playing football.

"You got it from some colored kid, didn't you? Don't lie to me." She'd wanted to send us to private school but couldn't afford to. I deduced from her tone that whatever small glory I might eke out of this would come from avoiding confession. Otherwise, at great sacrifice, money would be found for the safer school—I'd be offered sympathy, control, nets of protection. My weakness would be public. My father was right.

"Football," I maintained.

"If it isn't Jordan," the black guy said a week later. "Hey Jordan. You remember to bring my quarter?" He had my arm. He spun me around to face him. There were a few people in the hall—I was careful about not lingering at my locker—but they ignored us. The black guy smiled at me. I didn't know I'd grow eight inches and put on thirty pounds before the summer. I was skin and bones and mouth.

"Fuck off, asshole," I said, brave with despair. I jiggled my free arm. He pulled me closer. I was a dead man.

Then Hal Crosby came down the hall. "Leave him alone, man," he said. His tone suggested the two of them knew each other. The black guy let me go.

I didn't know why Hal Crosby rescued me. Never asked. I hadn't seen him before. He was sixteen and drove me home in his souped-up Chevy. I knew most high-school friendships were already sealed, exclusivity being the rule at that age, and it didn't occur to me the hoods might still be recruiting. Hal wore an old tweed jacket that would have been laughed off the grounds on anyone else. His hair grew down over his collar. He was tall.

"A quiet 'fuck-off, asshole' is a lot more effective than an excited 'fuck-off, asshole,'" he said, driving. "Better yet, don't cuss at all. Just make your face so calm only your mouth moves and say, ''Get your own quarter,' and then walk away. That way, they'll jive you that once but probably never again."

Pulling up in front of my house, he added, "The niggers don't want to be at Central any more than we want them here."

"That's real comforting," I said.

"Last year when they first came, we didn't have a normal day of classes for a month. They were that pissed."

I had heard about this—bottles thrown and white students jostled in the halls, angry demonstrations. The blacks wanted their segregated high school back—their all-black football team, all-black marching band, all-black pride. They did not regard integration as a hard-won victory. But police came to the hallways, the vacant black school was torn down, and the disruptions dwindled to insults and extortion, usually of lunch money carried by small white freshmen traveling alone. To me it seemed the blacks regarded integration as my fault personally.

"Thanks for the ride," I said.

"One more thing," Hal told me. "Never act spastic. Spastic is a dead giveaway, man. Look calm. Calm."

"Calm," I said, grinning.

Hal taught me the art of lifting sodas from the grocery store and of taking money from the girls' locker room while they square-danced in the gym. Hal's other friend was Frank. We played mailbox baseball late at night, Hal driving down the streets while Frank and I leaned out the window, trying to knock over curbside mailboxes with a bat. I had a ten o'clock curfew, but if my brother closed our bedroom door, no one checked.

My father was otherwise occupied. My mother had switched to evening shift at the hospital. Once, coming in late from work, she caught me. By then, Hal Crosby had rehearsed me well in the skills of deception. I looked into her narrowed eyes and held her gaze. There were some things you didn't tell the women.

All fall and winter, we stole small sums of money, drank the beer Hal took from his father, smoked the pot Frank bought on the street. The two of them treated me alternately as friend and as mascot. I stopped worrying about being caught. Hal was my protector, my mentor. By spring, we'd grown bolder. We cased a store on Conklin Street in the black public housing project.

"We ought to rob it, man," Hal said. "Get ski masks and gloves. They'd never suspect whites."

This made us feel high and heady, even after the impossibility of the project dawned. Black women shopped there all day; black men made deals for liquor and drugs at night.

"All the better," said Hal. "A challenge."

We bought dark turtlenecks, toy pistols. I don't know if we would have done it. Mixed with my euphoria was a vision of being caught and sent to jail. Even with Hal as my guardian, I was disturbed by that. If the others had their own misgivings, they didn't say so.

Martin Luther King's assassination stopped us. It prompted the residents of the project to knock out the windows of that store and others on Conklin Street, loot them, set them on fire. The newspaper blamed anger at the death of their leader, at the loss of an all-black high school, at their small grip on power and other slights of which we had no knowledge. Some blamed the hot weather. We didn't care. Glass crashed, flames shot into the air, we were released forever from our intended crime. Frank was busy that night, so Hal and I, jubilant, drove into the ghetto to watch the blacks tear their neighborhood apart.

The convenience store, fish market, and coin laundry were all burning by the time we arrived, but not so much that we couldn't see the smashed windows and the looted goods littering the pavement: rolls of toilet paper, racks of candy, broken soda bottles. The wind was blowing hard, whipping the flames around. Young black men were running, fists raised, shouting. The police had cordoned off an area to contain them, but they paid no attention. Hal gave a group of them the finger. No one noticed. They were absorbed by something larger.

The firemen went about their business. Hoses crisscrossed the street. Loudspeakers crackled, sirens wailed. Burning cinders blew into the clump of pines that separated the stores from the rows of barrackslike houses behind. Flames danced in the layer of pine straw at the base of the trees, then licked upwards to the branches. The sap hissed as it turned to steam; the needles flashed like burning powder as they ignited. Hal clapped me on the shoulder. I was glad Frank hadn't come. We cheered as the tops of the trees began blazing, sending down sparks onto the roofs of the adjacent houses.

Though firemen doused the roofs with water, a row of houses caught fire. Officials shouted for people to get out of the way. We ignored them. The smell of smoke made my heart beat fast, but I was too keyed up to be afraid. The blaze was to our right, to our left, more exciting than a robbery.

Soon the flames were hurling themselves into the night, screeching and cackling, a Halloween beast sending out curling wisps of smoke. Every hot color danced against the sky: yellow, scarlet, crimson, amber. The wind drew billows of flame from one frame building to another, sucking fire down the streets as if through a pipe. Hal and I ran from block to block, following the drama. Houses on three different streets were burning. A roof detached and sailed, a fiery raft afloat in the darkness.

"The ultimate fireworks, man!" Hal yelled.

The fire got louder. Voices on loudspeakers drowned in its roar. The looters stopped looting. The blaze was bigger than their anger. I had never been so high in my life. Not on beer, not on pot, not on nerves.

The worse it grew, the more we chucked each other on the shoulder and sped through the streets. We didn't notice when the flames got out of control, only that they were inanimate one minute, then suddenly alive, malignant.

"Let's get out of here!" I yelled.

When I turned toward Hal, he was lost in a shroud of smoke, and the voices behind me were so distorted against the howling that they might have been anyone's. The blaze was two enclosing walls, two armies approaching each other, battalions of flame.

When I turned to get my bearings, all the directions were the same. Smoke everywhere. Sparks falling, igniting patches of grass near the sidewalk where I stood. In one horrific moment,

I went from spectator to participant, lifting my arms over my head for protection. I couldn't move. A gut-rotting fear held me to the spot. My right hand was stung as if by a bee. I brought it down into my line of vision. The fine hair on the back of my hand was burning. *Burning*. Then I ran, panicked. The sparks from which my upraised arm had protected me rained on my face. I beat them away, but they came faster than I could put them out. The blaze was on both sides, above, everywhere. I was in the middle of an inferno. I screamed: "HAL!" The sound was so thin I could hardly hear it. And Hal couldn't, surely, how could he, over the hissing, crackling witch's voice of the fire? Guardian gone. No protection. My helplessness was so all-consuming, I won't forget it if I live to be a hundred. Then instinct made me drop, rub my hand on the ground, grind my face into the dirt and grass, put out the fire.

My eyes were gritty. My right eyebrow throbbed and stung. I was choking, breathing thick, smoke-filled air, breathing darkness. Coming up out of a nightmare. Someone pulled me, hands beneath my shoulders. Hal's hands? Time passed. Coughing again. Rubbing my eyes. Pain. And—slowly, slowly—my hand came into focus again, grotesque and swollen. I was still lying on the grass. A voice, but I couldn't hear it clearly. Not Hal's. I turned on my side and threw up.

"You're okay, son," the voice said. "A couple of nasty burns, but you're okay." A fireman. "Stay there for now. Ambulance'll be here in a minute."

The fireman disappeared into the commotion. I didn't want an ambulance. I got up. Somebody was lying right next to me. Hal? When my eyes focused, I saw it was a black kid. Where was Hal? The black kid didn't move. A big guy, almost the size of the one who'd demanded my quarters. It took me a minute to realize he was dead. Christ. A dead black kid a little older than me, with his pants and shirt so charred they clung to his skin like bits of paper. Snot crusted all over his nose. Eyes shut like he'd only gone to sleep. Except he had no eyelashes. They were burned off at the base, not a mark to show they'd ever existed. I felt for my own eyelashes. Intact. Then I felt above my eye, where the stinging was. Raw. But the lashes were there.

I couldn't stop looking at the dead guy. The skin on his cheeks was cracked like an egg, a burnt-black eggshell. Underneath it was a blood-red layer of face, seeping up through the cracks, a face as pink as mine under the cracked black skin. A wave of weakness passed through me. I figured firemen must have dragged us out of the fire about the same time, me and this dead kid who might be the one who'd wanted my lunch money all those months ago before Hal showed up. If he'd been knifed, or shot in a fight, I might have thought it served him right for the weeks of terror he caused me. But he was so utterly destroyed, so completely worse off than I was, in a permanent way, that I forgave him.

The pain in my eyebrow began to expand, taking over my whole mind. My vision was foggy from smoke and the sight of the dead guy. The throbbing in my hand was also intense, but the fact that I could see the hand, however red and glazed, limited the pain somehow, kept it in its boundaries. But I couldn't see my face. I believed, irrationally but with total conviction, that the damage in my brow would grow as the pain had, take over my eyes, leave me deformed and blind. I believed if I could reach Hal, my talisman, I might prevent this.

Through the blur of my vision, I saw the two walls of fire meet. A soaring flame leaped into the sky—a sudden last fountain of light—and then died away as the two fires canceled each other out, leaving what would become half-a-mile square of ruin.

I began to move toward Hal's car. That's where he'd be. Waiting for me. It would be all right. No one looked at me as I walked, raw hand clutched to my chest. They didn't look at me or at each other, though there were dozens of them, black and white. As if in a film with the sound turned off, they were mutely watching the end of the fire, the sky turning to smoke. Most of the Conklin project was gone. My hand and face throbbed, but I moved toward Hal. The ground beneath me was wet from the hoses. The smell of ash rose into the air. Hal would know what to do. I got to the block where the car was parked. Soon the burning pain would stop. The car was gone. Hal was nowhere.

I kept walking, unsure where I was headed. I found myself in the emergency room of the hospital where my mother worked. I asked to see her. The hand and the brow and my terror by then seemed to occupy my whole mind, my limbs, my chest. There were some things you didn't tell the women, but that night there was no one else to tell and too much for a fourteen-year-old to contain. So I told my mother in words and tears about our trip to the ghetto and the fire that had escaped like a wild beast from its cage; I spoke and sobbed, and the longer I went on the freer I felt, as if speech were a balm that could ease the pain.

My mother listened stony-faced, with what I didn't recognize until years later as the cold retroactive anger of a parent whose child has escaped mortal danger. "The only reason you got out was because you were lucky, you know that?" she said, face close to mine, shaking my shoulder. "You know how many people have died in here tonight?"

I realized then I had been talking quite a while, and that no one had rushed in with medical treatment while I rambled, and that my burns were not as severe as I'd thought and wouldn't blind or kill me. I understood what my father meant about not telling the women, how fragile was the masculine shell we had constructed, how easily pummeled and shattered, how small we would find ourselves inside it. I was ashamed of my weakness.

"How many firemen killed?" I asked.

"None. One brought in for inhalation, but he'll be all right. Why?"

I didn't answer.

Later, when the hair in the middle of my eyebrow refused to grow back and the scar on my hand was shiny and tight, I took these marks to be reminders of a number of things about that night, but chief among them the weakness of confession. It seemed obvious to me that the firemen had faced the inferno armed and therefore had escaped. That was the important lesson. If my mother could not see that for herself, she had no right to know. I was finished explaining to women.

· *Part One* ·

1988
Fall

·

ONE

*W*hat happened when Cassie Ashby was fourteen had less to do with the black man and more to do with the white one than people thought. The white man was her stepfather, Royal P.A. Ashby, who in Cassie's opinion stumbled in from his Wright County commissioners' meeting every Tuesday primarily to show he was so weary from carrying the town on his hairy shoulders that he could barely stand up long enough to get a beer from the refrigerator.

Every Tuesday, Royal pulled off his tie and opened his collar, releasing an extra inch of neck skin he'd stuffed in there—tan, loose skin so flabby it jiggled when he swallowed and made Cassie feel as if a hand were clutching at her own throat, cutting off the air. Having taken a swig from the beer before he could bring himself to close the refrigerator, Royal made his way into his study and slumped into the chair behind his desk. Cassie followed. Her mother, Betty, sat on the sofabed, where Royal often slept when he was "too wrought up" over some vote to go upstairs. He sighed.

"You have no idea what it means to be in power," he said.

Cassie certainly did not.

"I almost threw up on the bus again," she ventured, hoping he might at least be amenable to compromise in his power-monger mood. "I know Tiffany Galloway would drive me if I asked." Tiffany was a junior of great beauty and wildness who lived two blocks away and drove a red Honda Civic to school, breathing fresh air on the way instead of exhaust and gymshoes.

"Maybe we ought to consider it," her mother said.

The bus ride took forty minutes, meandering through Festival Beach, across the drawbridge, and finally to Central High in downtown Festival. It would have been shorter except that the bus passed North High on the way and went seven extra miles—"in order to deposit the correct number of white middle-class students into the black ghetto." That's how Royal explained it at cocktail parties. "The federal busing mandate was lifted in nineteen eighty-one, but we're afraid if we don't continue, the government will step back in." Then he'd sip his drink meaningfully, allowing his guests to contemplate the dangers of putting Wright County, North Carolina, into the hands of anyone but Commissioner Royal Ashby.

"I thought we'd discussed her getting a ride before," Royal said, rising from his desk and moving toward his wife, suddenly all charm. Betty, too, suffered from motion sickness. "Honey, I believe you have a genuine problem—I've seen it in action. But this child here..." He waved the beer at Cassie.

"I'm hardly a child, Royal." Cassie fingered her earrings. Sometimes when he was unbearable, she walked across the drawbridge to a little store called Jewels and had another hole pierced in her ears. Royal said only foreigners did this more than once, but Cassie had had her earlobes punctured more times than anyone she knew.

"Cassie, when you're in the position of making rules like I am," he intoned, "you have to be careful about breaking them. The rule is that freshmen ride the bus, and I think you should." He rested the hand without the beer on Betty's shoulder. "I'd say that even if the Galloway girl didn't have the reputation she does. If you don't ride the bus, people will think you're getting special favors because you're my daughter."

Cassie rolled her eyes, but Royal ignored her.

"It was different when your mother got seasick all the time," he went on. "All I had to do *then* was sell my boat."

"You never sold that boat because Mama got sick on it," Cassie said. "You sold it because real estate was bad and you couldn't afford to keep the damned thing."

"If that's how you choose to describe it, maybe you should ponder your choice of language in your room over the weekend," Royal said stiffly.

"Because I said *damn?* Because I'm supposed to be a credit to my stepfather, the important politician? Because if I hear anything nasty like the F-word, my mind is supposed to be too pure to retain it?"

Betty stood up. "You know what I can't understand?" she said. "I can't understand how two people can live under the same roof and take so much pleasure in being ugly to each other."

◆　◆　◆

It was late September and still hot. There was no autumn in Festival, not like in Baltimore when Cassie was little, where there had been air of the exact chill and dryness to let her hear individual leaves swishing against each other on the trees. Here, the sun didn't lose its bite, it only got yellower.

The bus was close and damp. Cassie's head pounded, her stomach churned, her tongue grew thick and dry. Curley Johnson, the bus driver, gave her a seat by the window and let her keep it open regardless of the weather.

"Me, I get to suffocate, and she gets a window seat with air blasting in," said Kyle Carter, the last passenger to be picked up. He lived next door to Tiffany, whose red Honda sat in the driveway. Kyle was a head taller than Cassie, blond and tan from surfing. He wore Gotcha shorts, Billabong T-shirts, nothing generic.

"You never passed out yet," Curley said, waiting for him to sit down. Curley was eighteen or nineteen, not easily rattled.

Kyle slipped into the seat across the aisle from Cassie and stared over at her with his usual mixture of lust and disdain. She knew what she looked like—tall enough, thin enough, good legs. When he singled out a spot on her cheek to examine as if it were crusted with food from her breakfast, she was grateful to be by the window, not on the aisle where Janet Biggs was, right across from him. Kyle tossed his head, flipping a wedge of pale hair out of his eyes from his hotshot surfer haircut.

Later, after the trouble began, when everyone wanted to know what Curley looked like, Cassie would say, "Like any other black guy." Maybe they called him Curley because of his hair. The truth was, she never much noticed. Between looking out the window and trying not to throw up, it was Kyle she was aware of those mornings, swaying back and forth across the aisle from her and Janet, grumbling every time they crossed a rough spot on the road.

"Too pretty to go to school," someone cried. Others murmured assent. Heat shimmered up from the road and a thin cool rose from the waterway as they crossed the bridge.

"I'll tell you what," Curley said. "You raise forty dollars, and I won't take you to school. I'll take you to Sand Dollar Beach." Sand Dollar Beach was the other beach town, south of Festival, a honky-tonk place with cheap motels and sidewalk arcades.

"All *right!*"

They started raising money, peeling dollar bills meant for lunch out of their wallets, handing them forward to Janet Biggs, who was always treasurer of everything. Janet got up and stood in the aisle, marking the sums in a notebook.

Kyle slipped into Janet's seat to torment Cassie further. He positioned himself so his calf touched Cassie's, its bleached hair grazing her skin. He didn't look at her face, didn't move closer or farther away, just sat limb to limb, staring at Cassie's smooth leg as if it were deformed. Cassie focused on Janet, pretending an interest in the collection of money. She wouldn't have moved if she'd been under the blade of a guillotine, wouldn't have given Kyle the satisfaction. On the periphery of her vision, the wedge of hair on his forehead was so white it hurt her eyes.

"Illegal to stand up on the bus," Curley told Janet. Janet sat down in the aisle, letting people hand their money down the rows. Everyone was laughing, happy. Coldness began to spread from the pit of Cassie's belly into her limbs. Her throat felt sour. She turned toward the window. Fumes came up from the road.

A red car zipped around them, a strand of black hair escaping the driver's window, flying in the wind. Tiffany. She was going fifty easily. The speed limit was twenty-five. She switched lanes, cut off the bus. Air brakes hissed. The bus lurched. Cassie swallowed hard.

"Only thirty-seven dollars," Janet said. "Curley, will you take us for thirty-seven?"

"Hey, a deal's a deal," Curley said.

"Anybody got another three dollars?"

"Not me, I'm clean."

"Come on, Curley," someone said.

"No, man, I can't do it. I'd like to, but I can't."

A general groan.

Kyle tossed the wedge of hair back from his face. Cassie's stomach contracted. A rush of saliva came to her mouth.

"Hey, you can't say we didn't try," Janet laughed. She was giving the money back, parceling it out.

"I gave you a five!"

"Like hell you did!"

The bus turned onto Bishop Street, three blocks from school.

"What'd you give me, Becky?"

"Ninety cents in change." Central High appeared in the distance, old brick baking in the sun. Janet worked quickly, consulting her notebook for the right amounts to return. Cassie's mouth tasted like oil. She felt ragdoll limp, muscles and innards melted away except for stomach and throat, where everything was poised to come up. Her limbs were loose and heavy. But she didn't move her leg.

They turned into the parking lot, went over the speed bump. "Home free, Miss Carsick," Kyle said. He was looking at her straight on now. At the sweat on her face. At her skin slick as wax. He gave her an eyeful of hate. People stood, heading for the doors. She forced herself up, locked her knees so as not to sink, kept her breakfast down by an effort of will. She followed Kyle onto the sidewalk, into volumes of fresh air, not throwing up. It was the hardest thing she'd ever done.

◆　◆　◆

All day, she dwelled bitterly on a single fact: four years before, she'd been living contentedly in Baltimore, where she might still be if she'd only reacted more quickly one afternoon when she was ten.

It was a Saturday. Her mother had taken her to a park across a finger of bay from the Inner Harbor, as if for their usual outing. The trees were orange and burgundy, luminous in the sunlight. They sat on a bench, munching popcorn that scratched Cassie's throat. The throat had been getting sorer all morning, but she didn't say so.

Her mother rose and walked over to a railing that separated the park from the water below. Honey-colored light sparkled up from the waves and caught in her hair. "I've been wanting to talk to you about Royal," she said.

"What about Royal?" Cassie asked.

Her mother worked for the convention bureau and had met him at a political conference. Since then, he'd been flying to

Baltimore on weekends, bringing Cassie T-shirts with yellow and aqua fish and "Festival Beach, N.C." on them. He told such wild stories about hurricanes and eighty-degree Christmases that Cassie hardly noticed how he ruffled her hair and whisked her mother off to dinners and shows. The relationship had grown more serious after he discovered Betty had been a Powell in Raleigh before Cassie's father took her north and died.

"He's asked me to marry him," Betty said.

"Are you going to?"

"I wanted to discuss it with you first."

"He's kind of old."

"Older than I am. But not *old*. He's a good man."

A shower of bright leaves drifted across Betty's shoulders, then swept down the bank into the water.

"He wants to make a better life for us. He has a house. A business."

In this, Cassie heard the voice of compromise. She chewed but couldn't make her popcorn soft enough to keep it from scraping her throat.

"He claims to have a car that runs more than two days in a row," Betty continued, smiling. The buildings of the Inner Harbor gleamed across the water as she returned to the bench. "What's the matter?" she asked. She put her hand to her daughter's forehead. "Fever," Betty concluded.

Later, Cassie sat in bed drinking tea, the sun slanting into the window, an ancient gold. Though she recalled how sick she'd felt, the memory wasn't unpleasant.

But somehow, when she was still safe, she'd failed to say the words that might have forestalled this. What should she have done? She could never decide.

So the wedding was at Christmas. Royal moved them south to his beach house, making Cassie a friendless newcomer at Festival Beach Elementary School in January. The temperature was closer to forty degrees than eighty. The sky was filled with harsh white light. The wind off the ocean bit clean through her skin.

Kyle Carter, then just one of twenty strangers in her new class, circled her on the playground as if he were looking at a dog up for adoption at the pound. The others watched with amusement.

"You look like your mother, I bet," he said.

"Some."

"Man, I can't believe it."

He kept circling.

"Believe what?" Cassie asked.

"That Commissioner Ashby dumped Peggy Tischer to marry somebody who looks like *you*."

The bystanders erupted into laughter. Cassie felt her face go red. She was too stunned to speak.

Janet Biggs detached herself from the group and came to her side. "He's just mad because he's kin to Peggy Tischer."

Cassie didn't care. There was nothing wrong with her mama. Nothing wrong with *her*. She moved so close to Kyle that he started to step back. Then she spat in his face. The kids who'd been laughing at her a second ago started to cheer and clap.

Royal's voice had drifted up the stairs that night, not his suitor's voice but rougher. "She's your daughter and I appreciate that," he said to Betty, "but there are certain things you can't allow."

"She was trying to defend me," Betty said.

"There's a way to do that and a way not. Let her get away with spitting on someone, and what do you think she'll try next? She's liable to become a *real* pain in the ass."

Betty and Royal grounded her—her first taste of his child-rearing techniques. She had not been grounded before. She knew then that politicians told hurricane stories and bought T-shirts and promised warm wind off the sea—but that had nothing to do with the true selves they revealed after you voted for them. It was Royal, not Cassie, who was the pain in the ass.

She dubbed him Royal P.A., for "royal pain in the ass," as if the letters were his middle initials. Though she referred to him as Royal P.A. any time she mentioned his name, no one thought to question her.

"Please come get me," she wrote her grandmother Truitt in Baltimore then. "You drive south through practically all of North Carolina to the town of Festival, then turn left and go over the Intracoastal Waterway to Festival Beach. You can see the house from the drawbridge because it's the tallest one on the waterway, a disgusting gray wood—'weathered,' he calls it—with ceilings so high the wind blows through the front room. Just don't come in winter unless you want to freeze your you-know-what."

Cassie's grandmother failed to act. She wrote back that stepparents required some adjusting to and Cassie ought to be patient.

◆ ◆ ◆

On the way home, the drawbridge was open, its gray-green grids a wall in front of them, letting tall-masted sailboats pass in the water below. The bus idled and rocked, which for Cassie was worse than moving.

"Curley, let me off here," Cassie called.

"Only a couple of minutes till you're home," he said.

"What's the matter?" Kyle asked. "Bus too much for you? Stomach too delicate?"

Hearing that, Curley opened the door. Cassie stumbled onto the pavement, dizzy. She remembered her mother plying her with Cokes on road trips. There was a Hardee's by the bridge, and she found herself inside, ordering.

A voice behind her said, "You look awful. You okay?"

She turned to see eyes so pale blue they might have been blind. Long dark lashes, hair a black sheet. Tiffany Galloway was the only person Cassie knew who lived at the beach and didn't get tan, claiming she had Irish skin that looked better white. Cassie felt sure it was only a matter of time until Tiffany was discovered by that film studio up in Wilmington.

"The bus makes me sick. I couldn't sit there waiting for the drawbridge."

"Here," Tiffany said, motioning to a booth. Cassie sat. Tiffany unwrapped a straw, scrutinizing Cassie through long blue eyes.

"If the bus bothers you so much, why don't you get a ride? Plenty of people drive," she said.

"Because Royal P.A. is big on the rule about freshmen riding the bus."

"Isn't there an election or something? I bet he's too busy to notice."

Cassie sipped her Coke, considering this. Although Royal P.A. maintained it wasn't necessary to campaign much after being in office so long, it was true he'd been gearing up for the November election. He'd accepted speaking invitations, prepared a brochure, had big board signs made for the top of his car.

"I could take you sometimes," Tiffany said, studying her. "Not Thursdays. Thursday, Brian doesn't have classes."

This was Brian Ivey, dark and handsome. He'd graduated from Central High and now went to Festival Community College. Cassie had heard Tiffany cut school to sleep with him but, until now, she hadn't believed it. Brian and Tiffany were famous for their colorful fights at football games and in other public places, after which they lovingly made up.

"Thursdays I could handle," Cassie said, though the whole idea was out of the question. She imagined Royal looking out his study window just as the red Honda pulled up. She would be grounded forever.

"Just give me a call." There was harsh light in Tiffany's eyes. Tiffany knew Cassie wouldn't.

"Speaking of the devil," Tiffany said. Brian Ivey was walking toward them, sliding into the booth, putting his hand on the back of Tiffany's neck, around her silky hair, in a gesture so intimate that Cassie had to look away.

"What've we got here?" he asked, meaning Cassie. He checked her out with eyes the exact opposite of Tiffany's, so dark the pupil was indistinguishable from the iris. Tiffany introduced them and gave him a summary.

"You have to ride the bus, huh?" He said it sympathetically, which she wouldn't have expected from someone so old. "Then you must be a freshman."

Tiffany twirled her straw between her fingers, impatient. "A freshman. That means she'll be an Azalea Princess in the spring." Sarcasm in her voice. Cassie didn't know what to say. Two years ago, when Tiffany was a freshman, she'd missed an entire month of school. It was her absence from the Azalea Festival Court of Princesses that had drawn attention to her long furlough. There were rumors she was in a drug program, had complications from an abortion, got suspended for blackmailing another student. No one really knew. She narrowed her eyes at Cassie. "I can just see you in a hoop skirt and crinolines."

They were both zeroing in on her, Tiffany with her blue gaze and Brian with his black one.

"Not me," Cassie said.

"Oh yes you will. Any daughter of Royal Ashby's..." The Court of Princesses was made up of the freshman daughters of every prominent family in Festival and Festival Beach.

"Stepdaughter," Cassie felt obligated to say.

"Yes, but he adopted you, didn't he?"

"In an election year. For the publicity."

They both hooted.

"He arranged for the papers to be signed right before the election. The *Festival Herald* covered it as a news event—no kidding—COMMISSIONER ASHBY ADOPTS," Cassie said defensively.

It was true. "She was always like a daughter to me from the first time I met her," Royal had been quoted as saying. Cassie, intending to be daring, had whispered to a reporter, "Like hell." She had been ignored.

"Adopted for the publicity," Brian repeated, shaking his head.

"I can understand how that would piss you off," Tiffany said sharply, "but somehow I don't think you'll get out of being an Azalea Princess."

Cassie had never even considered this possibility. Now she pictured herself riding on a parade float through downtown Festival, waving at a crowd that had gathered not so much to see the Princesses as the Azalea Queen, who was always some soap-opera star. She imagined standing among the azaleas on the garden tour, dressed like something out of *Gone With the Wind*. She imagined tourists gawking at her, drawn by the ads that ran statewide, announcing THE AZALEA FESTIVAL AT FESTIVAL. The event was such a big deal that years ago, the Chamber of Commerce had changed the town's name from Masonboro to Festival and the name of the beach to Festival Beach.

Though Betty was a member of the Festival Garden Club which organized the event, Cassie had never thought her mother's fondness for flowers would extend to wanting her daughter on public display. It was Royal who'd like seeing Cassie trussed up in taffeta, carrying a parasol against the sun. It was Royal who'd point out she was a credit to him, a sweet Southern belle.

"I'd rather die," she said to Tiffany.

Brian and Tiffany were still in the booth, touching shoulders, when Cassie left. She felt so warm with kinship and envy that she'd nearly forgotten her stomach.

She herself was not allowed to date until she was sixteen— part of Royal's effort to turn her into a flower of Southern womanhood. Having seen her own mother be taken in by

Royal, having endured Kyle Carter's staring, she mostly didn't care. Someday, when Royal deemed her ready to date the sons of contributors, boys from Carolina and Duke, she would refuse coolly. Royal's eyes would widen in disbelief. Her disinterest would serve her. But imagining Brian and Tiffany together on Thursdays when Tiffany cut school—their faces getting closer together, mouths opening, touching lips and tongues—that was something else altogether. She imagined them in a darkened room, the air conditioning cooling everything but their skin, little beads of sweat forming on Brian's forehead, dropping onto Tiffany's neck.

The sun was hot as Cassie walked, the street deserted. She was sweating herself, what with her heavy backpack slung over her shoulder, her arm bent holding onto the strap. She didn't notice Kyle coming toward her.

"Ah, Miss Carsick," he said.

He reached out as if to pat her stomach, then lifted his hand and cupped her breast instead—her breast!—as if she'd stuck it out there to amuse him. He never missed a step, just took a feel, then let go and walked on, a huge self-satisfied grin on his face. As if he'd read her mind and knew at that moment she was thinking about Tiffany and Brian and sex. She was too humiliated to say a word.

That night, she dreamed she was in Tiffany's house, in Tiffany's bed. Brian's hand was stroking her breast, rubbing the nipple. Maybe she was Tiffany. Her eyes were closed, but she felt the warmth of his tanned chest just above her, the approval in his dark gaze. When she opened her eyes, a wedge of white-blond hair was hanging over her, the expression beneath it full of disgust. The face was Kyle's, not Brian's. What he was doing was not an act of love or even sex. It was an act of hate.

◆　◆　◆

A seat on the bus had been slashed, a quick, long slice with a razor or pen knife. Curley stood in the doorway, letting everyone get just close enough to see.

"Listen up, everybody," he said, lifting a piece of white stuffing from beneath the gash. "We could spend a whole lot of time figuring out who did this, but we'd never get home."

The crowd mumbled. Anyone could slash a seat. Getting off in the morning, with everyone pushing out, a vandal could wield a knife big enough to carve beef and no one would notice.

"Like I say, we *could* spend a lot of time. But we won't. We're just gonna make sure it don't happen again."

He assigned every person on the bus a seat. Cassie got her usual place, with Janet Biggs next to her on the aisle. Kyle was assigned to the very back, opposite the emergency exit.

"This seat is your baby from now on," Curley said. "Anything happens to this seat, it's like it happened to your own baby. It gets dirty, you clean it up. It gets cut up, you pay the hospital bill. You hear what I'm saying?"

The next morning, everybody sat where Curley told them. Then Kyle got on. He stood hanging onto the back of Cassie and Janet's seat, tossing his hair.

"Against the rules to stand up," Curley said. "You got an assigned place, don't you?"

The bus was idling, vibrations from the motor shivering down the aisle. Kyle didn't move.

"We could wait here all day, man," a kid named Claud said.

"I don't think so," Kyle told him. "They don't like these bus runs to come in late. They might fire him if he stays here too long."

Titters.

"They might fire his black ass," Kyle said.

Curley moved the gear shift, putting the bus into park. He stood up to face Kyle. He looked tall and powerful. Beside him, Kyle was gawky. "Sit down, bleach boy," Curley said.

Not beach. *Bleach.* All that surfer-cut hair, whiter than sand. Cassie laughed. Everybody laughed.

"Nigger," Kyle whispered under his breath. Curley was still standing there, solid and unmoving. The passengers went dead quiet. Finally Kyle turned, walked down the aisle, and sat.

The next day, Kyle went to the guidance counselor and told her this story: The previous afternoon, after everybody else had gotten off the bus, Curley pulled off the road across from Kyle's house, but didn't open the door to let Kyle out. Instead, he threatened to accuse Kyle of slashing the seat unless Kyle did certain things with him. Then he put his hands in a certain place on Kyle's pants. Kyle broke free and triggered the door release so he could get out. Curley didn't come after him once he was on the street.

This was a rumor for six hours in school. Then they got on the bus and found a woman driving.

"Where's Curley?"

"I think he's been suspended."

When Kyle got on the bus, he was walking with a kid named Jeff, saying louder than he needed to, "...first time I've ever had a guy's hand there, man—and the last. Now when it comes to girls' hands..."

He winked as he passed Cassie's seat, then sat down with Jeff two rows back and laughed about Curley's suspension.

◆　◆　◆

That was Friday. Saturday noon, Royal P.A. dragged Cassie and Betty to the Elks picnic in Festival Beach Park. The smell of burnt chicken rose from the grills. A crowd gathered around the table where they were selling beer. Betty wore a tailored dress and Royal a suit—campaign clothes—though the temperature was in the eighties and hardly any wind came off the ocean. "You wear what you have to, not what other people do," Royal often said. "It's one of the obligations of power."

"I'll be damned if I'll wear church clothes to a picnic," Cassie said, though she never went to church. She dressed in a skirt and blouse, sneakers with socks, and earrings so long that they grazed her shoulder, a different stud in every extra hole in her ears.

They made separate rounds, Royal alone, Betty with Cassie, squinting against the sun, shaking hands. In the distance, Royal talked animatedly with the Carters, Kyle's parents, patting Larry Carter's arm as he pumped his hand. The Carters were big contributors.

"It must have been difficult for Kyle, saying what he did," Betty mused. "A lot of boys would be afraid to admit if some man made a pass at them."

"He'll do anything for attention," Cassie said. "Besides, he was lying."

"I doubt it, Cassie. Why would he lie?"

"Because he smart-mouthed Curley and Curley called him a bleach boy."

"A bleach boy?"

"Bleached hair."

"Lots of boys bleach their hair these days."

"Everyone laughed."

"Well, regardless, they'll fire the bus driver and that'll be the end of it. That's all they do unless there are witnesses."

"Why should they fire him if he didn't do anything?"

Betty didn't answer. Royal was coming up to them, Ashby-for-Commissioner button on his lapel, beer in hand, arm around the shoulders of an old guy Cassie had never seen before.

"Ron Trask, you remember my wife Betty and our daughter Cassie."

Stepdaughter, Cassie thought. Betty told the man how nice it was to see him. It was Royal's rule that they always say how nice to *see* people, never how nice to *meet* them, because maybe they'd met them before and forgot. Cassie nodded to the man but didn't smile or say a single word.

At home, Royal pulled off his tie and got another beer, this time from the refrigerator.

"What did the Carters say?" Betty asked, moving around him, taking a package of hamburger from the freezer.

"What could they say? The kid was upset. The bus driver's out." Royal took a swig of beer and sat heavily at the table. Interesting, how he could drink all afternoon, guzzle it down, and never say the first wrong thing, never show there was a drop of alcohol in him until after he got home. Drinking was what turned your neck into flab and showed you had no control over your body. It was as gross and disgusting as smoking pot or doing drugs. She looked at him with disgust.

"I guess you believe it," Cassie said.

"That the bus driver's fired? Damn right."

"That the bus driver did what Kyle says."

"Doesn't matter whether I believe it or not, it's a done deal," he told her. Bright sun poured into the kitchen from the west, glistening up from the Intracoastal Waterway behind them. In the light, Royal's face was slack and drunk and happy.

"That driver could no more have pulled off the road around here than drive into the ocean without somebody noticing it."

"What'd he look like, this bus driver?" Royal taunted.

Cassie kept her face expressionless. "They all look the same, don't they? Dark brown skin. Kinky hair. Smooshed-in nose. Just the type who might have the hots for Kyle."

"Cassie!" Betty said.

"No, Mama, look—he agrees with me. That's what they all look like, right? With real big you-know-whats that make them go around raping…"

"Cassie, stop it!"

But she didn't care. Once, in Baltimore, she'd had a friend Betty didn't know was black until Cassie brought her home. Cassie never thought to mention it. Down here, a person's color was the first thing you'd discuss. A lot of the Central High blacks lived in Bishop Gardens public housing and spent their time at school clustered in the hallways or the cafeteria—loud, laughing too much, and pushy. It was true Cassie didn't like them. And the ones who might be all right didn't pay attention to her, or she to them. That was how it was. The only black she really knew was LaMonica Reilly in her geometry class. But she was sick of Royal's acting like he was some precious white marble statue, guzzling beer and sounding righteous.

He finished his beer and moved to the refrigerator for another, smiling, enjoying her outburst. "No, Cassie, you got it all wrong," he said. "I don't think it has a thing to do with flat noses or big lips or even the size of their *you-know-whats.*" He leaned toward her, holding the new beer in his hand. "No sir, I think it's more that they're different in every way."

"Sure, Royal. Different in every way."

"Yes ma'am, *different.*"

"What he means, honey, is in this community the blacks are mostly welfare blacks and the whites are middle-class," Betty said quickly. "It's a question of economics and value systems, not just color."

"Oh no indeed, that's not what I mean at all," Royal said, sitting down. "I mean things like not being able to say the letter 'R.'" Smiling now, playing with her.

"That's crazy," Cassie said.

"Now wait a minute—is it really? You ever heard a black person say the word *poor?*"

"What's this, Royal? Twenty questions for bigots? Of course I have."

"I doubt it." He popped the beer can and watched the little mist come out of the opening. "You want to know why? Because they can't. They can only say *po'*. 'I don't have no money, I'm really *po'*.'"

"Royal, enough," Betty said.

"You ever hear a black person say he had four of anything?" Royal asked Cassie. "Or fourteen? No ma'am, you never did. Not a nigger in this town ever had those amounts. Most those po' niggers ever had was *fo'* of anything, *fo'teen* at the most."

"Nigger? *Nigger?*" Cassie screamed.

Royal stopped smiling. "Let me tell you something, Miss Cassie. In a place like this, you spend a lot of time with blacks, some of them good and some of them niggers. If it hurts your ears with those gypsy earrings hanging down, well, that's too bad, but it's the damn truth. Some of them are plain niggers. And a lot of times, you got no way of knowing which is which until something happens, like with that driver, Curley."

"Let me tell *you* something, Royal. Curley says the letter 'R' better than you do, especially when you're drunk. And he no more put his hand in Kyle Carter's pants than you did."

Royal paused, putting the beer can down on the table, turning the drunkenness off. "You're mighty sure of that, aren't you?"

"Yes, I am."

"You spend forty minutes riding on the bus with him and you know all about his morals, right? No, Cassie. You don't know the first thing about him outside of that bus." He picked up the beer again. "For all you know about him or any other black person in this town, they could still be living in Africa and talking a different language." He was holding the can as if he might crush it, but all he did was take another drink. "Your life has no more to do with theirs or theirs with yours than if they were still living over there in Africa. So what that bus driver did or didn't do to Kyle Carter—you really don't rightly know."

"So a bleached-haired white kid opens his mouth against him, and that's that."

"Yes." Royal was looking at her straight on. "The balance of power, Cassie. It's not as if they're sending him to jail."

Then he couldn't fight the alcohol a second longer, couldn't keep from breaking out into the most evil grin Cassie'd ever seen, worse than Kyle's when he touched her breast. She had to grin back so he wouldn't imagine he had the better of her, but she wasn't smiling, not really. She was planning how to shift the "balance of power" away from Royal P.A. Ashby if it was the last thing the arrogant bastard ever saw her do.

TWO

I didn't believe a damn word the girl was saying.

I mean, for godsake. On a Monday morning, after the fact. What could possibly be the point?

She'd told the secretaries it was an *emergency*, she had to speak to the vice principal right away. When they said Mrs. Lerner was free, she said no, she wanted Mr. Edge. Jordan Edge was in charge of discipline.

"I understand you have an emergency?" I said to her. Except for the hodgepodge of earrings, she looked to be one of the upscale kids from the beach, dressed in the regulation denim skirt, the athletic socks and sneakers. I expected her to wither. She didn't. Didn't even turn her eyes down to look at the floor.

"It's about Curley Johnson, the bus driver you fired," she said. "I ride on his bus."

First thing I thought was, oh Christ, another one claiming the driver had his hands in her pants. Just what we need. A black bisexual pervert bus driver.

"He couldn't have done what Kyle Carter says he did. I mean, it was supposed to have happened a couple of days after that seat in our bus was slashed, but it couldn't have. Not any day that week."

"Oh?"

"No sir."

I'm used to hearing "no sir" said in several tones of voice— every child in North Carolina learns to say *ma'am* and *sir* practically from birth—but her voice was neutral, and I couldn't tell if she meant "no sir" or "no shit" or something in between.

"Kyle Carter gets off at the last stop on our route, and I'm supposed to get off at the stop just before that, but most of that week I didn't," she was saying. "Either I got off with Kyle or else I got off at my own stop and walked right over to see him after I put my books in the house. Either way, there wasn't time for Curley to stop the bus and do anything."

"You got off at Kyle's house instead of your own," I said, repeating it to accentuate the absurdity.

"Yes, sir."

She gave me a level gray gaze she might have practiced in front of the mirror, looking like the Azalea Princess she would no doubt be, except for her earrings. An enormous contraption of brown beads and feathers that reached nearly to her shoulder dangled from her right ear. A string of additional holes were pierced in that same ear—four, maybe five of them—filled with round studs in various shades of brown. The other ear was more modest, only two holes, one with a fake diamond, the other with an orange smiley-face. And no other jewelry—no rings, nothing at the neck, just the cacophony of earrings.

"Sit down." I stood behind my desk as she slipped into the chair, putting lots of official dark wood between us. "The bus driver never said anything about your being a witness," I said.

"He probably wouldn't remember. It was the end of the run. If you ever rode a bus..."

Her name was on the note the secretary had given me: Cassie Ashby. I realized she must be the politician's kid, Wright County's colorful commissioner. Wouldn't know it to look at her.

"Why did you come to me with this?" I asked. "Why didn't you go to one of the guidance counselors?"

"What, to somebody like Dr. Howard, who talks twice as soft as he has to because he's afraid he's going to scare us?"

There I detected a thread of honesty. "You want to grace us with a few more details?" I asked.

"Kyle and I don't normally get along. I mean, not at all. On the bus, he's always after me physically."

Very good. *Physically*. She didn't bat an eyelash. "I mean, staring at me all the way to school. Touching me if he gets the chance. Trying to harass me." *Harass* I recognized from the freshman English text. I hear *harass* every fall for a month, until they finish the vocabulary unit. Then it drops from their speech as if banned from the language. She was staring not into my eyes but above them at the bare burned spot in the middle of my eyebrow, which the students believe came from a knife fight with a black man—a story I do nothing to discredit.

"Also, I get carsick on the bus," she said. "I mean, not just a little woozy, really sick. So a couple of weeks ago, I asked if I could get a ride with someone who drives. But my stepfather said no."

Stepfather. That explained the lack of resemblance. "I'm assuming this is all relevant?"

"Yes, sir. Well, Kyle just kept lording it over me on the bus. So when Curley assigned us seats and Kyle was supposed to sit in the back, I think he started all that with Curley mainly because he wouldn't be able to bother me any more." She lowered her gaze from my eyebrow to the scar on my hand.

"Then when Curley made everybody laugh by calling him a bleach boy...if you knew Kyle very well, you'd know he'd say just anything to get back at Curley for that."

She looked up, waiting for me to respond. I let the silence go on fifteen seconds, maybe twenty. This usually scares the bravado out of them. Along with the story about how I acquired my scars, there's another one around school that in my job as a volunteer firefighter I once punched out a man who was trying to get back inside a burning building. This is not true, but I assume it's what students think of as we sit there looking at each other.

"Your analysis of Kyle's character hardly constitutes proof," I told her finally.

"No. But also that week, I decided it was ridiculous being sick half the day just because Royal said to ride the bus. I figured if I got a ride, Royal would never know unless Kyle told him. I mean, telling Royal would be just his style. So I got off at Kyle's stop those couple of days after school to see if I could make some kind of deal with him not to say anything."

This sounded unlikely, but I was curious. "What kind of a deal were you trying to make?" I asked.

"I offered to do his geometry homework all semester. He said he'd think about it, to come back the next day."

"And?"

"I don't think he really wanted to make a deal. I think he was just flattered at my coming over there. At thinking he had power over me." Very flat, very smooth; I could hear her practicing it into a tape recorder, playing it back to herself.

"And if all this was going on that week, why do you think Kyle went ahead and accused Curley, knowing you could prove he was lying?"

"Because he didn't think I'd do anything. I mean, for one thing, Curley's just the bus driver. And for another, if I wanted to get a ride, then I wouldn't exactly get Kyle in trouble, would I? Not to mention that this isn't the easiest story to tell…I mean, about how I was trying to get around my stepfather."

"So what brings you here?"

"It didn't seem fair to fire someone for no reason."

"And maybe a little revenge against Kyle Carter?"

"If I thought something had really happened on the bus, I wouldn't defend Curley just to get back at a jerk like Kyle."

"I see." Despite the earrings, she looked the sort who might have principles.

"Are there other people who get off at your stop? Who would have known you'd gotten off at Kyle's?" I asked her.

She shook her head. "A lot of kids get on and off at the lower end of the beach. But up where we live, there aren't that many houses."

This, at least, was true. My ex-live-in girlfriend, Mary Beth, A.K.A. Marta the Bitch, aspired to live at the north end of the beach, where we often went on outings. The lots are dominated by fancy houses high up on stilts with a view of both the ocean and the sound—an assortment of rectangles, triangles and A-frames, framed by phony little gardens of yuccas and geraniums when nothing really wants to grow on the beach but sea oats.

"So no one saw you," I said to Cassie.

"No."

Too bad. The truth was, we already suspected the Carter kid was lying and would have liked a credible witness. A dozen times while he was in my office he'd tossed his head to fling hair out of his eyes, daring us to doubt him. He'd told his story to Molly Sampson, the bus coordinator who hires and fires all the drivers, in the exact words he'd used to me alone—and ditto when the bus driver was summoned. Curley had sat pale and unmoving, and then offered his only defense: "No *sir*, I wouldn't do a thing like that. I wouldn't and I didn't."

He'd graduated from Central High in June and was driving two bus runs a day while taking classes at the technical school. He did an elementary run early, then the high school run. If he were going to molest a kid, why not a younger one?

But Kyle stood half-smiling, never backing down, an arrogant blond peacock. His parents arrived at school. In soft, articulate tones that spoke of old money and prominence, they threatened legal action and publicity. It was only October, too early in the year to risk a racial incident. While the Carters were suing the school system, the NAACP would be crying discrimination. Curley would be caught in the middle. Molly asked Curley if he wanted to fight this thing or let it go. Curley quit.

"Just for the record, the bus driver wasn't fired," I said. "He was given an opportunity to resign—no investigation, no questions asked."

"You'd never hire him back, though, would you?"

"It's not likely."

She narrowed her eyes. "You don't believe me, do you?"

"I didn't say that."

In a move she hadn't learned overnight, she made her face completely expressionless. I assumed her skills were copied from the commissioner. He was much on the TV news lately, gearing up for the election—a wily man with a dry wit. I could imagine him showing Cassie how to look blank, how to overstate a case so everyone thought she was joking, how to lie outright when the need arose. Kids would bad-mouth a stepparent over some minor skirmish, but they were closer to them than they thought.

"Frankly, I'm not sure whether I believe you or not," I said. "I'm not the only one who would have to believe you. There would be an investigation. You'd have to speak to Mrs. Sampson."

She sat perfectly still and blank.

"The bus coordinator," I explained.

"Oh." A little animation began to creep back into her face then, as if she thought we were finally getting somewhere.

That's when my pager went off. Saved by the bell. Crackling at first, then the dispatcher's voice: "Attention North Festival, apartment fire at twelve-eleven Bishop Street, district two..."

The pager didn't phase the girl. She didn't startle, didn't jump. I've seen others nearly leap from their seats, depending on what they're in my office for, but she was fine.

I stood and reached for the turnout coat and helmet I keep on a hook on the wall. "We'll have to continue this discussion later," I said.

The way she reacted to my dismissing her so quickly, she might have been slapped. Her body jerked back before she caught herself. The feathered earring began to bob and dance just above her shoulder. Obviously one thing she hadn't anticipated was a fire interrupting.

Gotcha, I thought. You can never tell what will throw them off, just when they think they have you all wrapped up.

"Yes, sir," she said. The earring was still dancing when she stood up to leave the office.

It gave me no small satisfaction, watching that earring.

◆　◆　◆

Five minutes later, I was at the fire. My arrangement with the school included leaving any time there was an alarm, no questions asked. This was because Wright County has never seen fit to hire more than a skeleton staff of paid firemen, relying largely on volunteers. I only took advantage of my position once, in the early days with Marta, running by her place for a quickie after a grass fire that took all of five minutes to put out. I didn't enjoy it enough to make it a regular practice. After that, I went back to work as soon as I could—probably a good thing, because Marta proved not to be worth it.

The twelve-hundred block of Bishop Street is at the other end of the mile-long stretch of lousy neighborhoods that begins at Bishop Gardens near Central High. The apartments are ancient, three and four stories high, siding falling off, needing paint. Most of the trees in front had been cut down when the road was widened, so the street looked raw and menacing even outside.

I could smell the fire before I saw it—that combination of burning paint and plaster you can't describe because it's different from anything else. Smoke was banking down the street a block before I got there. First thing I knew, my heart was sitting in my throat the way it had twenty years ago when the town of Festival was burning down all around me and there wasn't a damned thing I could do. Exhilarated or afraid or both, I obeyed the speed limit by force of will, feeling the adrenaline, hoping my excitement wouldn't lapse into fear and paralysis. It hadn't since the night I was fourteen, but the memory still haunted me.

I parked the car and ran through the smoke toward the pumper. Clem, the captain, was there, and about half the men. The building in front of us had three floors, the second-story windows broken, flames shooting out and smoke billowing heavy. The tenants must have told each other and neighbors about the fire first, then called 911 as an afterthought. Mothers with their babies and preschoolers jammed the sidewalk, the kids half-dressed and barefoot. The older children were in school, but there were a couple of men, some teenaged boys. Welfare blacks.

I pulled on boots, pants, coat, helmet, gloves.

"Air pack," Fetzer said behind me.

Fetzer Laney sold lumber for Lowe's and helped coach Central High's wrestling team during the season, the best friend I'd had since I became vice principal. Fetzer was divorced, obsessive, one of those men who make a career out of being a volunteer firefighter—and a genuinely good one. Usually we ended up working together, but that day, Clem paired me with Andy Wilson, a new guy I hardly knew. I shouldered the air pack and pulled on my mask, judging I was fifty, maybe sixty pounds heavier with all that on—overstuffed but well-protected.

Fetzer had laid two lines from the hydrant to the pumper. I took the nozzle of the heavy one-and-three-quarter-inch hose and began hauling it into the building. Andy picked up the hose behind me. Clem walked in with us, holding his portable radio. I always felt better once there was something to do, could always count on my heart to stop dancing around, attend to the business at hand. We climbed the stairs and flaked out the hose on the second floor. Both apartments at the front were burning, flames shooting up to the ceiling and snaking down the corridor toward where we stood. I was already sweating under my gear.

When I turned on the nozzle, the vibration of water came flowing through the hose, through my fingers.

"Let's go," Clem said.

I aimed into the hallway, turning the nozzle so it would fog the water out at a thirty-degree angle. Steam rather than water would control the fire here, hot as it was. The wider the arc of water, the more steam it would create. The air grew so thick with smoke and steam that my mask got fogged up from sweat. I couldn't see a thing. I moved one hand down to crack the bypass valve on my air pack. This was against regulations because it drew down on the air supply, but everyone did it. A puff of extra air flowed into my mask, cooling me, clearing the facepiece a little.

I started around the bend at the top of the stairs, fighting the weight of the hose. If Fetzer had been on the line behind me, he would have been pulling on the hose to take some of the strain off my arms, but Andy was letting it go slack. We inched our way forward toward the apartment on the right.

We crept in, Andy and the captain behind me, all of us on our knees. Everything was burning freely in front of us, heat radiating from the walls of the entryway—a pulse of pure heat. The captain yelled something, but I couldn't hear. Behind face masks, above the roar of fire, the rush of water and hiss of steam, we had to scream to make ourselves heard.

"Ceiling's down," he yelled again. "Floor upstairs is beginning to go. Be careful, it'll come in pieces."

I nodded and gestured for us to go in a little more. Heart pounding harder—from nerves, adrenaline, effort. Under my gear, I could feel sweat dripping down my sides, my shirt wringing wet.

We pushed the line in a few feet.

"Shit," Andy said. The flames were almost directly overhead in front of us. Two more steps and we'd be underneath them. Our helmets were designed to deflect chunks of debris, but there was no telling what might come down, or how much; it was lunacy to get underneath it.

The captain was talking on the radio to the chief outside. "Fire's in back of us," the captain yelled. "Gotta turn the line." Slow-motion now, making a one-eighty with all that weight of hose and water in our arms. My mask was beginning to fog up again, but I could see where the fire had come out of the apartment across the hall, into the corridor behind us. A cardinal rule: never let the fire get behind you, never get trapped between two fires. I could almost see the flames flapping between the buildings of downtown Festival twenty years ago, two walls of blaze moving toward each other as if drawn by magnets, me and Hal Crosby in the middle of it. And later vowing never to let it happen again, never to face another fire unarmed.

I adjusted the nozzle to make the water come out almost straight, two hundred gallons a minute aimed point-blank into the hallway. Then, as we got closer to the door, I opened the fog-nozzle once more to create a wider angle, less for steam this time than for protection. The greater the circle of water, the less possibility of fire angling around to our side. It took forever to move out of the apartment, make our way back to the landing. A steady ache in my arms now, with Andy still not pulling his weight on the line. After a few minutes, the fire in the hall gave way, and we turned again, went back into the apartment.

The captain was on the radio. He finished listening and turned to me. "Somebody says a little girl's still up here. You and Andy do a search. Fetzer and Gibbs are coming up to relieve you on the line."

By the time he got the sentence out of his mouth, Fetzer was taking the nozzle from me, all the burden of the water-charged hose out of my arms. In the glow of the fire, through the mist of my mask, I could make out a couple pieces of cheap furniture in the room, an old TV. Nine times out of ten, they'd say somebody was inside and there wouldn't be. But kids do crazy things in fires, hide behind furniture, get under beds. I made my way to the sofa while Andy went to the chair beside it. We felt underneath, we felt along the wall. Nothing.

To our left was a bedroom, engulfed in smoke but not flames. We went in buddy system, two guys together in case something happened as we groped around in the darkness. I would have felt safer working with Fetzer. We started at the right and moved left, all the way around the room, sweeping our hands out in front and along the walls. Me first, Andy behind me. A closet. Sometimes kids went into closets, curled up in the farthest corners. With the air pack on, it was awkward getting low, feeling into small areas. I remembered being trapped. Rerun of twenty years ago again. Heart thumping. Down on my knees. I felt around on the floor, into the corners. Shoes. Some clothing. No child.

"Nothing," I yelled.

Andy closed the closet door behind us and marked an X on it with chalk, so we'd know, later, we'd been here. The chalk mark seemed redundant at the moment, since it was impossible to see. Nothing but smoke in front of us, a solid gray.

A bell sounded in my ear, dull at first, gradually louder. "Shit." It was the warning signal that I had only five minutes of air left. We wore thirty-minute packs, but breathing this hard we were lucky to get twenty. "No hurry, we can finish here. Almost done," I said to Andy.

Around the wall again. A bureau. Nothing under it. A bed. I squatted and stuck my leg underneath, made a quick sweep with my foot. Empty. I was sweating, listening to the commotion outside.

A second bed. A sweep with my foot. A solid mass.

"I've got something."

Heart beating in my throat now, memory of a blackened mess of trousers, bare arms charred, face cracked like old wallpaper and eyelashes burned off so clean they might never have been there. The bell would ring until the air ran out, but it was unimportant now, background music. I drew my leg out from under the bed and stuck my arm under. Something soft. The give of flesh?

"What is it?" Andy asked.

I pulled. It came easily—spongy, no weight.

"It's nothing," I said. "A pillow." But my pulse was still in my throat, my temples; sweat was rolling down my belly.

We finished circling the room, made our way out into the glow of the fire. I saw Fetzer, Clem, felt our camaraderie. Felt calm. I took a deep breath. Nothing came.

Breathed harder. Nothing. Sucking in on a vacuum.

Nerves.

No. The bell on my pack had stopped. I was out of air.

"His alarm started back in the bedroom," Andy said.

The fire was mostly on the floor above us now, pieces of the ceiling falling, smoke dense and dark. Nothing but poison to breathe if I took off my mask. I unscrewed the air line from the regulator of my pack, and stuck the tube attached to my mask inside my coat, under my arm. Foul smell, but another twenty, thirty seconds of air, easy.

"Get the hell out of here!" the captain yelled. "You too, Andy."

We made our way out of the apartment, down the stairs. Outside, I pulled my mask off. The sun was mid-morning high, blue sky smiling down even through the blot of smoke. The air that had seemed close and oppressive earlier tasted cool and dry.

"Must smell good to you after thirty seconds of armpit," Andy said.

"Yeah. Straight off a cold mountain stream."

Two more pumpers and a ladder truck had arrived; the pale spaghetti of fire hoses was everywhere. The top floor of the apartment was burning, the whole front of the building charred. The crew on the roof finished cutting into it for ventilation, and a cloud of heavy smoke rose from the hole, gray and acrid.

"So much for your fresh mountain stream," Andy said. I didn't laugh.

Coming out of smoke like that, it's easy to develop an appreciation for clear daylight. We took off our coats and gloves, laid them beside us as we sat down on the curb across from the building. Two little boys stood in the street, barefoot and transfixed. The breeze blew their skimpy shorts and T-shirts against their black skin. I was reminded of the Ashby girl, holding that still or trying to—and the earring giving her away. The wind cooled the sweat on my arms, my neck. It must have been eighty degrees, but I shivered.

"Best fire we've had since I been here," Andy said. He pulled a cigarette from the folds of his clothes and lit it.

"No such thing as a 'best' fire," I said. I could never understand how anyone could come out of the stench and poison of a burning building and deliberately inhale smoke. I studied him for the first time since he'd come into the unit: a small wiry guy, young, too cocky for the lousy job he'd done. Reminded me of some of the kids at school. I pointed to the scars on my eyebrow and hand. "Your idea of a 'best' fire is my idea of how I got those."

Andy dwelled briefly on the scars, then looked at me with new respect. "No kidding, man? When?"

"Ever go to Conklin Park?"

"Yeah, sure. With all the azaleas."

"It used to be public housing. Looked like barracks—quarter-mile square of junky old frame. They burned it down after Martin Luther King was killed."

"You weren't old enough to be fighting fires," he said.

"Old enough to be curious. A bunch of us went down there to see it. I was fourteen. We got a little too close."

I gave Andy a brief version of the fire, leaving out the rush of emotions that had filled me that night, omitting my experience with the corpse and the sense of panic and shame that had filled me. I concentrated instead on statistics.

"A dozen people killed altogether," I said, "and a lot more hurt."

"But the dead... How many white?"

"Two."

"Should have been *no* whites. Should have been just those blacks stupid enough to set their own neighborhood on fire." He took a last draw on his cigarette and flicked it into the gutter.

I didn't point out that race wasn't the issue. "They never tried to rebuild it," I said. "Nobody wanted to. That's how they ended up with the park."

Andy shook his head.

"I'll tell you what—it turned me around," I told him. "I was gearing up to do hard time. After that, at least I knew what I was mad at."

"Blacks," Andy said.

He sat there so calm and wiry and sure of himself that I was reminded of the cocky Carter kid and his trumped-up story about the bus driver. His expression made me think I ought to tell the Ashby kid I believed her. Let her defend the driver. What the hell.

"No, man," I said to Andy. "Not blacks. Fire."

THREE

Alona Sue Wand was twenty-eight years old, but sometimes she felt like she'd lived forever, what with fighting with her husband, Elliott, half the night and when she finally fell asleep, having that dream that always left her in shivers. So when she got to the shop and found Cassie Ashby sitting on the front steps, the first thing she thought about was truant officers. Not because she had any firsthand experience with truant officers, but because the idea seemed as nightmarish as her dream. In her mind, truant officers were more like police than school officials, barging into Jewels while Cassie Ashby was examining long wires strung with beads. She could see them handcuffing the girl, taking her off in an armored car. And maybe carting Alona off, too, as an accessory. FESTIVAL WOMAN ARRESTED AS ACCESSORY IN ACCESSORY STORE.

Pulling out the key to the shop, Alona said as warmly as she could, given that Cassie was a truant but also one of her best customers, "Correct me if I'm wrong, but aren't you supposed to be in school right now?"

"I had a dentist appointment earlier. I thought I'd stop here before I went in."

"Well, *that's* certainly a lie," Alona said, smiling and cocking her head so that the whole long fall of her hair tumbled to one side.

"I like your hair down like that," Cassie said. In retaliation, Alona reached back and gathered it into a pony tail, which she held with one hand until they were inside the shop, where she secured it with a clasp from one of the display cases. Only then did she notice that Cassie didn't have a single earring in either of her ears, which wasn't like her.

"Well, what can I do for the truant?" Alona said. "Just want to look? Or are you planning to fill up those empty holes?"

"Actually, I wanted another hole pierced—here," Cassie said. She pointed to the cartilage high above her right earlobe, which was the first available spot. There were three holes in the lobe itself and two more in the lower part of the cartilage. Alona had told Cassie when she pierced the last one that she absolutely wouldn't do any more.

"Honey, you know I can't."

"They told me at the mall some people get as many as eight. This would only make six."

"I see they didn't offer to do it for you at the mall," Alona said.

"I didn't ask."

"I'll bet!" Alona smiled again, and Cassie did, too.

"This is the last one I'll ask you for. After this, I'll stop."

"Why not do the other side instead?" Alona lifted a strand of honey-colored hair to confirm that Cassie's left ear still had only two puncture marks.

"That's not the look I want," Cassie said.

"Yes, but with so many in the right ear—you could get an infection."

"I never did before."

Being in the strange mood that always came after the dream, Alona didn't want to argue. She felt too vulnerable. She could just imagine Cassie getting one of those infections high up on the cartilage, the kind that could settle in no matter how sterile the earrings and the equipment. She could just imagine Cassie's father, the county commissioner, taking it into his mind to sue her. It made no more sense than thinking truant officers were likely to charge in, but in her present mood, she couldn't help it. Anyway, Elliott was sure to drop in any time to finish their argument. All she needed was a teen-aged truant in the shop.

Cassie was scooping up beads from one of the small bins Alona had set around the store. There were different-sized beads in some of the bins, and ribbons or tiny shells in others, to encourage customers to choose combinations for custom-made earrings. Cassie let a handful of yellow beads run through her fingers. She seemed in no hurry to leave.

"How long were you sitting out there on my doorstep anyway?" Alona asked.

"Not long."

"How'd you get there?"

"I walked over the drawbridge from the beach."

Alona could believe it. She had spent her younger days walking over that bridge every time she wanted to go to the beach, because her grandmother, Emma, wouldn't drive her. Emma loved the ocean but was deathly afraid of bridges. She never ventured over to Festival Beach unless one of her friends took her, and then she closed her eyes and hunched down in the back seat of the car. Nowadays, almost no one went over the drawbridge by foot because of the traffic, but Alona felt a brief kinship with Cassie as she imagined her standing on the walkway above the green water, her feet picking up the vibrations of cars speeding across the metal grid. She saw Cassie buying a sweet roll at one of the fast-food places that had sprung up everywhere, then depositing herself on Alona's steps to wait for her to open. Jewels was in one of the remodeled cottages soon to be torn down to make way for a shopping center. It was close to the road but surrounded by enough shrubbery to let Cassie sit for an hour without drawing attention.

"Did you see the turquoise?" Alona asked, pointing down into one of the cases.

Alona didn't keep much in the way of gemstones, what with the cost of inventory, but she had a few things for tourists and matrons. Cassie's mother occasionally bought her an expensive gift, usually in the off-season (for which Alona was grateful) and always in a close-to-the-ear style. Otherwise, Cassie adorned her right ear with the longest, loopiest earring she could find and her left ear with another, not matching (she never wore a pair) but equally long. She filled the other holes with studs or tiny specks of jewel. "Long but light," Cassie would demand. And Alona was glad enough to oblige.

She steered the girl toward inexpensive ribbons and feathers, or bits of rose quartz, which were useful for the healing and meditation she sensed the girl might need. She tried to guide Cassie away from stones like opals, which anyone who studied gemstones knew were too distracting for teen-agers.

Though she liked to be accommodating, today, after her fight with Elliott and her dream, Alona wanted Cassie out.

Last night, as always, the dream had lasted no more than a minute before it woke her up. She saw herself as if on a movie screen, walking toward herself. Her hair was flowing in a thick mane behind her, lit by a great shining light. She walked toward herself until the light got so unpleasantly bright that it woke her. That was it. The entire dream. Always. Not something she could convince her friends was the worst thing that ever happened to her, but in a way, it was.

She'd started having the dream when she was six, right before her mama, Dottie, went off to work in Raleigh and left her with Emma. At first, she thought she was dreaming about the kiss of God, because she knew that if God kissed you, it would feel like light. But later, she changed her mind because of the things that often happened. She had the dream before she graduated from high school and before Emma got sick; she had it twice before she met Elliott. Looking back, she saw she'd had the dream before just about every major event in her life.

She didn't remember exactly when she'd stopped believing the dream was about the kiss of God and begun to regard it as a nightmare. She hated waking with her mouth dry and her skin unnaturally hot. She hated feeling each dream was a milestone on a journey to some secret destination. She didn't know where she was going and so had no power to alter the route or slow herself down. That was what frightened her. She was getting closer all the time to some unknown place she might not even want to visit.

"Cassie, why'd you cut school?" Alona asked.

"I wanted to get my ear pierced," Cassie said. "Please."

She sounded desperate. She sat down on the chair by the door, where customers could wait while Alona custom-made their earrings. A stack of magazines was piled on an adjacent table so clients could be comfortable while she was working. Alona thought this was a nice touch, unusual for a jewelry store.

Cassie, seeing that Alona was not going to rush for her piercing gun, flipped through a magazine and picked up another. She looked as if she might stay there for hours, reading and staring out at cars until school was over. Alona didn't see how she could get any work done with things this way, not today.

"How about if I drive you to school? You won't miss all that much. I could close up for a while this early."

"No thanks."

Cassie didn't seem about to budge. She went through the whole stack of magazines and settled on what looked like one of those copies of *Time* or *Newsweek* Alona brought in when Elliott finished with them. Cassie stared at the cover and then turned to a page inside. Alona wouldn't have thought a news magazine could hold Cassie's interest, but the article seemed to absorb her. The solidity of the girl reading over there made the idea of truant officers grow larger in Alona's mind. She felt she had to get Cassie out, whatever it took.

Alona's worktable was covered with strands of wire, piles of beads, earring backs and other findings, a glue gun, several sizes of tweezers. She selected a strand of silver and twisted it into an uneven triangle, long and thin. She threaded a chunk of turquoise onto the wire, pushing it into the middle, securing it with a twist of her fingers. She held it out, examining it. It looked understated and dramatic. Alona looped the other end of the silver into a hook that could go through a pierced ear, letting the turquoise float free between the strands of metal.

"Come here," she said to Cassie, holding the earring aloft.

The girl was so engrossed in the magazine that she took a moment to look up. Her mood seemed to have grown less desperate. Cassie came to the work table, curious but still apparently distracted, still holding the magazine in her hand. Alona pushed Cassie's hair back and fastened the earring in place. From the display case, she chose four tiny turquoise studs, which she secured in the other holes in Cassie's right ear. This was costing her a fortune, but maybe it would be worth it. Turquoise was the stone of friendship. It might rid her of Cassie Ashby for now without costing her the girl's business. For the left ear, Alona chose a single turquoise stone and a silver stud.

"A gift," she said, handing Cassie a mirror.

"Is this a bribe?" the girl asked, looking at herself.

"This is a bribe," Alona told her.

Cassie didn't look as overwhelmed as Alona had hoped. "Can I have this, too?" the girl asked, holding up the magazine she'd been reading.

It was an old *Newsweek* with a drawing of a half-naked black woman on the front, kinky hair hanging down her back and some jungly trees behind her. "The real Eve?" the blurb on the cover read.

"Sure," Alona said. If she'd known the magazine would intrigue the girl so, she'd have offered it in the first place and kept the turquoise to herself. "I'll drive you to school," she added, turning the OPEN sign on the front of the shop to CLOSED.

In the car, Alona relaxed. A tunnel of old oaks arched above them, making the air seem a little cooler. The images of truant officers and lawsuits over ear infections dimmed. Alona began to feel almost magnanimous.

"Boy problems?" she asked. Cassie was a pretty girl—and anyhow, why else would she cut school?

"Not the kind of boy problems you think," Cassie said.

"Is there more than one kind?"

"If you're into heavy sex, probably not. If you're into being raised as the all-time vestal virgin Southern belle Azalea Princess, there are several."

"You want to fill me in on how this relates to pierced ears and cutting school?"

Cassie clutched the rolled-up magazine in her hand and looked out the window.

"Let me guess. The person raising the vestal virgin Southern belle happens to be your stepfather, and he doesn't like pierced ears." This would explain why the girl's mother always bought subdued pieces in precious metals her daughter couldn't resist.

"Only on gypsies," Cassie said.

"Ahh." In that case, Alona's notion might be right after all, that the commissioner would sue her over an earlobe infection. On television, he seemed friendly and forgiving, but you could never predict. She drove a little faster toward Central High.

"I'm trying to help out a friend," Cassie said. "Let's just say I'm not being encouraged."

"Hmmm." Alona didn't want to take a stand against parents, especially not a mother who bought jewelry.

"An *innocent* friend," Cassie continued, "being accused of doing something he didn't do."

"I see." Cheating? Stealing? Sex? Probably sex, since that would certainly be upsetting to a politician in an election year. Perhaps Cassie's friend had been accused of getting someone pregnant. The commissioner wouldn't want Cassie involved in any attendant publicity.

"So you were going to take comfort in mutilating your ear a little more," Alona said.

"I don't think of it as mutilation." Cassie looked sullen. "I don't see how you can make your living designing earrings and talk about pierced ears as mutilation."

The girl had a point. They came out of the tunnel of oaks into a raw stretch of treeless road. Suddenly there was far too much sunlight.

"But you know what?" Alona forced herself to say. "Parents usually understand better than you think." She had no idea if this was true. They turned onto Bishop Street, a straight shot to the school. She would be free in less than five minutes.

Cassie exhaled so completely it sounded like someone had stuck a pin in her. She looked like she might faint or throw up before they got there.

They were driving past the slummy low-rise housing project, Bishop Gardens—a joke of a name. No green anywhere, just sand and cinderblock and pavement. It was ten-thirty in the morning, and black men were gathered on the sidewalk in groups of two or three, most so young and strong-looking they surely could have been working. The sun was shining down with dizzying fierceness. They were probably doing drugs. This was no place to pull over for someone to be sick.

Then Cassie unrolled the magazine and spread it on her lap, tracing the outline of the black lady's kinky hair with her finger. The activity seemed to calm her. She turned a little less gray.

"You'll see going to school was the right thing after all," Alona said forcefully.

"Yes. I suppose."

A light turned red. They had to stop directly under the gaze of the loitering men, each one looking so menacing that Alona understood why when there was a murder in Festival, it was usually black men killing other blacks. The men didn't look exactly as if they would burst into her car, but their expressions were unsettling, and worse, they reminded her of something. Or maybe this was the effect of the strange mood the dream had put her in.

The sun was relentless. Her sunglasses were back at the shop. She squinted into the glare. You wouldn't think light could be so troublesome. Maybe people in the projects had so much misery because this brightness hit them the minute they walked outside. Maybe it kept them from thinking straight, from exploring alternatives to standing on the corners. She felt muddled from it herself.

"You'll see. This will turn out to be nothing more than the usual run of parent and boy problems," Alona said to Cassie when the light turned green and she was flooded with the freedom of being able to step on the gas.

Immediately she was sorry for her choice of words. *Boy problems* reminded her of her troubles with Elliott.

The speed limit was twenty-five, but she accelerated to forty.

Now that she thought of it, those staring men on the corner put her in mind of Elliott—or rather, of the heavy-lidded look on his face last night when she told him she was too tired to talk anymore. He got that look a lot lately, and it always made her think he was going to punch her. Of course, he never did; Elliott was not a violent man. He just gazed at her mutely. Much as Alona hated that, if she'd known she was going to have the dream last night, she would have tolerated it. She would have stayed awake to finish their argument, no matter how long it took or how Elliott stared. If they'd finished the fight and made love as usual, she would have been too tired to dream.

The school was finally in front of them, half a block away.

"You're going to have to sign me in," Cassie said.

"What do you mean, sign you in?"

"I'm over two hours late. I need an excuse. You can tell them you're my aunt and you took me to the dentist."

"After I bribed you to leave my store? After I loaded you down with fifty dollars' worth of turquoise and silver?" It wasn't actually fifty dollars' worth, but she probably wouldn't know.

"They won't let me in without an excuse," she said.

"Fat chance."

Cassie's face was smooth and calm. The *Newsweek* was clutched in her hand, the earrings gleamed in her ears. Alona sighed and figured what the hell, she was getting rid of her. She pulled into a visitor's space.

"I'm doing this on the condition that you never ask for any more holes in either ear. The subject should never come up, even in a whisper."

"Never," Cassie agreed.

◆   ◆   ◆

Alona hadn't been inside Central High for years. Each summer, vandals broke the windows and scribbled graffiti on the old brown brick, and each year, the damage was repaired a few days before the semester began—never sooner, because of the surrounding public housing and high crime rate. Right now, in early fall, the exterior bricks looked newly washed.

Inside, the cinderblock hallways had been painted a cheerful yellow. Cassie led Alona down the corridor into the attendance office, where a reception area led to the vice principals' offices. Usually the principal was white and the vice principals black, partly for racial balance but mostly because the vice principals had to handle the discipline problems. In this neighborhood, the delinquents were black.

"This is my aunt. She wants to check me in," Cassie said to a woman sitting behind the counter.

The girl was beginning to look nervous, which made Alona nervous, too. Maybe Cassie was in trouble, and it had been a mistake to come here. The attendance woman only thrust a pad across the counter, with columns for Cassie's name, Alona's initials, and the reason for tardiness.

A man—white, not black—emerged from one of the assistant principals' offices. He would have been good-looking except that part of his right eyebrow was missing—a spot right in the middle which made him look threatening. He was broad as well as tall, and he wore a short-sleeved dress shirt but no tie or jacket, as if he expected to be noticed for his strength and not his mode of dress.

"I thought you chickened out," he said to Cassie. It seemed an odd thing for a vice principal to say.

Cassie grimaced. The man got a smile in his eyes, not on his lips, as if he were enjoying her discomfort.

"This is my aunt," Cassie said.

He turned to Alona, still with the amusement in his eyes. He seemed to know at once Alona could not be the girl's aunt and to be waiting to see what kind of lie Alona would tell in Cassie's defense. He seemed to see right through her—to be expecting something as feeble, as foolish, as Cassie's own story. The patience in his gaze told her catching a grownup in a lie would be twice as entertaining as catching a kid.

She thought about lying for two or three seconds. She felt perfectly lucid, not at all foggy as she'd been outside in the sun.

On the one hand, she saw a hundred dollars of profit, maybe more, going out the window—in the off-season, too—if Cassie got riled at her. On the other hand, the contempt that would come to the assistant principal's eyes if she lied for the girl more than balanced the loss of money.

"I'm not her aunt," she said finally. "I found her sitting in front of my shop this morning, so I drove her in."

The man got serious. He stuck his hand out to shake hers. "Jordan Edge," he said.

His hand was warm and dry. He smelled like shaving lotion.

"Alona Wand." Her hand felt so warm inside his that a current might have been running through it. His shaving lotion was stronger than Elliott's, so spicy it went straight to Alona's brain. She wasn't even sure her voice sounded normal, what with his warm hand and his scent and his fierce face.

She didn't expect to react that way. She thought she'd outgrown being the type who could barely touch a man without being affected by it. Years before, if she ran into some guy from school who gave her a friendly hug, it would send her reeling. Even if he was ugly or fat, she could hardly keep from imagining herself belly to belly with him, kissing and hugging for real.

She didn't often give in to her impulse, because she knew the trouble it could cause. Her own mother had been an unmarried teen-ager when Alona was born. When Elliott came along, offering both sex and security, Alona could hardly believe her luck. And now, married and working in her shop, she seldom talked to other men at all, much less touched them. It was mostly women who came in for earrings. Whole days went by when the only males she noticed besides Elliott were the teen-aged baggers in the Food Lion.

But this Jordan Edge was putting her off balance with his big, warm palm engulfing hers like a blanket. Looking down at their two hands, she noticed that her fingers, next to his, seemed impossibly slender and delicate. Then she noticed that the back of his hand was covered with brown hair, except for one round spot where no hair grew at all—a perfectly smooth scar as big as a quarter. Such a thing should have been ugly, but it wasn't, not like the spot on his eyebrow. No, this place was so smooth she imagined it'd feel just like silk. She was already moving her left hand toward it, to touch it, when she caught herself.

"Come into my office," Jordan Edge said, turning his attention to the girl. Then, looking at Alona again, "Thanks for bringing her in."

Alona smiled at him. "I don't know what this is worth," she said, "but whatever it is, Cassie isn't chicken. If she was, she'd have gone to the beach and not to my shop."

Her hair was still in the clip she'd put in before, but she could feel it coming loose a little and hanging hot against her neck. Jordan Edge was staring at it. The way he was looking at her, her hair might have been as bright as it was in the dream.

◆　◆　◆

Elliott was sitting in front of the store when she got back. He was dressed in his gray suit, ready to go to work, looking uncomfortable in the heat but drinking hot coffee from a carry-out paper cup all the same.

"I thought you'd flown the coop," he said.

Even at the end of summer, his face always looked pale—a sort of pale responsible look, like a doctor or a banker, which she'd liked in the beginning but which seemed too serious now.

She got out her key and opened the shop again. She'd turned off the air conditioning a week ago and vowed to be finished with it until spring, but the store seemed unbearably dark and musty with Elliott in the doorway. There was not enough air in the place for both of them to breathe. She flipped the air conditioner back on.

Elliott sat on the tall stool she used for piercing ears. "I thought it might be nice to continue our discussion. The topic was having a baby, if you recall," he said sarcastically. "I thought we might finish up before I have to be at work." He was manager of Custom-Fit Shoes in the mall, and always had to be there the busiest hours, usually noon to nine.

"I thought we *were* finished."

"Only because you fell asleep," Elliott said. The heavy lidded-expression came to his face again, like the look on the black men's faces in Bishop Gardens. Alona turned away, gazing at the bins of beads. Women were supposed to want babies and men not, so she didn't know what he expected her to say.

"I'm not trying to push you," Elliott said. "I'm just pointing out that since you're about to lose the building—" he gestured around at the walls of the shop, "—maybe this would be a good time to consider living a more normal kind of life."

"And I'm saying there's nothing abnormal about the life we live now."

"You're saying you don't want children."

"I'm saying not yet."

"It's been three years."

Alona scooped up a bunch of tiny shells with holes in them and sat down at the worktable, threading them through strands of metal. She twisted the metal into braids and loops, making a shell-studded string.

"With Emma sick when we got married, those weren't exactly normal circumstances. I wanted you to have time to get over it. But now...things are different. We're older."

Older! That was the problem exactly! The very idea of being somebody's mother made her feel old. Elliott took a sip of coffee from his paper cup, as if he needed caffeine and sugar to speed him up, when she herself had something fast and bubbly running through her veins, zipping her along. She would be old before she knew it, even without a baby to remind her. No! She intended to make collages, draw designs, watch shapes form beneath her fingers. She intended this part of her life to last until she had no desire for it anymore. And maybe then she would think about having a baby and maybe not.

Or else it was her dream making her feel this way, always jolting her closer to that destination she sensed in the eerie light that shone on her hair. No matter. Watching Elliott sit there trying to plan her life, she had the conviction that if she had a baby just because he wanted her to, she'd be starting something she couldn't possibly complete.

"Elliott, couldn't we just let it go for a while?"

He sat back in the high stool until he almost tipped it over.

"For a while," he said. A smile began to play at the edges of his mouth. "But keep in mind that I may have to consider starting my family with Sally Battle instead."

Maybe it was the air conditioning, but a wave of such relief washed over Alona that she could breathe easier than she had all day. They never joked about Sally Battle when they were fighting. She looked up from the earring she was twisting together.

"Sure, make your move," she said. "Just remember, I'm a respectable woman, and Sally Battle is your basic floozy. You said as much yourself."

"I'd never say a fine woman like Sally Battle was a floozy."

"You said she hardly ever made a sale to a female customer. It seems to me that's because fat ladies don't relate to a floozy. Otherwise they wouldn't mind. It's true." It was, in a way. The shoes at Custom-Fit came in sizes and widths either too big or too small for the regular stores to carry, so most of the customers were either abnormally tall or short or fat.

Elliott considered this. "Flooze, maybe, but that big white bosom..."

"Big white bosom and round hips and a fat stomach to match," Alona said. She kept her eyes down on the shells so Elliott wouldn't see she was smiling. He was cute when he tried to tell her other women were out there waiting for him, tried to make Alona argue how inferior these other women were, to remember she and Elliott were happy in their...the term that came to her was *cocoon*.

Cocoon! Even in the middle of joking, he looked so serious. He was sitting right where the women sat while she sterilized their ears. He was as white-lipped and tight as they were before she got out the piercing gun and had it over with before they knew what happened.

"You ought to let me pierce your ear," she said. "Then maybe you wouldn't look so grim all the time. You wouldn't look like somebody who's about to fit people with sensible black shoes."

"No thanks. I'll stick to wedding rings and gold chains."

He'd never worn a gold chain in his life. She examined the earring she was making, skinny braids of silver and gold wire set at angles to each other, dotted at intervals with tiny white shells. It was a miniature mobile, six inches long, maybe more.

Elliott put his coffee cup on the display case. She supposed the argument was over and she had won, but suddenly she was exhausted, and not just from last night's lost sleep. She hadn't expected marriage to be so full of tension.

Even when she was little, she'd admired men. She'd loved their whiskers and muscular arms and the way they stared at her hair. Emma said it was the reddish color that made people take notice, changing with every light, but Alona knew it was the length. When Emma made her have it trimmed, Alona worried herself sick that boys might not look at her the same way—though of course they did. With all those strong feelings about men and with her determination not to get into trouble the way her mother had, Alona had thought when Elliott came along that he was everything she was looking for, that married life would be pure bliss.

Now he stepped around the counter to where she was sitting. The heavy-lidded look was still on his face. Alona didn't turn to him but instead strung a final shell onto the earring she was making. She took the gold hoop out of her right ear and put the new earring in. It came all the way down to her shoulder. She knew by the feel of it she'd never sell it to anyone else.

The clip in her hair was still askew, the way it had been in the attendance office at the school. Elliott undid it and let her hair fall free. He scrunched a lock of it in his hand, a gesture of affection. He didn't seem upset anymore, so the lidded look couldn't be anger. Still, it made her uneasy. She couldn't help thinking of the vice principal and of the amusement in his eyes when he thought he might catch her in a lie. It was nice to see a man enjoy himself, even at her expense. Even nicer if he stared at her the way Jordan Edge had done.

"Alona," Elliott said.

He kissed her and she kissed him back. She never let herself do this until they were finished fighting because she couldn't argue effectively after she'd been kissed.

When she opened her eyes and stared into the dark heaviness all over Elliott's face, she recognized it for the first time for what it was. Why, it had nothing to do with those staring men at Bishop Gardens; it was something else entirely. She'd recognized it in movies but never in her own husband. It was the look couples wore before and after they embraced—and not just desire, either. The heavy lidded look was love.

Her ear began to burn, and her neck, every place the new earring touched. All this time, Elliott had been talking to her, wanting to make up with her, wanting her to have his baby, all because of love. And all this time she'd been making an earring designed to get men to look at her—not Elliott, either, but men like Jordan Edge.

FOUR

*T*he next time we worked a fire together, I told Fetzer I had no way of knowing the woman was married.

Fetzer said, "What do you mean, 'no way'? You shook hands with her, you could have noticed if she was wearing a ring."

"I shake hands with twenty, thirty relatives a week. I don't notice rings—it's all I can do to remember their names."

The fact is, I didn't catch her name at all. What had distracted me was the kid, Cassie, coming into school just when I'd decided she was cutting. She was two hours late, wearing dress-up earrings appropriate for the prom, carrying a magazine rolled up tight in her fist as if she'd been fending off dogs. It occurred to me that I was doing neither the bus driver nor Molly Sampson any favor by allowing a truant to testify just because I'd been annoyed with Andy Wilson after yesterday's fire. I was mulling this over when Cassie's lady friend introduced herself. I didn't catch her name, just that the kid had ended up in her shop that morning and now here they were. All this as we were shaking hands, and Fetzer thinks I should have noticed if the woman was wearing a ring.

In midhandshake, the woman's eyes fell from my face— where I assume she'd been studying my misshapen eyebrow— to the scar on my hand. Her gaze homed in on it, and while our right hands were still clutched together her left came up slowly, as if to touch and examine it with a forefinger. This in a fraction of a second. Then she stopped the hand in midair and finally drew it back. That's when I actually noticed her. I cut off the handshake and took a look. She was in her twenties, attractive, wearing a full denim skirt and sandals. Long hair caught up in a clip that wasn't holding, strands escaping down her neck. Reddish gold, wavy. Great hair.

I told Cassie to come into my office, already trying to recall what the woman said her name was, coming up with nothing. As Fetzer would say: "Always the egomaniac, Jordan, even when it comes to romance. If she hadn't almost touched you, would you have looked at her twice?" Maybe not, but it happened.

Cassie sat down across from my desk, hanging onto that magazine the way you'd clutch at something if it was all they gave you while they were setting a broken bone.

"Change of heart?" I asked her.

"No. Why would you think that?"

"Cutting school, for starters."

"I woke up late. I missed the bus." She felt the tip of her earlobe with an index finger, running it over all the little turquoise studs.

"You always come in late without any books?" I asked.

"I had my mind on getting a ride. I walked across the drawbridge. I knew I could get a ride in if I went to her store."

Her store. Not "a ride in with Sally," "a ride with Anne," just "her store." By now a whole string of names for the woman was dancing through my head. Alexi? Arlene? An "A" name, I thought, but with more than one syllable.

"Mrs. Sampson will be coming down any minute to hear what you have to say," I told her.

"Fine." Defiant.

But when Molly Sampson actually came in, Cassie's bravado evaporated. Molly was fifty-five years old, a white-haired drill sergeant with a voice deeper than most men's. It served her well in her dealings with the drivers, most of whom were not yet out of their teens. Molly remained standing while Cassie sat—a tactic I liked to use myself.

"Okay, Cassie, let's hear what you have to say," Molly boomed.

Cassie tried to speak, but she turned the dead pale color that in freshman girls often precedes fainting. She squeezed the magazine in her hand so hard her knuckles looked like translucent marbles. Then, as if the pressure in her hand reminded her of something, she unrolled the magazine and stared down at the cover. Color returned to her face in a single rush. I couldn't see what she was looking at, but I assumed she had notes written there, cuing her what to say. I admired the presence of mind it took to prepare a crib sheet, and was grateful I wouldn't have to scrape her up from the floor. When she rolled up the magazine and began, she managed to repeat in almost every detail the story she'd told me the day before.

Though having one unsupported witness meant having essentially no witness at all, I sensed Molly was sympathetic toward Cassie's position. After all, Curley was jobless largely because the Carters were influential. And though the Carters weren't pressing charges, word of the accusation was out. No parent in Wright County would let Curley Johnson drive a child to school even if he agreed to castration.

When Cassie finished, Molly said, "You know, the most I can do is put this in the record. Nothing will really change except the paperwork. I hope you understand that."

"Why?"

"Because no one wanted this to go any farther, either the driver or the Carter family. No one wanted the police involved."

Mention of police brought a momentary stillness to Cassie's face. "You could offer Curley his job back," she said finally.

"It's very unlikely he would take it."

"But you could offer. It could be in the records that you tried."

Molly said nothing.

"I bet if there was something about this in the papers, you'd try." She paused briefly. "I might call the paper myself."

Molly looked at me. It occurred to me then that it didn't matter to the girl whether the bus driver got his job back or not, only that the story was made public—*ASHBY'S DAUGHTER DEFENDS BLACK DRIVER IN MOLESTATION CASE.* Apparently Cassie was so angry with the stepfather that she intended to embarrass him publicly. A politician's daughter taking up for a black man three weeks before the election would work pretty well. I imagined it would cost him more votes than he'd care to give up. I also thought Cassie Ashby was as much a rich little shit as Kyle Carter, and that the bus driver deserved better than he was being offered.

"You think calling the paper will help get Curley's job back?" I asked Cassie.

"Why wouldn't it?"

"Because it'll throw suspicion on him," I said.

"That doesn't make any sense." She looked puzzled.

"Listen, Cassie, I don't know what game you're playing or with whom," I said, "but right now, all anybody knows about Curley Johnson is that there's a rumor—a *rumor*, hear?—that he quit his job because he was accused of messing around with a white boy. Nobody knows anything for sure."

She didn't look quite convinced, but the morning was almost gone, I didn't have the shopkeeper lady's name, and I wanted a swift end to our conference.

"Two weeks from now, they still won't know whether he's guilty, and by then they won't care, either," I told her. "You call the paper, and it'll be a whole different thing. Once it's public— even if he's completely innocent—what kind of job do you think he's going to be able to get? You think anyone's going to hire him to drive buses or do anything else?"

"He's right," Molly told her.

Cassie's mouth opened a little and her lips began to look chapped, as if the revelation was oxidizing her skin.

"I think I'll leave the two of you," Molly said, and to Cassie, "I'll put what you said in his record."

Cassie sat motionless as I wrote out a pass to get her into her third-period class.

"The woman who brought you here this morning—what's her name?" I asked, holding the pass casually aloft.

"Alona."

Alona. I'd been right. An "A" name. More than one syllable.

"What kind of store does she have?"

"An earring store mostly. It's called Jewels," she said. "It's just on the town side of the drawbridge. Not far from my house." Defensive again. Good.

I handed her the pass.

Alona. I liked it. Not a name you heard every day. Not like Mary Beth.

As Fetzer often pointed out, it wasn't really the name *Mary Beth* that bothered me those three years we were together. There were deeper troubles behind my turning Mary Beth first into Marta and then Marta the Bitch. But if I had it to do again, I'm not sure it would be different.

"Every third female in North Carolina must be named Mary Beth," I teased her early on. "Didn't you ever wish for something exotic?"

"Like what?"

"Like... Marta." It was the first thing that popped into my mind. She laughed. Marta stuck. It didn't seem so terrible.

Marta the Bitch came later. She'd moved in by then, and there were two fires in a week, both in the middle of the night. I was up, dressing, and she was murmuring from the bed.

"Honestly, Jordan, I think you're really one of those locker-room types who keeps a woman but really prefers hanging with the *boys.*" And later: "What do you *do* out there that makes it so all-consuming? How do you feel?" Her tone was disapproving, as if the way I felt at fires weren't lonely enough without my being quizzed afterward and made to feel guilty for going.

"You knew what you were getting when you moved in with me," I said. "Don't be Marta the Bitch."

Fetzer said don't push it. I said, "Fetzer, since when do you get off criticizing anybody for pushing it?" Fetzer had long ago eschewed the Laney family fortune in order to become a lumber salesman at Lowe's, and had gone through two marriages to women he thought would help him drop several social rungs from the one he'd been born into. For recreation, he fought fires and coached wrestling the way some men rode bulls, in an effort to reduce his life to a test of physical bravery.

So I said to him, "What's the big deal about Marta the Bitch? Same initials as Mary Beth, just a few different letters, so what, what can she do?"

"Well, she could move out is what she can do," he warned.

And eventually, after her inquiries grew more personal and my insults more pointed, she did move out. Though Mary Beth and I hadn't married, Fetzer refused to condone the split.

"You're more of a shit than I thought you were, Jordan," he told me, looking pained to say it. And maybe it was true. But I couldn't have spent my life calling some prying woman Mary Beth.

By contrast, the name Alona appealed to me immediately.

I had no further time to dwell on it, though. A locker had been broken into and a case of M&Ms a student was selling for band had been stolen. At a school like Central, you don't leave anything valuable in a locker. There was an incident in the hallway, a shouting and pushing contest between two of the Bishop Gardens boys I have privately termed The Trash. After lunch, at which I handled the usual disruptions, a student was sent down for accusing the typing teacher of being gay. I dealt out the required detention. I spent my required hour pacing the hallways with my walkie-talkie, a policy that was the brainchild of Bob McRae, the principal, though it had yet to make the lockers safe for storage or the halls safe for students. When school was over, I monitored the parking lot as several hundred hormone-crazed drivers honked and braked their way into Bishop Street, five lanes of cars miraculously merging into two. Then I got into my Beretta and left through the back gate reserved for faculty and staff.

When I walked into Jewels, the stuffy air made me think of a nineteenth-century sweatshop, except that Alona was definitely twentieth-century, sitting at her workbench, three-quarters turned away from me with her hair hanging down her back, like a vision of a fully-clothed Lady Godiva.

First thing I said was, "Your air conditioning broken?" But when she looked up she was already smiling, just slightly, like the joke was on me, she'd been expecting me all the time.

"My grandmother thought it was self-indulgent to run the air conditioning after the first of October," she said. "Ever since she died, I feel guilty if I use it."

"You call not smothering the clientele self-indulgent?"

"Only if you value the family legacy." The sly smile again. "Anyway, there are no customers in October."

"What about me?"

She cocked her head so that her earring swung—a mobile of wires and tiny seashells even longer than the Ashby kids' feathers. "You looking for earrings for a lady friend?" she asked. "Or for yourself?"

The shells and wires almost touched her shoulder, drawing the eye to bare tanned skin, red-gold hair, a white tank top that fit tight across her chest, outlining small high breasts and darker circles of nipple. There was a sheen of sweat in the hollow of her throat, making the top look uncomfortable and constricting. When the image came to me of pulling the shirt up over all that hair, it was not just to get a look at her in the raw but also in the interest of setting her free.

"Actually, I had the air conditioner on this morning during a fight with my husband—to ease the emotional heat, you know? So I suppose I'm not completely true to my grandmother's legacy. Then Elliott left, and the place seemed noisy with the unit going."

Hear this, Fetzer: not until then did I know she was married. I had the feeling she mentioned the husband to taunt me.

I noticed a stack of magazines on a table by the door, and saw a way to switch the topic to business.

"I was curious," I said, "about the magazine your little friend was clutching in her fist like a talisman. Did it come from there?"

"Yes. An old *Newsweek*. I wish I'd known she wanted it so much."

"Why?"

"Because I was trying to bribe her so she'd let me drive her to school." She gestured toward strands of silver on her work table and pointed out tiny chunks of turquoise in the case. I remembered the fancy earrings Cassie was wearing. "And then she picked up the magazine off that stack and started reading it, and I swear, I think that was the only thing she really wanted."

"*Newsweek?*"

"Not that I begrudge her either the magazine or the earrings," she added quickly. "I just wanted her out of here. I kept having visions of truant officers appearing on my doorstep."

"Truant officers?"

"Yeah, sure. The guys who come and haul you back to school." She lifted her hair off her neck to cool herself, then let it drop back heavily. The room was stifling.

"Nobody would actually go looking for her unless she'd been out a week," I said.

"Well, maybe I was paranoid because Elliott and I were fighting." Smiling. Dangling the fact of the husband before me again.

"Even if you were the kid's mother, all you'd get would be a phone call from the computer," I said.

"From a computer. Figures."

"This is the attendance office at Central High School," I said, mimicking the recording, "calling to inform you that your student missed one or more classes today."

"How personal. How caring." She gazed into the distance as if confirming to herself some truth she had long suspected. She had the half-asleep quality that in my experience usually means a woman, married or not, is on the prowl.

I tried to concentrate. "This *Newsweek.* Why'd she want it?"

"Haven't the faintest." She lifted her hair again and rearranged it. She couldn't keep her hands out of her hair.

"She kept looking at the cover," I said. "As if she had notes written there."

"I didn't see her make any notes. I doubt you could read notes on such a busy cover anyway. A drawing of Jane of the jungle, with all these trees and leaves behind her. Only Jane was black. The article was about how we all go back to some original black mother. Or something like that. I never actually read it." She narrowed her eyes at me. "She said she was defending some innocent friend. Some boy. I didn't understand exactly."

"A black bus driver."

"Oh. Well. Maybe some kind of black connection." Her earring swung when she moved; the tank top cut across her chest. A trickle of sweat ran down the side of her neck, pooling on her collar bone. I felt sweat on my own back, under my shirt. Heat was gathering all around us like a red circle. An ancient air conditioner sat gray and silent in the wall.

"Let's go someplace cooler, and I'll tell you the whole story," I said. I never meant to make this offer; it was forced out by the heat.

Her eyes widened. Gray eyes. Nice. She looked as if she'd been waiting for my invitation, was amused to see the form it had taken.

"What did you have in mind? A walk across the drawbridge in the rush hour? To catch the breeze from the water?"

"I was thinking more of Joyner Creek."

"No thank you. I've been there once or twice, and each time incurred the wrath of the security guards."

"That shows how long since you've been there. They haven't had a security guard since the place was sold. Anyway, they wouldn't bother you if you're with me. I live there."

"Sure."

"I do. In the caretaker's cottage."

"The caretaker's cottage. Really?" Still skeptical.

But it was true, and I suspected she was curious to see if I'd really take her there or elsewhere, and how I'd proceed with the seduction.

The Joyner place was one of the last big tracts of undeveloped land along the Intracoastal Waterway in that part of town—three hundred acres of pine forest, along with the ruins of the main house and the clearing for my cottage. Joyner Creek ran through the middle of the property and emptied into the Intracoastal. The estate had recently been sold to a developer who was rezoning it for a golf course and luxury housing. But rezoning could take months, and in the meantime, I lived on in the cottage I'd rented, which Marta had never liked because of its isolation, tucked into the woods a quarter of a mile from the Waterway, accessible only by an unpaved road. I had rented the cottage cheaply at first from the Joyners, who believed Central High's assistant principal might discourage wild beer parties in the woods or on the beach or creekside. The developer was letting me stay on until building could begin.

"All right," said Alona. "Show me."

The cottage was not five minutes' drive from Jewels. The road into the Joyner place paralleled the Intracoastal for a few hundred yards, then turned inland and split into two sections, one going back to my cottage, the other into the woods by the creek. Alona kept her hand on the car door, as if on guard against my spiriting her toward the cottage, so I carefully took the fork into the woods, bumping along on the hard-packed sand. There'd be time to get her to my house later, I reasoned. With regard to married women, my policy was that they, not I, had the obligation to be faithful to their husbands.

Most of the estate was pine and scrub oak, except along the creek, where stands of shade trees grew. I parked the car half a mile from the Intracoastal, and we walked along the creek bank. The soil was rich and black there, not the usual sand, and there was more than pine straw underfoot—tufts of grass and fallen leaves from the gray-barked trees that arched over the creek.

Though in town the heat had been unremitting, I judged that in the woods it would soon grow too cool for Alona's tank top. I'd wait until she shivered, then put my arm around her.

We spoke briefly about the Ashby kid defending the bus driver, then went on to vaguely personal matters—how Alona was going to lose her shop to developers and how I was going to lose my house. We walked along the creek bed and then away from it, into the flat sand, through the pines. She said I didn't look like an assistant principal, I was the wrong color. I told her they didn't promote me for my skin tone, they promoted me for wrapping a kid's balls in ice. Her hair moved when she laughed, catching the light that fell through the pine needles.

"It's true. He OD'd on downers and somebody'd called the ambulance, but his pulse was about stopped. They asked me for help because I had firefighter training. So I had them bring ice up from the cafeteria and I gave the kid a jump start until the medics came. Afterward, the authorities were very grateful."

She put a hand to the back of her neck, lifting her hair as she'd done earlier, then dropping it against her back. She was so small-boned that the hair seemed the weightiest part of her.

"If that's true—and I don't believe it for a minute—what happened to him then?"

"He lived. He's still out there somewhere, far as I know."

"And that's how you got your job." She seemed pleased to think I might be lying.

A strand of pine straw had lodged itself in her sandal. As she bent to pluck it from between her toes, her hair fell away to reveal the back of her neck, white and frail and delicate.

"It's not only how I got my job, it's why I didn't get fired. All this happened when I was in a tenuous position for other reasons entirely."

When she rose, I was close enough to feel the heat from her skin.

"They were going to fire you? I thought you had to commit a crime before you could get fired," she said.

"I didn't have tenure then. I was just a typing teacher, and the girls' basketball coach."

"Girls' basketball!"

"You think it's funny? We had two decent players on the team, and one was a ball hog who'd take it downcourt and never pass, just shoot, and not hit more than one in five. We were 0 and eleven in the middle of the season."

"Tragic," she said, walking on.

I guided her away from the creek. We would make a circle through the pines, all the time approaching the clearing where the main house had been. From there, it was a hundred yards to the trees that hid my cottage.

"Go ahead. Laugh. But a ball hog is frustrating. The wrestling coach is a friend of mine, Fetzer Laney, and I started handing her this motivational stuff Fetzer believes in. 'There's no "I" in team. No glory except in teamwork.' I set up a system where they had to pass twice before they could shoot. Hell, what did I know?"

Alona rubbed her knee as if to scratch a bug bite, lifting her skirt with the motion. I could see her ankle, part of her calf. I wanted to see the rest. I had to work to concentrate on my story.

"One game we were only one point down, and the ball hog took it down court three, maybe four times, and didn't pass once, just kept shooting and missing. So I called time out and gave her the devil. I said, 'Pass, Kristi, pass. Don't think you have to do it all, let them help you, remember there's no "I" in team.'"

"A regular Dean Smith," she said.

"Oh, I was." Bugs hummed in shafts of sunlight. The light came lower from the west, and soon it would be dusk. I wanted her in my cottage before she decided she ought to get home to the husband. "Finally, with two seconds left, she brought it down, and for the first time all season, she passed."

"And some other girl took the shot and missed it," Alona said, grinning.

I nodded. "Afterward, Kristi came up to me and said sweetly, 'It wasn't my fault coach. There's no "I" in team.' Cute, huh? You'd have been proud of me. I didn't punch her. All I said was, 'No, but there is a "U" in stupid.'"

Alona grinned. Wrinkles settled around her eyes when she smiled. A little welcome imperfection against the flawless hair.

"That's when I almost got fired," I said.

"Oh, Jordan. They wouldn't get rid of you for a small thing like that."

Jor-dan. A long first syllable.

"They wouldn't unless the kid cries to every counselor that you're trying to humiliate her and crush her self-esteem and have been all season. They wouldn't fire you unless the kid happens to live on Festival Beach. You forget what a *system* the system is." We skirted the ruins of the main house, moving back toward the creek where it bent and cut around behind my cottage. "Fortunately, the administration saw my heroism with the ice pack as more important than my mouth."

We were both considering my heroism. We almost walked into the snake before I saw it, a blacksnake hanging from a tree in front of us like a long slice of discarded tire. Alona was still absorbed in my story. I touched her elbow and guided her around the snake. I had not touched her before.

She stopped walking. I felt her recoil, though I was sure she'd been waiting for my move all that time. She turned and looked back at the tree.

The snake was long, five or six feet, though not very thick. I've seen them as big around as my fist. He was just hanging there, a long black rope. The sound Alona made was not an utterance, just an intake of breath. Any other woman would have turned to me, let me hold her against the danger. But this one held her breath all alone—not looking at me, not depending on me in any way, holding me outside of her somehow in a way I'd never seen any woman do before.

A second later, her mind must have caught up with her, she must have seen it was just a blacksnake, couldn't do her any harm, so she shivered a little and then said, sounding no more moved or upset than if she'd gotten pine straw between her toes again, "Christ. Enough walks in the woods for *me* today." And she started walking back toward the car.

That was the end of it. All that come-on, the bravado, the little jokes, and when she had the perfect excuse to let me protect her, take her back to my house for a drink to cool her off and some loving to keep her warm, she pulled back into herself like a wary crustacean. No apologies, nothing. I drove her back to her shop. She didn't go into the store but straight to her own car.

The last thing she did was call out, "I'll say one thing. That certainly cooled me off, Jordan Edge."

I told myself my policy toward married women hadn't changed. It was up to them. If they said no, so be it. But as I watched Alona drive off toward home, toward the husband she'd been fighting with that morning, I couldn't help wondering if in a moment of danger she'd let him get any closer to her than she'd let me when she was face-to-face with that snake. I didn't think so. I thought she probably held him apart from her, too, and retreated into the place where she was entirely single. In a way, she was no more attached than I was. Which made it a different game entirely.

FIVE

Cassie knew she never would have gotten through that day, much less the week, if it hadn't been for Black Eve. She'd gone to Jewels out of a pure failure of nerve, because though she didn't know exactly what Royal P.A. would do if she defended Curley Johnson in front of the bus coordinator, she knew it would be terrible. Her determination to act, back when Royal was so drunk and obnoxious, had deserted her. In fact, with Mr. Edge not seeming to believe her at first and then later telling her she'd get to see Mrs. Sampson the next morning, her stomach felt so jammed that she couldn't bring herself to get on the bus. All she could think about was having another hole pierced in her ear at Jewels.

And then, right on the cover of *Newsweek,* was Black Eve. Like a sign.

What the article said was this: In the course of evolution many different pre-humans died off until finally one female was so strong, genetically speaking, that her offspring lived on, down through the generations, to this very day. She was a woman who looked pretty much like anybody, if the cover of the magazine was any indication. And—get this—she was black.

Which meant that if some people couldn't say the letter "R," it certainly wasn't Black Eve's fault, because she was the mother of everybody—of Royal P.A. Ashby and Curley Johnson both. The way Cassie saw it, Royal would be hard put to punish her for defending her own blood kin.

Then Alona made her the long turquoise earring—the very one Cassie would have chosen for herself if she'd had both her grandmothers' birthday checks in her pocket. All she had to do was let Alona drive her to school. It was as if Black Eve were giving her a present.

Even so, she didn't think she could continue after she got a look at Mrs. Sampson, who might have been a football player or a cop. The sight of her standing there made Cassie's voice come out a croak. Black dots danced in front of her eyes. She was passing out. But she didn't. Instead, she thought, *Black Eve!* And she knew Black Eve was more than just a sketch on the cover of *Newsweek;* she was a living idea that would give her strength. Black Eve saw to it that her voice returned to normal. Black Eve made Mr. Edge forget to give her a detention for being late to school. Black Eve got the word out even after Mr. Edge explained why Cassie couldn't go to the newspaper. Why, by the time Cassie got on the afternoon bus, the whole school knew what she'd done. It couldn't have gotten around that fast without Black Eve helping.

When Kyle got on the bus, he leaned over and hissed, "Nigger lover." Cassie didn't care. As long as everybody knew she'd defended Curley, Royal's downfall was assured. They would assume Royal shared Cassie's views. They would vote for somebody else.

Afraid as she was of what she'd be in for when Royal and Betty found out, it was still a little disappointing that the house was empty when she got home. Her mother didn't show up for an hour, breezing through the front door in a silk dress and good pearls and the dinner ring Royal had given her—clothes she wore in the daytime only when she was campaigning.

"Oh good, you're home," was all Betty said. "Don't forget the political forum tonight. I want to be a little early. They always get shots of the candidates' families for the eleven o'clock news."

Betty paused to examine her newly frosted hair in the hallway mirror. "Wear something nice," she said, frowning at Cassie's reflection. "That one earring is too long. You know Royal doesn't like that. The little studs are pretty, though."

Cassie knew then that her mother hadn't noticed the earrings were new, or that they were genuine turquoise Cassie couldn't afford. Cassie might have stolen them, police might be on her trail, and all Betty cared about was Royal's possible disapproval. "I want us to make a nice showing, to show his family is supporting him," Betty said, as if they three of them would be doing something pleasant together. What a crock.

"I have an English test tomorrow," Cassie said. "I have to study tonight."

"You can study before we go. After all the times he's put himself out for you, sometimes you have to reciprocate."

"Oh, Mama. He never puts himself out for anything but himself."

"What about when you promised to take that friend of yours out on the boat that time? He canceled a meeting with the state leadership to take you out that day."

Cassie knew Royal would never cancel a meeting with the state leadership even if she were dying.

"Mama, that was three years ago. How can you bring up things from before he sold the boat?"

"Well, other things, then."

But it was as if Black Eve had made her mother mention that particular incident. Royal had taken Cassie out on the boat so her friend Lee Ann Pembroke could water-ski. He had made a big issue about his "sacrifice," even after Cassie pointed out she could take Lee Ann herself if Royal would just let her. Royal refused. He claimed there was too much boat traffic on the waterway as it was, without children driving boats. He thought there should be an age limit for operating what he called "water craft," the way there was an age limit for cars. At a time when Janet Biggs was taking her brothers out to fish in her family's Chris-Craft, Royal had yet to let Cassie handle the controls of his boat even once.

But having Royal chauffeur Lee Ann Pembroke up and down the waterway was nothing compared to what happened afterward. When Lee Ann finished skiing and got into the boat, Royal let the motor idle for a moment while he did the most obscene thing. *He took off his shirt.* "Hot," he said, looking up at the sun. His neck hung slack and his stomach settled into what looked like rolls of pale sausage. And the worst thing was, he had more body hair than any man alive. Curly salt-and-pepper hair grew on his chest and halfway down his back. Little tufts of it sprang up from his shoulders. He looked like a semievolved gorilla. Lee Ann averted her eyes. It was the most mortifying event of Cassie's life. Royal knew exactly what he was doing. He had a whole collection of striped knit shirts with open collars that he called his boating shirts. He often brought an extra one to change into in case the first one got wet. Cassie knew the only reason he was sitting there bare-chested in front of Lee Ann Pembroke was to gross her out and show his power over Cassie.

"Cassie, go up and study for your English test right now, and then get ready," Betty said. "I mean it."

Despite the trouble she was about to get into over Curley, Cassie couldn't keep her mouth shut. "Just because you've been campaigning for him all day doesn't mean everyone else wants to," she said.

"For your information, I haven't been campaigning. I just came in from a Garden Club meeting is all."

"Oh. Garden Club. Even better."

She hoped her mother caught the sarcasm. Women didn't join Festival Garden Club only out of an interest in flowers. They got in through legacies from older relatives who'd belonged. It was that exclusive. And all they did was listen to a lecture on plants once a month and have refreshments served from silver pots and trays. Cassie knew Betty belonged strictly because Royal's mother once had. She knew Betty wasn't even in the running for the grand reward of membership: having her garden on the Azalea Festival garden tour one year. Much as Betty dug and planted and fertilized, plants did not do well in the sand and salt spray of Festival Beach. Belonging to Garden Club was ridiculous.

"Don't tell me," Cassie said. "You planned the whole Azalea Festival. Not only do the Princesses get to wear hoop skirts this year, they get a special little rhinestone tiara and silk parasols with fringe all around for the sun."

She hoped her mother noticed how unappealing Cassie found the Azalea Festival. She hoped her determination not to be a Princess sank in before the matter even came up.

"It was just a committee report," Betty said. "The program itself was on sasanquas."

"Huh?"

"Sasanquas. A kind of camellia that blooms in the fall. The ones that smell good."

Betty turned to look out the window at raw patches of sand scarring the grass, at browning shrubs and a single pine tree misshapen by the wind. Betty didn't seem to see that Royal's political office prevented them from moving across the bridge to more fertile soil, that they were trapped out here forever.

"Cassie, I know you're not interested in discussing flowers. Please, honey. Go get ready."

And because Cassie saw her mother's genuine grief at the dying of her plants, she did.

◆　◆　◆

At City Hall, more people were milling around in the lobby than sitting inside the auditorium. Most of them were volunteers for candidates, holding signs and giving things away. Cassie took an emery board saying CLINE FOR REGISTRAR OF WILLS, figuring at worst she could get her nails in shape while the boring talks were going on. There were imprinted scratch pads, matchbooks, buttons, even a bowl of fortune cookies with the state senator's name on a slip of paper inside.

"You could fill a shopping cart with this garbage," Cassie said.

Betty looked thoughtful. "Royal got those litter bags that fit over the radio knob in your car," she said. "He thinks the psychological value...having that bag in the car with you every day right before the election...he thinks when it's actually time to vote, it's as if he's become part of your family."

"Oh gag, Mama." Cassie could picture people riding around in their cars with little white trash sacks hanging from their radios, reading ASHBY FOR COMMISSIONER.

"Really, honey. It sounds simple-minded but that's how it works."

"Why not barf bags?" she asked. "You get even closer to a barf bag."

"Cassie, hush," Betty said, and led her into the auditorium.

Each candidate was allotted three minutes to speak. If they weren't finished when time ran out, a gong sounded to stop them. This happened to one of the first speakers, whose face turned violet with humiliation. With all her heart, Cassie hoped Royal would get gonged. But he finished about a second before the time was up, unbuttoned the jacket of his navy blue suit, the one he usually saved for official funerals, and stepped away from the microphone. He looked as if he'd been doing this for years, which in fact he had.

He came down from the stage and conferred with Betty. Their expressions grew grim. Then Royal P.A. led Betty and Cassie out into the lobby, clutching Cassie's arm like a claw.

"The three of us need to have a little conference when we get home." He spoke through clenched teeth, all the while nodding to the crowd. Heavy as he was, he moved with snaky ease as he reached out to shake hands with constituents. For what seemed forever, the three of them stood in the lobby greeting people, grinning like cartoons.

◆   ◆   ◆

At home, Royal checked his watch to see how long it would be before he could admire himself on the eleven o'clock TV news. He motioned Cassie into his study. He loosened his collar but didn't stop to get a beer. Cassie clenched the *Newsweek* in her fist and sat beside Betty on the sofabed. Royal was behind his desk, his voice as dark as the suit he was wearing.

"Our concern, Cassie, is with your capacity for deception," he said.

"Capacity for deception?" she asked.

"Don't be coy. It doesn't become you."

Royal's Adam's apple pumped inside his red skin. She thought *redneck,* but decided it didn't apply because it referred to the back of a neck, like a sunburned mason or farmer.

"What did you expect?" she said. "I told you I knew Curley never touched Kyle."

She kept her gaze on his throat. *Chicken neck,* she thought. She'd never seen a live chicken up close, but Royal's neck was exactly what she imagined.

"You never told us you were a witness," he said.

"I tried to. You weren't in the frame of mind to hear it. You were too busy talking about the letter 'R.'"

"The point is," Royal said with painful slowness, "you did all this behind our backs. Told this story at school without consulting us. Which brings us back to your capacity for deception."

"If there was really something to discuss," Betty added softly, "even if you didn't want to talk to Royal, you could have mentioned it to me." Hurt in her eyes. "If you felt like you had to defend that black man..."

"Mama, he's not even a man. He's just a couple of years older than us. I'm not doing anything wrong. Nothing unethical. In fact, just the opposite."

"Royal feels," she said tentatively, "that if you really wanted to do some good, you would have spoken up sooner." She was twirling the dinner ring on her finger, garnets and tiny chips of diamonds. She watched her hands as she spoke. "He feels by the time the weekend passed—after the boy was fired—it was more an empty gesture. And particularly right now...with the campaign. When it could be so embarrassing."

"That's really it, isn't it? That it could be embarrassing?" It damn well better be embarrassing, she thought.

"Not just embarrassing for Royal. For you, too. Do you think the election is all we're concerned about?" She looked up for a second and then back down at the ring. "In fact, Royal's fear, Cassie, is that it's probably difficult for someone your age, being dragged into the middle of a campaign. The pressures that involves." Her voice grew fainter. "And I'm inclined to agree with him, honey."

The hair on Cassie's arm prickled. Betty's soft voice might have been a cube of ice rubbing across her skin. "Oh, come off it, Mama," she managed. "Two hours ago you couldn't wait to drag me to my third political function in a week."

Royal sat back in his chair, more sober than Cassie was used to seeing him. "After hearing today what you did," he began, "particularly hearing it from strangers at a political forum..."

Cassie wouldn't look at him. "What are you getting at, Mama?" she asked.

"It's not as if your mother and I haven't tried to avoid this," he continued, not waiting for Betty to answer, "but we think this particular incident...we've reached the point..."

"We thought maybe the best thing..." Betty added, "...in spite of the expense..."

Neither of them seemed to be able to speak in complete sentences.

"We thought you'd be better off going somewhere else to school," Royal finished bluntly.

"Somewhere else?"

"Somewhere...away," Betty said.

"You mean boarding school?" Once before, when she wasn't turning out as Royal expected, he'd suggested a prep school where she'd be away from Festival and "the existing tensions." Cassie wouldn't have minded particularly, but Betty had balked.

"We were thinking of Caitlin Academy," Royal said flatly.

"Caitlin Academy!" Throat tight now, worse than when she watched Royal P.A.'s neck. Her arms were freezing.

"Caitlin seems the appropriate choice," Royal said.

Cassie wasn't sure she could get enough air into her throat to utter another word. Caitlin Academy wasn't just boarding school, it was reform school. You went if you were from a good family but incorrigible, like Katie Venable, who'd actually stabbed one of her brothers in the hand.

"I don't believe it," she said finally.

Royal only shrugged. Betty examined her ring. Cassie had to sound calm if it killed her.

"I mean really. Sending me to Caitlin Academy just for defending Cousin Curley from wrongdoing."

"Cousin Curley?" Royal asked, distracted.

"Cousin. Yes. Blood kin."

"Your blood kin, maybe. Not mine," he said.

Cassie unrolled the *Newsweek* in her hand and held up the drawing of Black Eve in all her glory, with the green forest shining behind her. Surely Black Eve would help. "She's everybody's great-great-grandma, yours and Curley's both," she said. "Which makes him at least a cousin, don't you think?"

"Which avoids the issue, doesn't it?" Royal asked.

"It's true, though. We all descend from one original mother who was genetically stronger than the others. And she was black."

Royal snorted.

"You shouldn't dismiss it before you read it."

"Some bleeding heart comes up with a theory like that at least once a month," he said. But Cassie knew that though Royal went to Baptist-by-the-Sea every Sunday and sometimes Wednesday nights, in his everyday life he claimed to be scientific.

"It's not just a theory; there's proof." Her impulse was to thrust the magazine at him, but she knew better and set it on his desk. Her calm was slipping. Royal would send her to Caitlin Academy. He would tell people: "Yes, she did make up a story about that bus driver, but she was under a lot of stress at the time. Now her mother and I are getting her some help." Her mother and I. Help. The more Cassie protested, the more deranged she would sound. Her mother was actually going along with it.

She looked down at the cover of the magazine to hide the sudden mist that glazed her eyes. Black Eve was as blurry on the page as Cassie's thoughts were blurry in her mind. She felt the depth of their kinship. She was Black Eve's descendant, a slave girl with nappy hair who'd been sold, wrenched from her natural parents, her natural life. It was almost too much to bear. Then strength came to her as it had in Mr. Edge's office, traveling all the way from the beginning of history, from a woman so strong her children lived on to this day, black and white, with a few sick mutations like Royal. Her vision cleared. In the small hopeless downturns in the course of things, Black Eve seemed to be saying, sometimes the only strategy left was indifference. And when Cassie looked up, her eyes were dry.

Royal didn't even notice. He was checking his watch.

"Almost eleven," he said, starting out into the living room to turn on the TV.

The video clip of the forum showed Royal sitting among the other candidates while the announcer's voice summed up the issues. Cassie went up to bed before the news was over, afraid that otherwise, displeased with the coverage, he might make yet more dire pronouncements about her fate.

In the morning, the sofabed in Royal's study was pulled out and rumpled. The unimpressive TV clip must have left him "too wrought up" to sleep upstairs with Betty. The *Newsweek* was on the coffee table, so he must have read the article. Cassie hoped Black Eve had haunted him all night. Now he was sitting in the kitchen scanning the morning paper for political coverage. Betty, in her bathrobe, stood at the counter.

"The country sends ninety-eight percent of its elected officials back to office," she said reassuringly.

Royal nodded and read on. Of course there was no reason for him to be concerned, not now. In the eyes of his constituents, sending Cassie away would absolve him of any responsibility for her liberal tendencies. He didn't utter a word about Black Eve or Caitlin Academy or even Cassie's capacity for deception. He didn't have to. With Betty's help, he'd already exercised the ultimate test of his power—to cast her out. The ultimate victory. Cassie didn't think she could bear it.

♦ ♦ ♦

In the afternoon, the buses that carried students home from Central High lined up behind the school. When they were all loaded, they started their motors simultaneously, like cars at the Indy 500, and pulled out in a great yellow line. Once, Betty had parked in front of the buses to retrieve Cassie for a dentist appointment, and every student noticed, on every bus up and down the block. She was mortified. So when Brian Ivey drove his Escort hatchback to the front of the line, and came to the door saying, "I'm looking for Cassie Ashby," she swallowed her shock and shouldered her backpack as quickly as she could just to cut short the hot beam of everyone's attention.

"I thought riding the bus might be a little uncomfortable today," he said, putting his tanned hand on her shoulder and ushering her to his car. His hand felt enormous. She couldn't breathe well enough to refuse.

She slid into his passenger seat, meaning to thank him for the ride, but nothing came out of her mouth. She was a freshman and he was a college student. He was Tiffany's boyfriend. His hair was hot-combed back from his face and his eyes were so black she could only imagine them staring into Tiffany's blue ones, not into her own. They drove off, turning onto Bishop Street, the whole long line of buses following.

"I heard what you did," he said. "I thought it was gutsy. I knew when I saw you that day in Hardee's you were the gutsy type."

So. He liked the gutsy type. Tiffany was the gutsy type, too. Brian must have had another fight with her. This was Brian's way of getting back. Everyone on the bus would know he'd given Cassie a ride.

Brian was looking at her, not at the road. It was all she could do not to lower her gaze. Royal said as long as someone held your stare, you had to hold it back. Otherwise they would have the better of you. Brian smiled and Cassie did, too, and it seemed about an hour before he looked away.

She covered a pimple on her chin with her hand. That put her in an odd position. She felt she couldn't move. To avoid another staring contest with Brian, she studied his sneakers on the gas pedal. They were so clean they looked dressy.

"I had a psych quiz today," Brian said. "Ever heard of the hierarchy of needs?"

She shook her head without raising her eyes, and he began describing the class as if it were a natural thing for them to discuss. Maybe he was talking to make her feel comfortable. That was what Royal did: said things to get people off their guard, and then, *wham,* moved in to ask for their vote. But Brian probably wanted only vengeance against Tiffany. Oh well.

If Royal were home when they got there, he would be polite to Brian. No one on earth could be more courteous in public and then do such an about-face later. After Brian left, Royal would say something like, "Who's the olive?"—referring to Brian's dark complexion. To Royal, that automatically meant Mediterranean ancestry. Cassie would point out Brian was an Ivey, the son of the people who owned the Waterway Restaurant, where Royal always took company for dinner. She would point out Brian's family had been in North Carolina longer than Royal's, and that Royal served on committees with Brian's father all the time. Then, relieved as Royal would be to see Cassie with someone from the right background, he'd ground her for getting a ride home instead of taking the bus. "Just one more example of why you belong at Caitlin Academy," he'd say. Cassie saw this scene very clearly.

But no one was home when they got there.

"How about coming out to the beach with me then?" Brian asked, gesturing toward the back where his skim board lay.

Oh. He'd been on his way to the beach anyway.

She didn't understand the invitation. Tiffany never went to the beach—she didn't want to tan or risk sunburn. She wouldn't see them; she'd never know. This would be a private date. Royal wouldn't allow such a thing for two more years, and surely it would be impossible at Caitlin Academy.

"Sure," she said.

She debated putting on a bathing suit but changed into shorts and a top. She never swam in October because the water was cool even when the air was hot. No sense putting on something skimpy just to show off. Besides, girls with tans probably didn't appeal to Brian. Cassie was not at all black-and-white like Tiffany. She was shades of brown and beige this time of year, her skin a little darker than her dirty-blonde hair.

She sat on the beach while Brian rode the skim board. With a flick of his arm, he sent it skimming along the tiny waves at the shoreline, then ran after the board and jumped on. He went for twenty feet, thirty, and then did a three-sixty turn to stop, squatting low so as not to fall. She knew he was an athlete. He used to play soccer for Central High. On the edge of the waves against the clear sky, he looked solid, muscular. The sun brought out a hint of red in his dark hair. Only a true bigot like Royal P.A. Ashby would call Brian Ivey an olive.

After he was finished, Brian threw the board onto the beach, jumped into the waves and swam out beyond the breakers to wash off. When he came out of the ocean, he didn't shake the wetness off. He walked toward Cassie with a thousand drops of water clinging to him, mainly to the hair on his chest and legs. It was a normal amount of hair, nothing like Royal's excess, but because of its darkness, it seemed like a lot. Cassie moved away a little when he sat down close beside her, not so much to escape the wetness as the hair. She couldn't help it.

The tide was coming in and all the water birds were feeding, the brown pelicans and the gulls. It was too noisy to talk. Brian lay down on the towel and closed his eyes, letting the heat dry him off. Golden light picked out the places on his face where he'd have to shave tomorrow morning. Cassie didn't think she'd ever been this close to a boy who shaved. The closeness made her think of the dream where Brian had been rubbing her breast, only when she opened her eyes it was Kyle, not Brian. Of course, Brian hadn't had these whiskers in the dream. Just then, Brian's hand came up and rubbed Cassie's back. It was as if he knew she was thinking about rubbing.

"I have to get going," she said, standing up away from his hand. "I'll walk home. I can use the walk."

He laughed, as if he'd caught her. It wasn't an evil laugh like Royal's, but it did give her the shivers.

"Thanks for the ride," she said.

"My pleasure."

As she walked away, all Cassie could think about was Royal's long-ago trips to Baltimore, when she and her mother met him at the airport. Royal would put his arm around Betty as they walked to the car, massaging her shoulder. It always embarrassed Cassie, though she didn't know why. Now it seemed she'd been aware, somehow, that Royal was rubbing her mother's shoulder because it was the only part of her body he could massage, respectably, in a public airport.

She sensed Brian watching her as she walked off the beach, giving her a look as intense as Kyle's but less hostile. It was the kind of look that would make you feel powerful if you didn't want so much to put distance between yourself and the whiskers and the rubbing.

◆ ◆ ◆

She was surprised to find Brian waiting for her again the next day. This time he made less pretense of talking as they drove. He didn't go over the drawbridge. He turned onto the side road just before it, into the parking lot at the Waterway Restaurant.

"Come on," he said.

For a minute, she had the alarming thought he was going to take her inside to meet his family, but he didn't. He led her around back to the weathered gray pier on the Intracoastal.

At that time of day, there were hardly any boats in the slips reserved for customers. Royal used to like to impress people by boating up to this dock and taking them to lunch, but now, between mealtimes, the dock was deserted and the deck above it empty of the customers who usually sat drinking cocktails as they waited for tables. The glass walls of The Waterway overlooked this area. For all Cassie knew, people could be inside spying on them. Brian's father or mother could be there, or the kitchen help who would report Brian's activities. He would tell Cassie's name and word would get back to Royal. Brian led her down the pier to a Boston Whaler similar to the one Royal used to have, a seventeen-footer.

"Hop in. Today we take the water taxi," he said.

Inside the boat, Brian opened the battery case and retrieved an ignition key. Royal had never kept his own spare key on the boat, maintaining that no matter how well it was hidden, it could only invite thieves. Cassie thought how trusting the Iveys must be, keeping a key where anyone could get it.

"Isn't there somebody you should tell that you're taking the boat?" Cassie asked as Brian started the motor.

"They'll know," he said in a rich-boy voice she hadn't heard before. His tone reminded her of Kyle.

They sped under the drawbridge and past the Joyner estate to the north, then east toward Festival Beach. Southbound boat traffic heading for Florida was heavy at this time of year. Brian went fast, dodging between other boats. The prow rose and fell when they crossed wakes, slapping the water hard. He was enjoying it. When he cut the motor to an idle, they were directly opposite Tiffany's dock.

Cassie understood. Brian wanted Tiffany to see them together. He reached into his pocket and pulled out a bag of marijuana and some paper and began to roll a joint. The queasiness in her stomach was probably seasickness. She could never stay at anchor very long.

Brian finished rolling the joint and lit it and held it out to her. She pictured Royal P.A. half drunk from beer, half out of control, more than half disgusting. Her heart beat in her neck, in her ears, everywhere but in her chest where it ought to. Brian's dark gaze bored into her, offering. She had no more power than a slave girl. She took the joint and lifted it to her mouth.

"I hope Tiffany's watching," she said after a while.

She felt a little floaty, but she wanted to show her sophistication and how she knew what was going on. Her voice was hoarse and unfamiliar. Brian didn't answer. The joint was nearly gone. He squeezed the button to get the boat out of neutral, eased the gearshift forward, drove her home.

She climbed onto the pier, relieved to see no cars in the driveway.

"Dock-to-dock service," Brian said. He looked so pleased when he took off, you'd think he knew something she didn't.

The next day, Tiffany stopped Cassie in the hallway. Cassie expected some threat about leaving Brian alone. She wanted not to care. She hadn't really done anything.

Tiffany was dressed in a black skirt and black top, black Reeboks and black socks against her long pale legs. Cassie couldn't help thinking how gutsy the outfit was and how good it looked on Tiffany, and how she, Cassie, was also gutsy in her way—the sort to avoid being an Azalea Princess and defend black bus drivers and hang out with guys like Brian Ivey—and how, under other circumstances, she and Tiffany might be friends.

She could almost see how it would be, when Tiffany leaned over to whisper in her ear, as if they were sharing a secret.

"You little whore," she said.

Cassie tried to laugh. It came out sounding as if she were being strangled.

SIX

*A*lona was standing with Elliott outside the Adams Park fire station waiting to vote, which in a way was touching because his being there with her had nothing to do with voting and everything to do with her grandmother, Emma, who had died on just this day—election day—two years ago. Alona knew Elliott was trying to keep her from feeling mournful while she was waiting in line, but the weather was so much like that other election day—balmy as spring, and the air tasting so much like water that she couldn't help it.

And besides, Emma was a source of contention between them. After her death, Elliott maintained that anybody who said balmy days made the water call to you, beckon you down off the bridges, probably did die the way the police said. Alona said that Emma's fear of bridges was no crazier than Elliott's fear of eating bread not absolutely fresh from the store and his habit of throwing out any he thought might be going bad. Then Elliott said, "The difference, Alona, is that Emma had the kind of phobia that can drive you to suicide if you're not careful." And Alona yelled that never in her life had Emma been in any way suicidal.

They couldn't talk about Emma any more than they could discuss having a baby. So although Elliott was doubly gentle with her as they stood in the line, his hand held protectively at her waist, still Alona couldn't help feeling a little resentful.

"I didn't think it would be this crowded," Elliott said, noting the line that had backed up past the big open doors of the firehouse and across the lawn where they were standing. The fire trucks had been parked temporarily at the curb—no doubt the same kind of trucks Jordan Edge drove when he was being a volunteer firefighter at that other fire station across town.

But she had no intention of thinking about Jordan Edge today. Her plan was to dwell exclusively on Emma, in the most cheerful possible way, which was only appropriate on the anniversary of someone's death.

"They can't come closer than a hundred feet to the voting booths," Elliott said, seeming to think Alona was staring not at the fire trucks but at a campaign worker on the edge of the lawn with a poster of Royal Ashby wearing a jowly grin. "Not a very good likeness," he said.

"It's not his looks I mind," she said lightly, "It's his position on pierced ears."

"I'm glad to see you voting on the issues."

"Oh, I am," she said.

They both smiled because they knew Alona never followed politics. It was Elliott who believed voting wasn't just a privilege but a responsibility, which included keeping up even if an issue didn't concern you. After he read *The Wall Street Journal* or watched the evening news, he told Alona more about the expansion of the sewer system or the state of public schools than she hoped to hear. Yet in a way, she admired his dedication.

That very quality had attracted Alona to Elliott when they first met, at Custom-Fit, after Emma's feet had grown so bony and thin from illness that she couldn't stand on the hardwood floors of the Waterway Restaurant in her old oxfords. Elliott had spent nearly a week tracking down inventory from other stores to soothe Emma's misshapen arch, and when he'd finally called to say the shoes were in and to invite Alona to dinner, Alona had no inclination to refuse.

In a way, he'd rescued her. Although Emma had been ailing a year by then, Alona still couldn't picture her as anything but the healthy, energetic sixty-year-old she'd been before. She couldn't imagine permanent sickness when her own worst illness had been a flu once that had made her so feverish and dizzy she felt as if she were letting go of something. Then suddenly it ended, not gradually but all at once, and wellness bubbled up inside her like fizz from the ginger ale she'd been drinking. She remembered being wide awake and restless, filled with a wicked hunger. She drank soup, nibbled toast, and then, tired of soft foods, gobbled potato chips until she felt ready to pop from so much salt. The next day she was fine. And for a time, her life was powered by the sheer joy of being well. Surely Emma had that to look forward to.

But Emma didn't recover. "It's just age is all," she assured Alona. "Like having your strength measured out to you all at one time instead of getting a new supply as you go along. I can wear myself out by nine in the morning or portion it out till ten at night." Though Alona's own energy always seemed an endless stream, she pretended to understand, even when Emma cut her hours at the Waterway Restaurant, saying, "I'm having too many of those nine-in-the-morning days lately."

So when Alona saw a TV show about how crystals had healing powers—different healing powers for different shapes—she was intrigued. She worked in a health food co-op at the time and bought three crystals meant to be worn as jewelry, close to the body. She made a necklace for Emma out of the largest one and a pair of earrings out of the others, knowing Emma would wear them to please her.

Then she thought, maybe other stones have healing powers, too. She experimented with bracelets and anklets, with neck-laces and rings. She noticed that when Emma wore each new piece, she always had a good spell. And then—the way Alona saw it—the energy of the stones wore off, even the energy of the jeweled bracelet she'd fashioned from chips of every stone she had collected.

"It's beautiful, and it's sweet of you, honey," Emma said then, "but I wouldn't do it justice. I don't go anywhere fancy anymore. Just to work and then for my swim."

"Anybody who can swim every day is not that sick," Alona pointed out. Emma had taken a swim in the Intracoastal every warm day for most of her life. "You'll go interesting places when you get better."

Emma pointed to the sky. "The only place I'm going is to the apartment they're getting ready for me up there."

"Don't talk like that, Grandma."

"It gets to the point," Emma told her flatly, "when there's just no other solution."

Alona stopped dating then, even though she was nearly twenty-five. She stayed home evenings on the pretext of need-ing to make more jewelry, which by then she was selling at the co-op and at Trader Charlie's in the mall. Emma had grown so weak that overseeing breakfasts at the Waterway Restaurant wore her out completely. She barely touched the wholesome dinners Alona fixed. All she wanted to do was sleep. Drugged by darkness, Emma slept through storms and the honking of traffic, through a car wreck to which police and ambulances noisily responded. Sleep so sweet she couldn't let go of it.

Though Alona prided herself on controlling her weakness for men in order to handle the situation at home, still her mood grew thick and cheerless. The earrings she spun while Emma dozed were gray and black, pewter and onyx. Her thoughts were equally somber. It wasn't until they went to Custom-Fit, until Elliott turned his serious level gaze to assessing Emma's feet, that Alona felt unaccountably comforted. He was the first man in a long time she had wanted to touch.

He courted her properly, with drinks and dinners and an interest in her jewelry-making. He made love to her as if he'd thought through what he was doing and intended to do it well. Slow hands, like in the song. And Emma liked him. It didn't occur to her until later that perhaps she'd only wanted Alona settled so she could continue her long dying at her own pace.

"Looks like you might be a little late after all," Elliott said now, wrenching Alona from her reverie. It was nine-thirty, and he'd promised they'd be finished voting in time for her to open Jewels at ten. Now that they'd made their way from the lawn into the firehouse itself, they could see how slowly the line was moving.

"You wouldn't open Custom-Fit late," she said a little petulantly.

"Our lease with the mall says we have to be open mall hours. You know that."

"Just because my lease doesn't name my hours doesn't mean I don't *have* them." But he knew as well as she did she wasn't careful about hours, that she put out her CLOSED sign whenever she felt like it, even for a long lunch or a walk on the beach. If he brought that up, she'd have no defense. She moved slightly, so he had to take his hand off her waist.

"We could come back later," he offered.

"No. We might as well get it over with."

No point in being so touchy. After all, it was Elliott who'd convinced her to open the shop in the first place, Elliott who helped her find the building, set up her books, get through the first unprofitable months. If it weren't for that, Alona didn't know how she would have stood up to her grandmother's worsening condition.

But still, it had never occurred to her that marriage would give Elliott a say in Emma's illness. Emma stopped taking her medicine, saying drugs were unnatural. Elliott said she should listen to her doctors. Emma insisted her problem was only old age, "when you spend so much time nursing yourself, you can't even hardly go to work." After she finally quit her job, Alona could hardly bear how frail her grandmother looked. Elliott said she wouldn't be so pathetic if they got a nurse in the house and some oxygen for the days she had trouble breathing. They did that briefly, until Emma sent the nurse away, claiming she wasn't bedridden and could do for herself.

"She's a little unbalanced, Alona, you know that," Elliott said then, as if they'd been conspiring to pretend Emma was normal when they both knew she wasn't. Elliott found other cutting things to say, not always about the illness—like how wrong it was for Emma to have let Alona's mother, Dottie, go off to work in Raleigh when Alona was a child. "What a trauma that must have been for you," he said, even after she explained that Dottie was fourteen when Alona was born and Emma more the mother from the beginning. "I never even called her 'Mama,'" she told him. "Always Dottie." But Elliott thought it was wrong to call parents by first names. He thought Emma's permitting it was eccentric.

Other times he tried to comfort Alona by saying it wasn't pathos that shone out of Emma, it was sweetness, as if she'd been burned clean. Alona said that was ridiculous. The glaze in Emma's eyes was pain and the sweetness only bland like when the tartness goes out of a lemon and it gets pale and dry—a helpless blandness, because there was nothing more to do.

They didn't stop arguing until summer came. Summer had always been Emma's favorite season. She loved the neon-pink crepe myrtle of July, the white-hot ocean sand she'd walk on whenever someone drove her across the drawbridge to the beach. To Emma, even the dense heat was no burden, "Why, it's just something you wear for a couple of months, it's your gown," she'd say.

But Alona feared the shimmering gown of summer was too heavy that year. When Emma went down to the Intracoastal to paddle briefly through the water, her swim was a gesture. She abandoned her strong crawl in favor of a timid breast stroke. Seeing her, Alona remembered the feeling of letting go she'd had during her own bout of flu. She tried to imagine letting go for years the way Emma was doing, and hoped it wouldn't happen to her that way when the time came, hoped she'd be able to let go all at once.

At the end, Emma seemed adrift on a thin film of energy, like someone floating on the ocean. When the tide was in, she seemed nearly healthy. She'd leave the house, walk, even shop. When the tide was out, she stayed in. So when Emma drowned on that balmy election day two years ago, Alona understood. She knew Emma had saved her last great effort of will to walk down to the sandy banks of the Intracoastal and slip into the warm waters to shed the out-of-season gown of heat. And though the tide swept out faster than Emma expected, and swimming proved too much for her, Alona thought it was the bravest thing her grandmother had ever done.

It was unthinkable to her, at first, that the police suspected Emma had jumped off the drawbridge. Any fool knew she wouldn't set foot on that bridge unaccompanied, and in any case, no one could jump without being seen. There was always a steady stream of traffic. Nor was Emma's body the first to be found against the bridge's pilings, swept there by the currents. The only "evidence" that Emma had jumped was that there was no sign—no purse or robe—to prove she'd entered the water at her usual place along the Intracoastal. Before long, Elliott was saying flinging herself from the bridge was the kind of thing Emma would do in desperation. Such a good swimmer wouldn't drown just going in for her usual dip. Alona knew that was ridiculous. She reminded Elliott how weak she was, how she'd been slowly dying for several years.

Elliott said, "Yes, Alona, that's just my point."

It was as if, ever after, that disagreement had hung between them.

Alona did not believe her grandmother was unbalanced. If Elliott tried to make a mockery out of Emma, how could she trust him? How could she be sure he loved her, never mind that he was standing next to her, touching her, while they waited to vote?

A volunteer was checking off names on the list of registered voters. Elliott steered Alona to the sign reading T THROUGH Z. "Elliott and Alona Wand," he said, in the take-charge tone he sometimes used at Custom-Fit, especially when someone was making a return—polite but not too polite. The volunteer gave them an approving glance, as if she were thinking what a nice young couple they were, him so serious-sounding.

There were still five or six people in front of them. It was ten till ten. She could hardly bear the thought of not opening Jewels on time. Waiting even a second longer seemed out of the question. She turned, so edgy she knew she'd have to walk right out, get on with what she was supposed to be doing.

Another fire truck pulled up to the curb, and two firemen got out. One was built so much like Jordan Edge that for a second her heart lost its normal rhythm. On closer inspection she saw he was rounder in the face. Jordan was a volunteer, anyway, not one of the two or three paid firemen who manned each station. What was wrong with her? She remembered she wasn't thinking about Jordan today, only about Emma.

"Here," said another volunteer, handing Alona a pencil and a ballot, motioning her into one of the booths. Finally.

The ballot was a computer card printed with the names of the candidates and circles to fill in. Alona was reminded of standardized tests in high school. Of computer-generated phone calls about student truancy. At least Jordan Edge had had a sense of humor about that. Elliott certainly didn't have a sense of humor about voting.

She wondered what he'd do if she told him she hadn't voted after all, only fed a blank ballot into the counting machine.

One thing was for sure: he wouldn't laugh.

She knew Jordan Edge would.

But even as she considered not marking a single name, she dutifully blackened circles, voting for the candidates Elliott had recommended. Her hand cramped from her very hypocrisy.

Outside the booth, Elliott waited for her, his gaze blue and patient. He took her arm, escorted her to the parking lot, kissed her goodbye. The touch of his lips might have been a reward for good behavior. She couldn't wait to get in her car. She couldn't drive fast enough toward her shop.

She felt irritated until she smelled the Waterway. Until she saw her parking lot, and Jordan Edge's white Beretta.

She knew at once the reason she'd been so jumpy about voting, so lax in her determination to think only about Emma. It was because the schools were closed for the election. Because she knew all along Jordan would be waiting for her. Because she feared if she opened the shop too late, he might go away.

◆　◆　◆

Jordan had been to her shop twice in the weeks since their excursion to Joyner Creek. She really hadn't expected it, after the fiasco when he tried to steer her around that blacksnake hanging from a tree. She was no more afraid of blacksnakes than she was of earrings. The woods behind Emma's house had been full of them. That particular snake startled her, true, but she could have handled it. What unsettled her was trying to decide if Jordan had wanted to hide the snake because it would interrupt his slow seduction, or if it was a purely unselfish gesture—as instinctive as putting ice down the pants of a student dying from a drug overdose. The thought of his protecting her made her feel so wobbly that she'd acted doubly cool toward him to hide it. She wanted to get away and sort out her thoughts. And it was a good thing she did, because by the time he dropped her at her shop, she'd decided the only reason she'd gone with him was because she was angry with Elliott.

Then Jordan came to see her again. It was Saturday and there were customers. He waited half an hour before she was free. She said, "What're *you* doing here?" and he said, "Looking at jewelry," and then more people came and he left.

The next time was after school, when it wasn't busy. He didn't pretend to look at earrings. Mostly, he talked about his job, and she talked about hers. Before she knew it, an hour had passed. He didn't try to touch her, though he did stare at her longingly. When he left, the store seemed dim and quiet.

"I thought if you had a business, opening time was sacred," he said now, as she got out of her car. "I thought maybe you were closed for the election."

"Why, were you worried?"

He kept in stride with her as she headed for the shop. "I thought maybe you'd take off and go with me to the beach."

"The beach!" She opened the door and snapped on the light as briskly as she could, to show the impossibility of accepting such an invitation.

Inside, he was as restless as Alona had been at the polls. He examined the bins of beads and shells as if he'd never seen them before, the carousel stands of finished earrings, the unmounted stones in the display case. When he spoke, his voice was so deep it made her think how seldom a man was in here—except Elliott, of course. But Elliott never paced, and he didn't wear such spicy aftershave that the odor made her dizzy. "Well? Are you coming with me or not?"

Her eyes were on the missing middle of his eyebrow, and she knew if they were sitting on the beach together, it would be the most natural thing in the world to touch it, and then to touch the scar on his hand. She didn't let her gaze drop, for fear of looking at his hand. "Why, this is likely to be my busiest day since Labor Day," she said.

"Oh?" He raised his partial eyebrow.

"It's true. Half the yuppies in Festival are off work today, and most of them will go shopping." She said *yuppie* deliberately because Elliott thought the term derogatory, especially if it described the people you made your living off of. But Jordan didn't seem impressed.

"It's November," she told him. "They say the Christmas season begins at Thanksgiving, but that isn't really true. Once it's November, psychologically it's Christmas season."

"Actually," he said slowly, with the edge of a smile dancing at his lips, "it's wrestling season."

"What?"

"Wrestling practice begins November first."

"So?"

"When school is closed for the day, Fetzer can't get into the wrestling room for practice. Fetzer Laney—the wrestling coach I told you about. He thinks nothing of calling me up and harassing me about it. That makes it difficult to stay home. That's why I'm inviting you to the beach."

"It's not very flattering to be thought of as a distraction from the wrestling coach," she said. She knew she should pick up some work, something to show she was serious about not going with him, but the most she could manage was to step on the other side of the counter so he'd feel like a customer.

"No insult intended," he said.

"And what about that?" she asked, pointing to the pager at his waist. "How do you expect to escape Fetzer with that?"

"Fetzer wouldn't call me on that. That's for fires. A labor of love."

"Love?"

"Not exactly *love*." He said it so she knew which kind of love he was talking about. She felt her whole body turning liquid. His eyes were brown, and the light bounced off of them so cheerfully she couldn't help comparing them to Elliott's cool thoughtful eyes that spoke of obligation and seriousness.

"I bet you like the beach," Jordan said.

"When I was a kid, my grandmother was terrified of bridges, so the only time we got out to the ocean was when one of her friends drove us," she said. "It was a bigger treat than movies. You wouldn't think that, living here."

"And here I'm offering you this major treat and you're turning me down."

"Oh, I got old enough to walk across the bridge any time I liked. And then, of course, I learned to drive." Here she was, contentedly thinking about Emma and the drawbridge, which was what she'd wanted to do earlier and couldn't.

"We'll stay at the beach for an hour," Jordan said. "Then you can come back and tend to all the yuppie customers lined up to do their Christmas shopping."

"No." But she couldn't help smiling. It was odd how insulted she was about Elliott making her open late, and now Jordan was asking her to close entirely and she wasn't insulted at all. Not that she meant to go to the beach with him. Or anywhere. She owed that much to Emma and Elliott.

"If I go alone," he said, "I'll think about Fetzer." He gave her a meaningful glance. "I'll think about wrestling."

"Vice principals don't have anything to do with wrestling," she said. "It would be the custodian who'd open the wrestling room. Or maybe I got it wrong. Maybe you *are* the custodian."

He narrowed his eyes, trying to look mysterious. "I'll tell you about it at the beach."

"You mean tell me about wrestling, or about your real job over there at the high school?"

"Everything," he whispered.

"Spare me."

"You really think an assistant principal doesn't have any-thing to do with wrestling?" he asked, persisting, opening his arms out as if to show his disbelief. He knocked into a carousel stand of earrings and sent it spinning. "The assistant principal is on the line for everything."

"Oh, Jordan."

He stopped the spinning cylinder of earrings with his scarred hand. "I mean it. Last year there was a kid who used to moan like he was dying while he was getting pinned, and then complained because he couldn't breathe. Fetzer asked him how come if he was smothering he could make so much noise. The kid said, 'I *couldn't* breathe; he was right on top my face.' And Fetzer said, 'That's what you've got teeth for.'" Jordan paused. "That," he added meaningfully, "is what I have to deal with."

"I don't believe that for a minute," Alona told him, smiling. "And anyway, what's that got to do with the assistant prin-cipal?"

"Ah! The next match, the same situation came up again. Only this time, not wanting Fetzer on his case, the guy opened his mouth and bit his opponent. I'll leave it to your imagination to decide what body part he ended up biting."

She wasn't going to laugh, but she did all the same. "Jordan Edge defends assailant of eunuch wrestler," she said.

"Fortunately, no. Our kid didn't do him any permanent damage."

"And what about the wrestling coach?"

"Fetzer? What about him?"

"Was he fired?"

"No."

"I bet you hate the guy."

Jordan shrugged. "He's my best friend."

Alona rolled her eyes.

"Now will you come to the beach?" he asked.

"Really I couldn't." Jordan's hands were resting on the counter next to her own, but she didn't dare look at them.

"Half an hour," he said. "I'll have you back in half an hour."

"Jordan, really." But suddenly she imagined herself sitting at the beach with him just as she'd once sat with Emma, watching the pelicans and the gulls while Emma swam in the ocean as if it were her very home, as if water and not language were her native tongue. Emma had loved the ocean so much and was so afraid of the bridge she had to cross to get there that going to the beach on the anniversary of her death seemed like a sort of tribute.

It seemed so simple and right that she knew there must be something skewed in her thinking.

Though she didn't lower her gaze, she sensed Jordan's hand resting on the counter inches from hers atop the polished glass, bristling with fine hairs except for the smooth place just below his knuckles, sleek as satin, gleaming in the pale light of the shop. It was all she could do not to touch it.

"For the last time, I can't go to the beach," she said. "It's a workday. I'm a storekeeper. I work in my store." She was proud of the resolve in her voice. She mashed her palm firmly into the glass of the display case so it would have to stay there like a suction cup and not travel toward Jordan.

"If not now, and if not the beach," he said huskily, "then you ought to come see my house. Any time. Whenever you can. Just come by."

He didn't move closer to her. His voice was thick and warm, but she knew he was going to leave. He'd go out the door and leave the rough edge of desire behind him, hanging in the muggy air of the shop all the time she was working. She wouldn't get a single thing done. She felt as if every bit of air were being sucked out of the room. In the vacuum that remained, she could hardly breathe. It was the vacuum that forced her hand up off the counter and over toward his. She had nothing to do with it. Her fingers moved, touching the round scar. Just as she imagined, the scar felt exactly like the cool silk sheets they sold for a small fortune in Belk's.

"Come to the beach," he said.

She knew you didn't memorialize someone this way on the anniversary of their death. You didn't betray the kindness of your husband. But she turned the OPEN sign on the door of the shop to CLOSED. She knew it was wrong. She couldn't help it. She didn't know how she could think such deep thoughts and still be so evil.

SEVEN

By election day, Cassie knew Royal P.A. was deliberately trying to torture her. She'd felt so bad when he first threatened to send her to Caitlin Academy that she didn't think there was anything more he could do, but now she knew better. What was worse than actually being shipped off to Caitlin was not knowing if and when the banishment would take place.

Because the thing was, although Royal never mentioned boarding school again, he made it clear he was still angry about her defending Curley. He'd come home from speaking to the Festival Junior League and said with chilling calm, "I was informed of your escapade again today at lunch." Then he fell silent. He said the same thing after speaking to the Lions Club and the Elks. Cassie heard that one lady asked outright if it wasn't his daughter who'd taken up for that colored rapist bus driver. So how could it be that Royal didn't mention Caitlin Academy even in passing? Had Cassie's mother nipped the idea after all, the way she'd done once before?

But no. The minute Cassie had settled on this comforting explanation, a brochure from Caitlin Academy appeared in the mailbox. The next day, on the memo pad in the kitchen, in Royal's handwriting, was the phone number to call for an appointment to visit. But so far as Cassie ever knew, no appointment was ever made. Nothing. Relieved, she decided Royal must be too busy to follow through. He had pre-election TV appearances on the "Kitty Lane Show" and "Carolina in the Morning." He slept in his study almost every night. Sometimes Cassie didn't think he slept at all, in spite of the fact that ninety-eight percent of incumbent officials were re-elected. It was as if a little blue flame of hate burned in his gut for anyone who might oppose him. A little blue flame of hate for Cassie.

Just as she'd nearly dismissed Caitlin Academy as no more than a threat, a message was left on the answering machine by Caitlin's dean of students, returning Royal's call. Cassie erased it. She couldn't ask her mother what was going on for fear Betty would interpret it as a cry for help. Cassie couldn't help thinking of Black Eve and likening herself to a slave girl being sold off. Royal was the white master. He might be selling her to owners miles away, perhaps in the next state. Or maybe not. Either way, there was nothing she could do. Since that's how it was, Black Eve ought to give her strength to endure whatever happened. But Cassie wasn't sure she would.

On election day, she didn't wake up until ten. The house was quiet and empty. She could almost see Royal P.A. sneaking out early, instructing Betty to leave his teen-aged political liability home. The question of who'd been inside Kyle Carter's neon yellow surfer shorts was not something he wanted to deal with today. Interesting how she could be sound asleep and still aware of what was going on between people who were awake and about their business. When Cassie finally opened her eyes, the hazy hot sun had found its way into every corner of her room. She had a headache exactly behind her eyeballs.

The pain came with her as she walked into the bathroom and remained after she'd splashed her eyes with cold water and started to dress. Cassie realized that Royal's dangling reform school in front of her all these weeks without actually sending her meant he didn't regard her crime as serious enough to cost him the election. After today, he'd be in for two more years.

A warm, sticky wind blew into her room from off the Intracoastal. The air was hard to breathe. There was only one thing she could do. She finished dressing, locked the door behind her, and walked across the drawbridge toward Jewels.

Going to Alona was a compromise, but she didn't care anymore. She knew that since Alona had refused to say she was Cassie's aunt at school that day last month, the dignified course would be to avoid Jewels entirely. But Cassie's head hurt, and the metal grid of the bridge vibrated as cars whizzed by, making her sway in one direction while the choppy gray water below went in another. And in view of Royal's imminent re-election,

Alona's lack of loyalty didn't seem so serious. Cassie liked the turquoise earrings Alona had given her. A person who meant to mistreat you wouldn't give you such a gift. She knew she could talk Alona into piercing one last hole.

The headache had relented a little by the time she left the drawbridge behind and walked past the billboard for the new shopping center. She turned in by the small houses where Alona had her shop. The sign on the door of Jewels announced that business hours were ten to six, like always, but a CLOSED sign in black letters was hanging from the door. Even the fate of her own ears seemed out of her control. She'd be damned if she'd give up so easily. She went out to the road and took the bus to the mall.

"I want another hole—right here," she told the clerk in Merle Norman, pointing to the cartilage high on the right ear. That would make six holes on the right side, which she could have had weeks ago if Alona had cooperated. Later, when she went home, she would put five different dangle earrings in the right ear, along with the gold stud in the newly-pierced hole, and two more long earrings in the left. The last time she'd done that, the weight had nearly torn her ear off, but she didn't care. If a reporter came by like they usually did on election day to ask the children of the candidates how it felt to wait for the results, she'd make sure they took her picture and got the earrings on TV before the polls closed. How could you vote for a commissioner whose daughter looked like a gypsy? How could you trust such a parent with power?

"Against our rules," the Merle Norman woman said, her mouth flashing bright lipstick which was supposed to be in style but only looked garish. You could wear true red if you were dark or if you were blonde, but this was a redhead with a face so flushed that adding more color made her into a clown, and Cassie had half a mind to tell her that. The woman should have been glad for a chance to pierce someone's ear.

"What rules?"

"It's too high up. On the cartilage. Too dangerous. It could pull right through. You already got enough holes in that ear, what do you want another one for, anyway?" The words came out of the shiny-bright mouth like spit or nails, hurting even more than when Alona had said them.

It was the same story at Trader Charlie's, The Accessory Shop, and the The Middle of the Mall, a little earring kiosk in the center aisle. She didn't know what else to do.

She was walking past The Foot Locker, where they sold athletic shoes and clothes, when a voice came out of the bright fluorescent interior. She would have recognized it anywhere. It was the same voice that had once said, "Bleach."

"Hey, Cassie Ashby," the voice said.

"Curley."

He was inside the store, in the blue-green fluorescent light. He wore black pants and a black and white striped top that looked like a referee's shirt. It was the outfit all the clerks wore. He made a thumbs-up sign.

"Thanks," he said.

He sounded like himself, but he looked like someone else. Thanks for what? She had never seen him out of the driver's seat except that one time when he stood up to Kyle. She'd never seen him in anything but jeans and a T-shirt. She knew black and white stripes were not only for referees, they were also for prisoners.

Except for that, she might have gone inside, drawn by his voice. The bright lights made a crazy-quilt of the objects in the store—T-shirts and jogging suits in Carolina blue, NC State red, UNC-Wilmington green. Curley stood in front of a paneled wall studded with shelves of shoes: Men's Running, Women's Aerobic, Walking. It was exactly as Royal and Betty had said. Curley was never going to drive that bus again.

"Thanks for nothing," she said, stopping short of the entry-way, put off by the prisoner's uniform she might have sentenced him to, for all the good she did. She couldn't make herself step out of the dim center of the mall into that hodgepodge of color.

"What?" he asked.

"I see you didn't get your job back."

"No, but..."

She made a thumbs-up sign to match his, cheerful as she could manage. "My mama's down there," she lied, pointing to the other end of the mall. Then she fled.

She walked a mile, maybe more. The air was close and too warm for November. It was one-thirty, and she hadn't had a thing to eat, which was making the headache worse. It was the kind of pain that never quite goes away without sleep. There was nowhere to go but home. Finally she found a bus stop and traveled back the way she had come.

The phone was ringing when she got in the door. "Where've you been? I've been trying for an hour," Betty's voice said. It was a statement, not a question. "I'm campaigning over here at Festival Beach Elementary, but we'll all go over to election headquarters about seven, right before the polls close. I'll pick you up, and we'll get a bite at Hardee's on the way."

"No," Cassie said. She just couldn't. Once the polls were closed, even seven dangling earrings wouldn't help her.

She waited for her mother to protest. There was a long silence on the other end. After a few seconds, Cassie knew Betty would make another round of the polling places and then meet Royal alone. Tonight they would make their entrance into election headquarters without her, and watch as the votes came in. They would smile for the reporters. People would whisper about Royal's daughter and the bus driver. But the votes would already be in.

She sat on the living room couch. On the coffee table was the old *Newsweek,* exactly where Royal had put it, with Black Eve staring out. Black Eve! A picture in a magazine. She turned it over so she wouldn't have to look at it. Though it was still afternoon and she'd been awake less than six hours, Cassie felt exhausted. Her eyelids were so scratchy she could barely hold them open, and her limbs felt weighted down. Maybe because of the humidity. She couldn't have moved from that couch if the house were on fire. A sudden heavy sleep descended.

When she woke up, the sky outside was dark. She'd left the sliding glass door facing the waterway open. Balmy air was drifting in. Someone was outside on the deck. Her mother? But it was election night. She sat up fast. The person on the pier came over and knocked on the screen. It was Brian Ivey. She wasn't surprised to see him. She was beyond surprise.

"What're you doing here?" she asked. Her voice sounded far away.

He stepped inside, sliding the screen shut behind him. "I brought the boat. I thought you might want to go out."

"No," she said. "I don't."

He sat on the couch beside her. They turned on the election returns. Royal and Betty were at headquarters, smiling at his supporters.

"He's in for two more years," she said. "Shit."

Brian slid his arm around her. "You don't know that yet. The polls just closed. Relax." She couldn't.

Brian started kissing her. She thought: well, what does it matter? It was a year and a half before she'd turn sixteen and was allowed to date, so Royal would be horrified if he found out. Good. She thought of something Royal would hate more. "Not here," she said to Brian. "Come in the other room."

She led him into Royal's study, onto the couch Royal had been sleeping on all week. If Royal was going to think she'd done forbidden things, this was where she wanted to do them. Right under his nose.

Brian pushed her down onto the couch and kissed her for a long time. Cassie would have liked it better if she hadn't been thinking of the whisker-hairs growing out of follicles all over his face, which felt like sandpaper against her cheek. She tried to pretend she was Tiffany so she could enjoy it more, but somehow she wasn't ready to be Tiffany; she couldn't help it. She wondered when was the last time he had shaved.

His hand crept under her shirt. He undid her bra one-handed more easily than she could have undone it herself. She began to feel queasy, just as she had that day in his rocking boat. He was so smooth that she figured he had done this a hundred times, with a hundred different Tiffanys.

"Relax," he said again. Brian thought Cassie was afraid, but for some reason, she wasn't. She let him kiss her some more. Though he was very skillful, she began to feel far away. The far-away feeling helped to calm her stomach. Out of nowhere, she remembered three years ago, the last time they'd had a big snow.

It was the only time since she'd moved to Festival that the snow had stayed on the ground more than a couple of hours. Some winters there was none at all or just a dusting that melted as soon as it came down. But this was a real snow, maybe three inches deep, and it was still there the next morning.

She'd gone with Janet Biggs to the public golf course. Everyone was there because it was one of the few places with hills. No one had sleds, but the boys took their boogie boards and skim boards, which were faster than sleds although harder to control. Most of them went down the small hills sitting up or lying on their bellies, but there was one who sledded on his skim board standing up, as if the snow were the ocean and the skim board a surf board going over the waves. He coasted all the way down a little rise without falling. He was a high school boy, much older than they were, dark and athletic. She was sure, suddenly, that the boy had been Brian.

Now he was touching her breast, moving his mouth down to kiss it. His hair felt crisp and wavy against her skin. As soon as his mouth was in place, his hand went up her leg and started to fool with her underpants. It was all very smooth. She was getting wet between her legs and at the same time recording this fact in her mind. She thought of the boy in the snow again. He had sledded the same small hill a hundred times. It was as if he were readying himself for some important event. Maybe he was preparing for a surfing competition by conquering the snow. Probably he had also kissed a hundred girls, practicing sex the way he practiced riding waves. All of it was a sort of athletic workout. What they were doing now was not like love at all, it was more like sports.

"Get off," she said.

"You want it," he said. "You know you do."

"No, I don't." She didn't like the way he said you want *it*. *It*. Something unmentionable. She didn't want *it* at all. "Get off," she said again.

He paid no attention. He was pressing into her. She was the slave girl, and Brian was the master, taking what he would take. She had nothing to say about it whatsoever.

Considering how quickly she knew what to do, Black Eve might have been whispering to her, in the dark cool part of her mind. Cassie pushed with her hands against Brian's chest.

"For Christ's sake, relax," he mumbled.

Royal said you couldn't be effective when you were angry, but it wasn't true. Cassie pushed harder, and when Brian still didn't budge, the words Black Eve might have been saying echoed in her head. She knew to hike her knee up, into Brian's crotch. He groaned and rolled away.

He was in pain, looking at her in hate and humiliation. And Cassie was smiling. She wasn't mocking him or even registering her delight that Royal's was not the only kind of power. Mostly, she was cheerful because of what Black Eve seemed to be saying to her. She was not a slave.

· *Part Two* ·

1989
Spring
◆

EIGHT

*T*he fires that plagued southeastern North Carolina that spring had been burning for almost two months before they got to us. Two months. They'd begun a hundred miles to the west early in February, spawned by out-of-season lightning on drought-stricken forest. Nothing out of the ordinary. Small fires lit up in any dry season. Usually they were quenched either by fire-fighters alone or with the help of the normal winter rains. That year, there was hardly any rain, not even much in the way of clouds, just an occasional misty drizzle.

It was an odd winter in a part of the South where winters are unpredictable anyway. In Festival it's often warm enough for the students to wear shorts through mid-November and occasionally after that whenever weather comes up from the Gulf and turns balmy. Then January and February are chilly, sometimes so frigid that the Garden Club matrons snivel about their gardenias being killed. In March, wind greets the daffodils and the air feels colder than it is. Then the azaleas bloom in April and spring settles in, and suddenly it's summer, humid as hell, and the town is full of tourists.

There are a few variations on the theme, but we weren't prepared for four months of clear skies and only a few dry cold snaps that came and went in the space of a couple of days. It turned out to be the warmest winter of the century—the strangest, driest, sunniest winter anyone could remember.

So the fires came gradually. Deceptively. West of us, in February and early March, they were controlled in one spot only to be discovered in another, sparked by careless trash burning, or set by arsonists, or their embers carried from one spot to another by the prevailing winds. By mid-March, they had inched out of the Piedmont, into the sandhills, onto the coastal plain. Here they were knocked down by local firefighting teams only to keep moving, unnoticed, in underground peat bogs until they came to a place of fresh vegetation and flared up again. In Festival, we basked in seventy-degree sunshine, not paying attention to somebody else's fires. We weren't thinking how, week after week, everything was conspiring to drive them our way.

I would have noticed them even less if it hadn't been for Fetzer. Around the station, after we'd put out a house fire or grass fire and were back cleaning up, there was often mention of the blazes to the north and west—where they'd cropped up most recently, how they were being handled. They were still so far away that they seemed noteworthy only in passing, except to Fetzer, who was already going every weekend to help fight them.

He'd seen them first on his way to the regional wrestling meet in February, driving the activities bus to Fayetteville with a dozen nervous wrestlers in the back. The way he told it, just south of White Lake the air started smelling singed, and black smoke burgeoned into the sky from a distance. That was enough to intrigue him. After the season ended, instead of coaching freestyle wrestling for one of the local clubs all spring, he helped them out just on Friday afternoons, and spent every Saturday and Sunday volunteering at the forest fires, wherever they happened to be at the time.

I was always surprised how much enjoyment Fetzer got out of those fires. If I stopped on my way home Friday at freestyle practice in Central High's wrestling room, body heat would be pulsing, and the odor of sweat would be hanging like a physical presence, and Fetzer would be striding through the middle of it, directing take-down drills the way he might conduct an orchestra, standing knobby-legged and happy in gray shorts, with the bill of his ever-present blue baseball cap pulled low over his eyes, *Lowe's Millwork Express* stitched on the front in what had once been white. I knew for a fact coaching freestyle didn't make him that joyful. He was what Marta had once referred to as "heavily into macho sports," by which she meant not only wrestling but firefighting—and it was true. For years he'd been avoiding becoming an officer in the company for fear he'd have to take the chief's place sometime and direct the operation from outside.

"I don't want to coach at fires, I already coach wrestling," he said. "If something's burning, I want to be in there among 'em."

And those afternoons in the wrestling room, anticipating a sport he could get tangled up in all weekend, he'd grin and make his way between bodies to where I stood, saying low so the kids couldn't hear, "Chasing tail this weekend? Or coming with me to chase fires?"

I was usually on my way to see Alona and had begun to take offense at the term "chasing tail," but I never said so then. It was impossible not to respond to Fetzer's pure good nature. He was the only firefighter I knew who was genuinely unafraid—a rare quality because fire is not a single thing, not just flame but heat and smoke and darkness, choking, being trapped, being confined—so many terrors that few men can escape being afraid of at least one or two and having that fear mingle with their anticipation.

But for Fetzer, the joy seemed unadulterated. Most weekends, all he got to do were small backup jobs for the units already on the scene, but sometimes a tree fell or the wind turned and blew flames onto a house he was spraying, and when that happened, he came back elated, buoyed up for another week hustling lumber and training three dozen unpromising post-season wrestlers.

In that way, the winter passed. Fetzer spoke of the fires four or five counties away as if they were a long-term enemy. Gradually they came closer and were mentioned more often on the evening news. Through February, into early March, the fires seemed unimportant next to our clear coastal skies and unseasonably warm sunshine.

The weather had been so sweet for so long that the students began exhibiting spring fever in the first timid days of the new season, weeks before we expected them to. I found myself dealing with infractions we usually didn't encounter until the last six weeks of school. It was all I could do to mete out punishments and devise strategies to keep Central High from chaos before the first of June. In the evenings, I was busy with

Alona, either before supper if it was an early night for her husband, or until nine or ten if he had to stay to close the mall.

I didn't think of fires, though we had our share of them in Festival that winter—maybe more than our share because of the lack of rainfall. Then came the day in late March when the wind carried the smoke into town not gradually but on the edge of a fast-moving front, into a sky that went from blue to yellow halfway between opening bell and first lunch. It might not have created such havoc if it hadn't been the end of the week, but everything was always exaggerated on Friday. Usually the kids were quiet on Monday from god-knows-whatever they did on the weekend and didn't wake up until Tuesday or Wednesday, even The Trash.

These were a group of guys nineteen and twenty years old who'd been hanging around for five years and were never going to graduate, being too poor, too black, and too irredeemable by then. Instead of going to class, they spent their time hassling freshmen in the halls and trying to deal drugs, which was harder than it used to be because we knew who to suspect: any male from Bishop Gardens who was supposed to live on his mama's welfare check but came to school in high-topped Air Jordans that cost a hundred and ten bucks a pair. They might have been streetwise, but most were either too stupid to notice we were monitoring their feet or didn't care. About half the original Trash had dropped out of school over the winter, and the remaining handful were usually controllable through mid-week. But the warm Tuesday before the smoke blew over us, two of The Trash had gotten hold of a freshman, twisted his wrist until it swelled like a grapefruit, and caused a general ruckus that ended with an ambulance and a police car at the door and the kid in the hospital overnight. Recalling my own woes in this regard many years ago, I took no small pleasure in suspending the perpetrators.

Two hours later, we got our first bomb threat of the year. Dan Taylor, the other assistant principal, suggested The Trash might be involved. I didn't argue, because Dan is black, but the truth was, The Trash tended to be more straightforward. We proceeded according to plan. At Central High, bomb threats were handled exactly like fire drills. The teachers were expected to keep a student body of twelve hundred outside in seventy-degree sunshine twenty minutes or more, all the time saying no, it's not a bomb threat, just a fire drill, while police and administrators—and *dogs*, for godsake—sniffed through the halls looking for an explosive we never found. We'd had at least one such incident every year since I'd been there, and so far nothing had blown up except a few tempers.

Wednesday brought a second bomb threat, probably from someone who'd gotten the idea Tuesday. By then, the atmosphere was so loaded we didn't evacuate the school, just checked lockers, the gym, the dressing rooms, leaving the kids in class.

Thursday, the weather was warmer yet, and I swear, you could feel restlessness shimmying down the hall between classes, radiating out from the students like waves of heat. But usually it was Friday we worried about. Black Friday, Fetzer called it, though that was easy for him to say, having to deal with it only during wrestling season and the rest of the year spending his time with the civilized lumber company customers who patronized Lowe's.

That particular Friday started out so clear that it was hard to miss the change when, at mid-morning, the sun began to look hung over, sickly and smudged as if blotted by a tissue, indistinct behind sudden yellowish smoke.

The kids in class were affected by it immediately. They began looking out of windows, sniffing as if for poisoned gas even though there was not yet an odor. When one of the science teachers used the sky as an example of what to expect during nuclear winter, a girl rushed out of his class hyperventilating until she almost fainted, blubbering about the possibility of contaminated water and post-holocaust vegetables. I gave her a paper bag to breathe into and said, "Look, if they were going to bomb us, you think Wright County, North Carolina, would be a prime target?" Then I sent her to Frank Howard, who always spoke in a whisper and whose specialty was weeping women.

All the students were antsy. I thought the science teacher would understand when I suggested he save his nuclear winter demonstration until after the students had adjusted to yellow haze instead of blue skies. Instead, he looked puzzled.

"Hormones," I said, which in a high school can be used to explain virtually anything.

Then came lunch. Except for The Trash, who didn't care about being caught (and God knows, we were relieved to have them off campus), twelve hundred kids ate elbow to elbow in the cafeteria in three shifts, starting at eleven in the morning. Six staff members were assigned to cover each shift, but since it took the teachers time to get from their classrooms to the lunchroom, it was often just me or Bob McRae, the principal, directing pandemonium at the beginning of each lunch period.

We averaged one or two fights a week, not always at lunchtime. Two was a lot, and considering what had already happened on Tuesday with the Trash and the freshman and the sprained wrist, we weren't really due. Ninety-five percent of the incidents were between boys—two blacks, two whites, you couldn't predict; a mixed-race fight was rare unless The Trash were involved, trying to extort money from whatever poor white sucker looked like he might ante up. And mostly the fights were less over matters of substance than of temperament or ill feeling such as filled the skies that Friday. When I took the combatants back to my office to talk to them separately and then make a value judgment about whether they'd cooled off enough to bring face to face, I was always amazed how seldom we established what the confrontation had been about—not because they were trying to conceal it, though God knows sometimes they were, but mostly because they didn't always know what had started it. The best I could usually do was get them to shake hands while I doled out the required five to ten days of suspension, which was a deterrent only if they cared whether they passed their courses.

Fights between girls were less frequent, though you couldn't rule them out when the atmosphere was as charged as it was that day. Girls seemed to have a built-in social monitor to judge how much aggravation they could endure before making fools of themselves by throwing punches and messing up their hair—especially white girls, who almost never fought in public. Black girls were quicker to go after each other, though they, too, refrained until they'd gotten totally committed, trading insults about their mutual boyfriend—invariably there was a boyfriend—and finally realizing there was nothing left but to exchange blows. Then they hissed and lashed out like dropped high-pressure hoses, and it was terrible to stop.

Walking to sixth-period lunch that Friday, I had all that uneasily in mind. But in spite of the yellow sky and the thin haze of ash in the air, I wasn't ready for the melee that greeted me—a crescendo of angry female voices that blurred into motion the moment I stepped into the cafeteria. I was already running toward them when I registered it was not two black girls or two white ones but three, maybe more, every color, clawing, kicking, pulling hair—black and blonde and frizzy and straight—a whirl of hands and clothing and noise. If they'd all been black or all been white their friends would have been egging them on or trying to get them to stop, but the onlookers were doing neither, only standing wild-eyed and bemused and silent, faces flushed, excited at the rarity and magnificence of the thing.

I made my way between the rows of tables, no quick progress given the layout of the place, listening to screeching and panting, cries of "Bitch!" and "Whore!" With boys, it was possible to step into the middle and make them part; that was what they were expecting and waiting for. But *girls*. The shouting. The ferocity. From the opposite direction came Amy Abbott, a small woman, an art teacher. She was yelling inaudibly, waving her arms. I looked for other help, someone who knew not one but two of us would need to separate them, each from behind, pinning their arms back so they couldn't scratch. A whirlwind of movement; Amy was still two tables away. Were there four of them fighting? Five? I had no choice but to step in the middle, myself alone against them, as Amy advanced all too slowly—and as the yellow sky hovered outside and the whole cafeteria looked on.

"Break it up!" I yelled, getting two white ones by an arm, trying to swing them apart. They were stronger than I expected. I shook them. Nothing. They kept coming. Scratching, clawing. Clawing *me*.

"Break it up!"

Clearly, I did not have their attention.

On the periphery now, Amy grabbed a tall black girl who'd been in the middle, who didn't seem to be resisting. The other black girls had disappeared. A fingernail scraped across my brow. A scratch. Pain.

"Enough!" Dan Taylor shouted. He forced his way through and managed to hook the dark-haired white girl by the elbow. He was six-three and two-sixty, but she didn't care, she tried to keep coming toward the dishwater blonde I had now gotten hold of. The brunette was butting her head forward and kicking out, angry to discover the rest of her body frozen in Joe's strong grip. Unable to reach the blonde, she turned and shouted at the black girl Amy was holding: "White nigger!" Summation and final statement. Then she went silent, breathing hard and staring the other two down.

It was then I noticed I was the most wounded of the three. There was a nasty fingernail gash down my arm and the scratch over my left brow—my good brow—was starting to bleed into my eye. The whole cafeteria noticed the blood about then, too, and I swear, I could feel their pleasure: Mr. Edge finally got it, and from *girls*. The dark-haired one smiled. *Smiled.* I felt like a damned idiot.

"All right, to my office, all three of you." I said, pretending I was unaware of the other two or three who'd been in the fray and escaped into the crowd. I figured if I tried to find them, I'd fail and look more foolish yet in front of sixth-period lunch.

The girls were so wild with disarray that I didn't recognize them until they sat before me in my office, looking too exhausted to start up again. The two white girls were beach kids—the dark-haired one, with wolf's eyes and a vampire outfit all in black, was Tiffany Galloway, an unsettled vixen with whom I had ongoing dealings because she cut so much school. As a freshman she'd spent several weeks in a private counseling center after physically attacking the girlfriend of a boy she liked in Raleigh. There would have been a court case and publicity except that the incident took place out of town and the other girl wasn't seriously hurt. I wasn't surprised to see her. The other two girls, I was. The blonde was Cassie Ashby, the commissioner's daughter, my old friend from the fall. A warrior in her own way, but hardly a scrapper. And the black girl was no Trash. She was an honor student. Role model. Azalea Princess. LaMonica Reilly. Christ.

I gave all three of them five days of in-school suspension. Ten is the max for fighting, but considering the perpetrators, I felt five would do. The gash on my arm stung, and my brow was bleeding through the tissues I kept using to blot my eye. There was a note on the desk to see Tansy Parrish, the school nurse, pronto, and I thought how timely; she could give me a Band-Aid while we were talking business.

"I didn't start it," the Galloway girl said. She gave me the clear innocent look of the pathological liar.

"You don't have to start it. You only have to be part of it."
I considered pressing to find out exactly how it *had* started, but
then I looked down at the note again and remembered Tansy
Parrish almost never couched requests in the form of an emergency.

"You should have stayed away from Brian," Tiffany said to
Cassie.

A boyfriend. Of course.

"I wouldn't date that spoiled piece of shit if he begged me,"
Cassie replied.

LaMonica Reilly remained impassive. In all my years at
Central High, I'd never seen a black girl in a physical fight with
a white one, and LaMonica was the last one I would have
expected to find in a fight, period. She was miles removed from
Bishop Gardens, more uppercrust than most of the white kids
in the school. A stately girl, not a cheerleader but head of the
math team. I didn't know what her role was and was damned
curious, but more than I wanted to ask questions I wanted to
be sure none of the three overheated again. I pushed the button
to summon an office aide and instructed her to take each girl
to the ladies' room separately to clean up, then deposit her in
in-school suspension. Then I went upstairs to the infirmary.

Tansy Parrish had come to Central High from a ghetto
school in Washington the year we started seeing regular drug
problems and decided we didn't want the Wright County
school system to get sued after some kid died on campus.
Specifically, Tansy was hired after I'd stuffed that kid's pants
with ice, and the board of education decided we'd better have
a more scientific approach to drug reactions, along with someone competent to carry it out.

Tansy was a good nurse and a better politician. What sat in
her office was no medical emergency, and not related to the
yellow sky, either, but rather a tactical problem. It was a freshman girl who'd fallen beside the soccer field and landed with
her hand on one of those prickly cactuses that grew wild in the
sand. She'd picked up a palmful of cactus spines, and the hand
was already red and bothered-looking. Some kids were more
allergic to cactus spines than others, as we knew from long
experience.

"Unless you have a better idea," she whispered, "I'm going
to have to send this one to the hospital." They'd give the girl

an adrenaline shot, just in case, and pick the spines out one by one with tweezers.

We were immediately of one mind. If we could have driven the girl to the hospital in a private vehicle, no problem. But that was against the rules. Another ambulance screaming up the driveway that week, after the one that took The Trash's victim off on Tuesday, after the bomb threats and police cars, a sky that looked like nuclear winter, and a handful of multi-colored girls trying to tear each other apart in the cafeteria—after all that, another emergency vehicle at the door might set off God-knows-what, and we'd be lucky to get through Friday afternoon dismissal without another fracas and all kinds of attendant publicity.

"Let's give her the glue treatment instead," I said, improvising.

The girl looked frightened but wasn't the crying type. "The glue treatment?"

"Elmer's glue."

Tansy produced the Elmer's but looked doubtful. I spread the glue across the kid's palm and let it dry. Then I peeled it off in one sheet, fast, the way my mother used to remove Band-Aids so the pain would be over all at once. Presto, just as I'd hoped, the cactus spines came out stuck to the sheet. A couple more minutes and the girl's hand would have been too swollen to let go of the pickers, but as it happened, the Elmer's did the trick. Almost instantly, the swelling started to go down.

"Christ, where'd you learn that?" Tansy asked.

"My mother was a nurse."

Tansy narrowed her eyes at me skeptically. I shrugged.

"You want me to clean up that cut over your eye?"

I might have taken her up on it except that Bob McRae called me to his office just then on the walkie-talkie, which wasn't his style. Later, I wished I'd opted for a bandage.

He sat at his desk in the same pose I often used with students, casual but well out of reach.

"I don't think we can suspend those girls," he said in the worried, questioning tone I'd come to know was neither. *We* couldn't suspend them; *I* already had.

"It's your own rule, Bob. Five to ten days for fighting, no exceptions."

"Under ordinary circumstances, I wouldn't even bring this up. You know I wouldn't, Jordan."

Bob was a small guy, ex-military, wore his hair in a crew-cut. You expected bluster from him and were always surprised to find him so agreeable, so milquetoast. He was also a distance runner, so you waited.

"You mean if LaMonica Reilly weren't on the Azalea Court," I said.

"Not just LaMonica. The whole mess with the Queen. The media looking for more dirt to dish. I don't want them finding it at Central High."

It was true that the Azalea Festival had turned into a publicity free-for-all the last couple of weeks, but I didn't see why that should affect school policy. A rigid wall of anger slowly began erecting itself around the inside of my head. It occurred to me that it was Bob's ass, not my own, that I'd saved getting those cactus spines out of the girl's hand, and ditto during lunch when I'd pulled the fight apart—all gestures that would keep reporters from his door, not mine—and now instead of gratitude I was getting dumped upon. Thanks to Jordan Edge, Bob McRae would retain his usual heroic stance and not have his name in the press for running a hotbed of fighting and disruption; thanks to Bob McRae, Jordan Edge would have the student body laughing at him because he couldn't suspend a couple of girls for fighting and make it stick.

"There are three dozen Azalea Princesses. You're saying if we suspend two of them, the press will come after us?"

"Damn right." Bob held up a hand to point out an imaginary headline. "AZALEA PRINCESSES FORCED TO RESIGN AFTER MELEE AT CENTRAL HIGH." He didn't smile. "And the kicker. BLACK PRINCESS AND COMMISSIONER'S DAUGHTER INVOLVED."

"Then what would you like me to do?" I spoke calmly, though anger pressed on my forehead from within. "Walk into the suspension room and tell them it was a joke?"

"I think we should give them each a week's detention."

"Perfect. Keep them after school for half an hour. You consider that punishment to fit the crime?"

"And tell them it's in deference to the Azalea Festival activities," he said softly.

"What about the Galloway girl? She's not involved in the festival."

"Let the Galloway girl off, too." By now his voice was barely audible. There's nothing like a whisper to carry a threat.

We stood there staring at each other for a while, both skilled at not dropping our eyes.

"Jordan, I'm sorry," he said finally. "But you can see our position." I assumed he was using the royal plural.

I understood him too well. If, instead of suspending the offending Princesses and their co-combatant, Tiffany, he had me give them all a week's detention, their crime would be assumed to be minor. Even if some student had the bad taste to mention the fight to a mother who then called the school to check, the administration's answer could be no—if the girls had really been fighting, they would have been suspended, that was the rule. No one could swear to the fight except the four hundred kids at lunch, and hell, they were teen-agers.

I expected Bob to address the fact that I'd lost real and not just figurative blood over this thing, but he ended the conversation so quickly that I wished I'd let Tansy call the hospital and order the second ambulance of the week, with God knows what aftermath. When the anger began to tighten around my head like a little band, I comforted myself with the thought that I'd soon be out of there, spending most of the weekend with Alona.

I left before the parking lot was empty, though Bob liked me to stay until it was clear, believing that somehow the students would be less likely to hotrod knowing it was the ferocious Jordan Edge they'd have to face. How this was supposed to work if he undercut me in front of them, I wasn't sure. I wished for a fender bender in my absence—statistically, most of them happened on Friday afternoon—and for Bob to be blamed, along with the unsettling, hazed-over sky.

Alona had been working late most evenings making jewelry to sell at the Azalea Festival in two weeks. She normally closed early only to sneak in a quick hour with me on the nights Elliott came home for dinner, but I was sure I'd find her at my cottage that day even though Elliott was working until nine. I thought so in spite of never having believed couples could sense each other's moods from a distance, through thin air. It had certainly never happened with me and Marta. But it was March, and Alona and I had been together since November, and we knew more about each other than most people did. We couldn't go anywhere because of the husband, so for lack of activities other than sex, we talked.

Alona knew the havoc the warm weather was wreaking at school. She knew the name of every kid on Fetzer's wrestling team. I knew the formula for putting a price tag on a piece of jewelry made of nothing but sequins and tie-dyed cloth. We didn't discuss the husband, of course, or Mary Beth. And rarely firefighting, especially after the time she asked me if I was afraid and I said yes, not too seriously, and could see she didn't believe me anyway. As my father used to say: there are some things you don't tell the women. But everything else—yes. So I expected Alona would note the change in the atmosphere and know how it would affect the mood at Central High, and that this would bring her to my house early to hear about it.

Fetzer would have said that was dangerous—"more what a guy expects from his wife, which is a mistake unless you're really committed." But I dismissed anything Fetzer said about commitment after he jettisoned two wives in order to spend an occasional evening with his current squeeze of the month. In my view, anticipating Alona's response was hardly like making the heavy commitment of other years, when Marta had wanted me home every evening and was pouty and resentful if I attended a sports event or social function at school.

"You think it's funny that Fetzer fills his time with so many activities he can't even think," she'd said then. "But you're no different, Jordan. Instead of work and fires and wrestling, you have work and fires and me. In that order."

Alona made no such accusations. She closed the store and eluded the husband when it was convenient; I saw her when I could. I relished having both the relationship and my freedom.

Nor did I take seriously Fetzer's contention that I'd soon grow jealous of the husband, because I'd checked him out at Custom-Fit one Saturday early on. Studying Elliott while browsing through the display of shoes, I decided he looked less like a salesman than a preacher or banker, or maybe a board-of-education bureaucrat with framed graduate degrees hanging on his walls. There was nothing more sincere—in an arrogant sort of way—than Elliott Wand selling shoes. I understood then why Alona wanted more, and after that, I never gave the husband another thought.

The fork of road to my cottage branched off near the entrance to the Joyner Estate and ran a quarter of a mile into the woods, curving back from the water and through the pines and pin oaks. The rezoning of the property had recently gone through after a year of hearings, and a backhoe was parked on the last curve of my lane. It wasn't until I drove around it that I saw my driveway was empty. Alona was not there to hear me make light of Bob McRae and Azalea Princesses and the humiliation and powerlessness of being hung out to dry.

A jagged white wallop of rage hit me. It was so unexpected that it was like being sucker-punched from behind. I got out of my car and stood in the woods beside the house. My hands were actually shaking. My vision was momentarily blurred. All the diffuse discontent that had been building in my head that afternoon focused itself on Alona. I pictured her not at work where she should have been, but at home with Elliott, in an apartment I'd never seen, surrounded by the same clean-cut modern furniture Marta the Bitch might have chosen, with Elliott's socks strewn carelessly across the floor. When the initial blast of rage quieted and tunnelled in, it joined my existing anger and grew more powerful, like a muscle flexing.

I didn't stay home even long enough to change clothes. I knew Fetzer would be leaving the wrestling room at Central High to join his fellow lumber salesmen at King Neptune's bar, before sleeping it off so he could spend the weekend fighting fires. I gunned the car down the lane, blanketing the woods with kicked-up sand. I think I knew even then, hours before what finally happened, that I was in trouble.

NINE

*I*f it hadn't been for the business about the Nigger Princess and the Nudist Queen, Cassie would never have agreed to be in the Azalea Court. Ever. But once she saw Royal's face the day he burst into the living room with those obnoxious racist comments, she wouldn't have missed it for anything.

And not just because of the slur about LaMonica Reilly, who'd practically *dragged* Cassie through the first semester of geometry before she caught on. No: Cassie was also furious with Royal for going after Tara Barry the way he did. For one thing, Tara Barry was the first Azalea Queen Cassie had actually heard of beforehand. She played the girlfriend on "Crest Ridge," which Cassie watched every Wednesday night. As far as Cassie was concerned, the only appeal of being an Azalea Princess was the chance to sit next to Tara at the festival. Not that she intended to do so. This was when Cassie was still saying to Betty, "Mama, I know how much it means to you, but I'm just not the Azalea-Princess type," and Betty was saying, "All I'm asking is for you to think about it, Cassie."

Then Royal came home that afternoon and deposited himself in his study, where he made phone call after phone call in which Cassie could hear the name "Tara Barry" being spoken in low and uncomplimentary tones.

"What did she do, commit some crime?" Cassie asked Betty, who was around the corner in the kitchen. Royal's face was drawn and white as he spoke, which it almost never was unless one of the other commissioners had outsmarted him.

"Worse," Royal said.

"She posed nude in *Playboy* a few years ago," Betty explained, walking into the living room wiping her hands on a dish towel. She raised a sly eyebrow. "Apparently nobody checked her background until after she was selected and the press got interested."

"Well, posing nude is how actresses get attention these days," Cassie said. "Really they're not wearing much less than lying on the beach in a bikini." She looked at Royal. "Are you going to outlaw sunbathing, too?"

Royal rose out of his chair slowly, as if the joints in his back were fragile and in need of protection. The top button of his shirt was undone, and more skin than ever sagged down his neck because of the weight he'd gained since the election.

"When you live in a small town that has one nationally known function a year—a family event celebrating the beauty of the azaleas and of your community," he said, "then you want everything about it to be consistent with your community's values. You don't want the whole country thinking you chose some tart to represent you who posed stark naked in a porn magazine."

"Nobody thinks of *Playboy* as porn," Cassie said. To Royal, pornography was anything with pubic hair showing. The same model could be almost naked on the beach, and as long as her bikini line was shaved, he wouldn't think a thing about it.

But Royal was no longer listening to her or, Cassie realized, even addressing her directly. He was mentally rehearsing a speech for the media. It must have annoyed him to look at Cassie and be wrenched suddenly back to his surroundings and to the fact that only his family was listening. That was when he flung himself out of his office into the living room and said with authority and conviction, "Well, we might have to have a Nigger Princess this year, but we damn well don't have to put up with a Nudist Queen."

Cassie was almost glad for the shiver of anger that ran through her just then, because she had been having spells of mildness lately, though not so much toward Royal. When she listened to the radio, all the songs were the color of ripe plums. Sitting in class, she'd become aware of the strings of a violin or guitar strumming just behind her, inaudible to anyone else. For hours after such episodes, she felt oddly pleasant and mellow. This had been going on ever since she kneed Brian Ivey in the balls on election day four months ago, and since Royal had failed to send her to Caitlin Academy despite his threats. Though she hadn't really gotten to direct her own life any more than usual, sometimes she felt she was. Even on the days Kyle Carter followed her onto the bus and winked at her or Tiffany Galloway passed her in the hall with her standard greeting ("How's the little slut?"), Cassie often failed to get upset. It was as if part of her had died. So when Royal's comments about the nudist Queen filled her with a wave of hate and anger, she felt as if she had been resurrected.

"Personally," she said, "I'd consider it an honor to serve on the court of someone as famous as Tara Barry, even if she did pose for *Playboy*. Better than those soap opera ditzes you usually get who no one's ever heard of."

"Does that mean you're agreeing to be a Princess?" Betty asked. "I hope it does."

Seeing the look of hope on her mother's face made Cassie realize they'd reached a moment of reckoning. The words *Nigger Princess* and *Nudist Queen* floated on the air. Royal looked self-righteous. She judged she could annoy him by placing herself next to Tara Barry and LaMonica Reilly every chance she got.

"I wouldn't miss it," Cassie said.

Next thing she knew, Betty had whisked her to an orientation meeting for the Princesses at the home of Rose Bell who headed the Teen Committee. Mrs. Bell opened by stating that she remembered with pride the spring years ago—"I won't tell you how many years"—when she was an Azalea Princess herself. She looked down, revealing a strip of dark eyeliner that placed her reign sometime in the '60s. Breathlessly, she added that it was the role of the Princesses to show Southern hospitality to both the celebrities and the other visitors who came to the events, "whether they be from out of town or from right here in Festival." Cassie looked around to see if there was anyone nearby to make a gagging gesture to, but all the other girls seemed rapt, even LaMonica Reilly.

"With three dozen Princesses, naturally, not everyone is required everywhere at once," Mrs. Bell said, naming the events at which the Princesses would appear. They would all be at the opening ceremonies and they would all work the garden tour, "which isn't really work, girls, it's an opportunity to model your gowns in some of the loveliest gardens in the South, with the azaleas in full bloom."

The function of the girls, she went on, was to *grace the gardens* so the visitors could *get the flavor* of antebellum Festival. Mrs. Bell's voice became light and drifty as she spoke, as if the idea of antebellum Festival had transported her. She gave each girl a list of the specific events she would grace—some at one location and some at others—"because we don't want to give you so much you'll end up absolutely exhausted."

But you could see by your list that the daughters of Garden Club members had the best jobs. Cassie's included meeting the Queen at the airport on Thursday, going to the coronation ceremony and riding on the Queen's float at the Saturday morning parade. She saw over her shoulder that LaMonica's list was almost the same as her own. This was because LaMonica was black, and the Garden Club wanted her to be visible. Cassie imagined Royal's face as he noted LaMonica and Cassie seated together in public, several days in a row. She felt so mellow that she planned how she'd tell the Queen "Crest Ridge" was one of her favorite shows. If Tara Barry's unbelievably thick dark lashes turned out to be real and not added onto or false, Cassie would compliment the lashes, too. She'd make Tara glad she'd come to Festival despite Royal's unfriendly attitude. She'd do this even though she knew this was exactly what Rose Bell meant by showing Southern hospitality.

It didn't occur to her that Royal's indignation over the Nudist Queen was any more than that, not after he'd failed to send Cassie to reform school. But that same week, Royal and the other county commissioners, along with three ministers and the presidents of two banks, held a press conference. They read an open letter demanding that Tara Barry be dismissed and another Azalea Queen chosen. This was a community of decent people, they said. The citizens of Wright County would not like decent young Azalea Princesses or the nation at large to think that a *Playboy* hussy was the role model they'd chosen to represent them.

"I know from personal experience," Royal said with a catch in his throat, "because among this year's Azalea Princesses is my own daughter."

Daughter! Cassie thought she would die from humiliation.

The next day, a Queen Committee spokesperson said a decision about keeping Tara Barry or replacing her would be announced as soon as possible. A *Festival Herald* reporter phoned Tara's agent in California, who said yes, the actress knew about the controversy and no, she wasn't resigning unless she was forced to; she'd done nothing wrong.

All of Festival was immediately divided. Some people wrote to the *Festival Herald* claiming that politicians like Royal Ashby were right-wing and reactionary. Others called the radio talk shows to defend morality and decency and the bravery of citizens like Royal who spoke out. These people usually opened their statements by saying, "Well, I just want to tell you I've been going to Fourth Street Baptist Church for thirty years, and this is the worst flaunting of public indecency I've ever seen in my life." Royal didn't mind being either defended or berated just as long as his name stayed in the paper.

In the meantime, while the fate of the Queen hung in the balance, other arrangements for the Azalea Festival went as planned. Betty insisted they rent Cassie's dress before all the good ones were taken. They could rent from Sarah Welby, who worked at home and sewed in lots of authentic details, or they could go to Janet Foy, owner of Janet's Ruffled Curtains, whose staff made up a stock of dresses when business was slow. The main deciding factors, finally, were that Sarah Welby's gowns were so old they smelled permanently of cleaning fluid, and that Janet Foy went to Royal's church.

This connection might have put Cassie off if one of her spells of mildness had not been upon her just then. She was listening to an R.E.M. tape on her headphones, with the bass turned up so high she could feel it beating in her blood.

Janet Foy's shop was so full of ruffles—bedspreads and pillow shams and ornamental wreaths as well as hundreds of curtains displayed on imaginary windows set around the walls—that as soon as she went in there, Cassie couldn't breathe. Mrs. Foy herself added to the effect, a woman as plump and fussy as the rest of the store, stuffed into a tailored business suit that might have been the only ruffle-free item in the shop.

"Of course! This is Royal's girl, Cassie!" Mrs. Foy exclaimed, rushing toward them and spewing pins that had been in her mouth. She clutched Cassie's hand. "I keep hoping we'll see you in church sometime with your folks."

"Folks?" Cassie asked. Everyone knew Royal was a regular churchgoer and Betty wasn't. When Betty accompanied him to Baptist-by-the-Sea half a dozen times last fall, it was purely for political reasons.

Cassie didn't have time to pursue this further because Mrs. Foy was pulling her by the hand and motioning Betty to follow through two rooms of ruffled curtains to a workroom with a big wooden closet at the back, which she threw open to reveal a rack of floor-length Azalea Princess gowns in every fabric and color.

Cassie did not mean to draw her breath in so audibly. She had decided she would not wear taffeta, or anything scratchy, or anything sickeningly bright. Nor would she choose a gown that had a shawl or parasol or other extra paraphernalia to go with it, as she'd seen some of the Princesses wearing in previous years. But as she was trying to remember all the taboos she'd set for herself, Mrs. Foy was guiding Cassie's fingers across materials soft as old bedsheets and no harder on the eyes than dogwood blossoms. Cassie found herself pointing to a gown pale blue like the sky in summer, with lace at the neck and hem but no flounces or ruffles. In an instant, Mrs. Foy was carrying it across the shop toward the dressing room, along with a floor-length petticoat with a hoop sewn into the bottom.

Once she'd slipped the petticoat on, Cassie came back to herself. She realized she was about to commit to an outfit she wouldn't have tolerated for a moment two months ago. The hoop was so wide that it barely fit inside the dressing room. The dress, in spite of its soft color and fabric, had such an enormous full skirt that it weighed a ton. Mrs. Foy gathered up the material so Cassie could move out among the sewing machines and ironing boards to show Betty how she looked. She took up so much space with her hoop and yards of skirt that she felt as if her center of gravity had shifted. She might have gained fifty pounds. Although she'd always thought *Gone With the Wind* was long and boring, suddenly she understood completely why Scarlett O'Hara was always so grumpy.

"Almost a perfect fit!" Janet Foy exclaimed, poking at Cassie's shoulder and at her waist. And then, turning to Betty: "Even if it needed hemming, that would be included in the price."

Mrs. Foy frowned, still looking at Betty, and lifted Cassie's hair off her neck. "They have to wear it up, you know," she said.

Cassie could see in the mirror that, above the masses of fabric, her pulled-back hair accentuated the too-longness and too-thinness of her neck, making her head look as if it were bobbing an unnatural distance above her shoulders.

"And no big earrings," Mrs. Foy said, fingering one of the heavy silver loops Cassie happened to be wearing. The earring pulled unpleasantly at her earlobe. Mrs. Foy smiled. "Maybe just some nice little pearls."

Cassie didn't like the way this Janet Foy was presuming to be in charge of things. She would wear whatever hairstyle and earrings she wanted.

"The only thing that's extra is the hoop," Mrs. Foy said. Cassie wanted to say she could live a long a time without the hoop, but Mrs. Foy continued to study her critically, as if she were some sort of judge instead of just the woman who *made the fucking dresses,* for godsake.

Cassie might have reassessed her whole position on being a Princess if, at that very moment, LaMonica Reilly and her mother had not come in. Cassie felt as she had in the fall, during those stressful days after she picked up the *Newsweek* in Jewels and convinced herself an ancestral mother named Black Eve was guiding her. Now that she was fifteen and could look back from a distance, all that seemed far-fetched. She still suspected Black Eve had gotten Brian Ivey off her that time, because without Black Eve whispering in her ear, how would she have known what to do? But the idea that some paranormal process had been at work seemed ridiculous. It was just that LaMonica's appearance right then reminded her that, as back in the fall, there were moments when coincidence seemed too small a concept to account for what was happening.

Both of LaMonica Reilly's parents were dentists. Dr. Amelia Reilly and Dr. Hubert Reilly. At various times in middle school, one or the other had come to a science class to explain what they did. During these visits, the black kids mostly exchanged glances and snickered, and the white kids were overly polite. LaMonica acted like she never noticed any of them.

Right now Dr. Amelia was wearing the sort of straight skirt and plain blouse over which she might have worn her dentist's tunic in the office all day, but the clothes looked expensive all the same. So did her engagement and wedding rings, and her braided gold necklace. LaMonica was pretty, but her mother was elegant. Even if one of Janet Foy's assistants had not brought the two of them in and said in a loud voice, "This is Dr. Reilly and her daughter, LaMonica. One of the Princesses," you would have known Amelia Reilly was someone important.

LaMonica said hey to Cassie and Cassie said hey back. A lot of the black kids in school, when you talked to them on the phone or heard them over the loudspeaker, even without seeing them you knew they were black. But LaMonica wasn't one of them.

"Is that your dress?" she asked Cassie. "It looks good on you."

Everyone could feel the atmosphere of the room cool off just then. Janet Foy, who'd been poking at Cassie just a second before, did what in one English assignment had been called "drawing herself up to her full height," and gestured toward the closet full of Princesses dresses as if they had been repossessed from girls who'd each shed several leprous fingers into their folds. Instead of taking LaMonica's hand as she'd taken Cassie's, Mrs. Foy pointed at the closet from a distance as she said to Dr. Reilly, "You go ahead and look through them, and if she sees what she likes, she can try it on."

Cassie noticed how LaMonica and Dr. Reilly also drew themselves up to their full height. They seemed to put more gloss into this gesture than Mrs. Foy had, which Cassie assumed was because they were black and had lots of practice. They began to search through the dresses as if Mrs. Foy didn't in the least concern them.

Mrs. Foy went back to poking at Cassie even more energetically than before. She pulled on the hem of Cassie's dress and then took a little tuck of the sleeve between her fingers. "You know, when I saw Royal's press conference on TV," she said to Betty, "it amazed me how all day I'd been saying the same things Royal did." She let the word *Royal* roll out familiar and easy, as if to show that a county commissioner and a curtainmaker were equal, going to the same church and agreeing on things. "I said I'd been making dresses for these young girls ten years, but I'd stop tomorrow if I thought they were setting up a nude role model for them to copy."

Janet Foy waited for Betty to agree with her, but Betty kept a noncommittal smile on her face, perhaps in deference to Cassie's standing there in a hoop four feet in diameter covered by fifty yards of cloth. Janet Foy let go of the sleeve and began to tug at the neckline. LaMonica and her mother spoke in low tones over by the closet. Mrs. Foy didn't once look in their direction.

"There are some traditions and some values you have in a community like this," Mrs. Foy whispered. "You like to see traditions carried on. You hate to see them tampered with."

If the Reillys heard this or suspected it referred to the tradition of white Princesses, which LaMonica was one of the few to break, they gave no indication. Smiling regally, Dr. Reilly pulled a peach-colored taffeta gown out of the closet with a huge swish, a greater swish than was actually necessary, and said, "For starters, I believe we'll try on this one."

◆ ◆ ◆

"I can't believe she'd talk like that right in front of them," Cassie said when she and Betty were in the car with the gown encased in plastic across the back seat and the rental contract tucked into Betty's purse.

"Oh, she's just a pill, honey. Anyway, the Reillys probably didn't hear. It didn't seem to bother them."

"Only because they were being polite. Really, Mama, how can you pass her off like that when we went there in the first place because she goes to Royal's church. Because she's some higher type of person."

"I never said she was a higher type of person because she goes to church. The main thing is, she has the best dresses." Betty looked straight ahead at the road, motherly and serious. Then she smiled slightly, as if she couldn't help it. As if the sight of the traffic amused her. "I happen to know Janet Foy is not only not without her prejudices, but also not completely honest."

"Oh, terrific," Cassie said, trying to sound disgusted but actually getting interested.

"Remember when I had her make those draperies Royal has in his study? She tried to charge me tax on labor. I never did tell Royal.

"I pointed it out, too," she went on. "I said, you don't charge tax on labor, do you? And she said, oh yes, some do and some don't, it all depends on the way your accountant sets it up. Well, anybody knows that doesn't make sense, anybody knows you don't charge tax on labor in the state of North Carolina. It has nothing to do with your accountant." Betty's voice had grown straightforward and careless, as if she were talking to a friend instead of a daughter. It was as if she'd been waiting all this time to tell somebody and Cassie was the one she'd chosen.

"Then what did you do?"

"Oh, nothing, I let it go," Betty said.

"You mean you paid it? But she tried to cheat you."

"Yes, but I have to see her in church, honey. Or at least Royal does. It was less than ten dollars."

"Ten dollars you didn't owe."

"Well, I didn't want to be ugly. I didn't think it was worth being ugly."

"Oh, Mama," Cassie said. She didn't add that sometimes she thought being ugly was all you could do.

◆　　◆　　◆

The peach taffeta gown was the one LaMonica did choose, as Cassie learned a few days later at the mother–daughter tea. This was a pre-festival event where the girls wore their dresses for the first time. It was also the day Cassie discovered the impossibility of sitting in a car or anywhere else with a hooped petticoat under your skirt. You couldn't fit in the front seat at all. Even in the back, the hoop wanted to ride up unless you pushed it down at all times with both hands. The second you let go, the hoop popped up like a spring, leaving your legs exposed and cutting off your view out the window.

"I hope you're planning to drive fast, because I don't know how long I can do this," Cassie said to Betty, holding the skirt down with both palms. They'd gone less than a mile and it seemed like twenty. "I feel like I'm in shackles." Cassie pushed the skirt this way and that. The tea was at one of those big houses in town with gardens someone had started a hundred years ago.

"Honey, slip the petticoat off and set it next to you till we get there," Betty said calmly. "You can put it back on after we park. I bet everyone else will have to do the same thing."

Cassie wasn't sure she liked her mother's complacency. She felt she had no choice but to do as she was told. Sitting next to the petticoat, she wondered if the hoops were actually hula hoops bought at K-Mart and sewn between sheets of fabric. They didn't say another word until after they'd driven all the way to the tea.

Coming from the stark endless yellow of Festival Beach and the withered dryness of Betty's yard, Cassie wasn't prepared for the scene before her when they entered the garden. Because of the unseasonable warmth, the azaleas were already in full bloom two weeks before the festival. The lawn was shaded by trees hung with Spanish moss, and beneath them were what must have been a thousand azaleas, the big Southern kind that grow tall as a person, pink and white and purple. Against the tall trees and the spring-green grass, the drifts of pastel color made Cassie draw in her breath.

"Lovely, isn't it?" Betty said.

The other Princesses and their mothers were chatting as they drank lemonade and ate tiny white-bread sandwiches filled with thin slices of cucumber. It was the kind of refreshment you would expect the Festival Garden Club to serve. Cassie had intended to find LaMonica and Dr. Reilly and go right over to them so Betty could report this to Royal, but LaMonica and her mother were surrounded. The heads of all the committees had made a ring around them as if they were all best friends.

LaMonica didn't seem at all uncomfortable closed in by so many white adults. She stood in the middle of the circle, talking and laughing as if she did this all the time. In a way, Cassie supposed, she did. At school, the black kids from Bishop Gardens didn't like LaMonica. They didn't like the way she talked or the fact that she was in all the advanced classes. On the other hand, the white kids found it easy to talk to her and ask for her help in class, but they weren't friends with her outside of school. LaMonica didn't seem to care. She didn't push herself on either group.

One thing that always bothered Cassie about this was that it made LaMonica seem ahead of her in some way, not just in geometry. It was as if LaMonica had lived longer and knew things Cassie didn't, even though they were the same age. LaMonica knew how to stand in the middle of a crowd of seven white women who were trying to be nice. She knew when to pull herself up around Mrs. Foy and when to ignore her. Even the peach-colored taffeta against LaMonica's dark skin looked lighter and more comfortable than Cassie's heavy blue cotton.

Betty left Cassie standing in the middle of the lawn and went to get refreshments. The mothers were performing this task because if the hoop-skirted Princesses had tried to serve themselves at the table, with all the room each one took up, only two or three of them would fit around. It was ridiculous. Cassie felt slow and cumbersome moving across the grass, not able to get through to LaMonica or even sit down in a comfortable way. Most of the other Princesses were standing, too. The chairs and lawn furniture that had been placed around were empty or occupied by adults. The only Princesses seated were on a concrete bench with enough room around it to arrange their skirts.

Cassie was going to point this out when her mother returned with sandwiches and drinks, except for the odd thing Betty did. She raised her punch cup toward the huge tree they were standing under, with branches overarching and new leaves light-glossy green above them. "The way you've changed so fast," she said, "you remind me of these live oaks, which you probably think of as evergreen."

Well, Cassie never thought of live oaks as evergreen or anything else, no more than she ever thought about plants in general, but her mother looked so pleased that she tried to seem interested.

"This time of year, the oaks shed their old leaves and grow new ones all in a couple of weeks," Betty said. "Just like you. So fast you hardly realize they've changed till it's over. With you agreeing to do this and now standing here in that dress—that's what I think of."

Cassie couldn't believe her mother would say such a thing. She stared at the trunk of the tree, which was as wide as her skirt, but instead of the embarrassment she expected, a wave of mildness went all through her, making her arms and legs feel as shimmery as they did when the plum-colored music played on the radio or the invisible strings strummed in the air of her history class. She didn't know what to think.

Then a voice said behind her, "I thought you were going to wear your hair up. It's traditional to wear an upsweep." Turning, she saw Janet Foy bustling toward them, dressed in a business suit too heavy for the summery weather. Cassie scanned the garden and judged that only about half the girls had their hair up off their necks. The ones with short hair—even the ones with geometric cuts—didn't comb it any differently than usual.

"Do you have a daughter here yourself?" Betty asked, polite but pointing out that this was the mother's tea.

"No, I just come as a festival official." She pinched at Cassie's sleeve to puff it up more, as if she had a right. Cassie didn't like the word *official*. A dressmaker was not an *official*.

"I like to see all my Princesses in their dresses."

"I don't think LaMonica Reilly has her hair up, either," Cassie said.

Janet Foy raised her eyebrows.

"I decided against wearing little pearl earrings, too," Cassie continued, pointing to the turquoise and silver in her ears, which Alona had given her back in the fall. You wouldn't think turquoise would go with this shade of blue, but it did.

Mrs. Foy looked to Betty for help. Betty had such a pleasant, fixed expression on her face that it was impossible to tell whose side she was on.

Cassie was about to ask in what capacity Mrs. Foy considered herself a festival *official* when Betty caught Cassie's eye and did another odd thing: she winked at her. Mrs. Foy barely missed noticing. Betty's wink seemed to say the Azalea Festival was an issue between mother and daughter and no one else, no matter how much Mrs. Foy wanted to horn in.

"You ought to try the petits-fours," Betty said, lifting a little square of iced cake from her plate. "Delicious."

Mrs. Foy looked suddenly a little foolish, dismissed like that, dressed in that formal suit to impress people and yet pinching up tucks of fabric at Cassie's sleeve. She began looking around as if to show how many other people she knew here at the tea. After a minute, she recognized someone across the yard and waved to them. "Remember me to Royal," she said as she moved off.

"So much for pious church ladies," Cassie said.

Betty frowned and guided Cassie to the far side of the tree, where people were less likely to approach them.

"Just because of our discussion in the car the other day," she said, "I don't want you to think I have any objection to going to church."

All of a sudden she sounded motherly and stern, when a minute ago she had been comparing Cassie to live oak trees and winking at her. Cassie couldn't understand it. She knew her mother grew up going to St. John's Episcopal mainly because Grandmother Powell insisted. Betty had once admitted she liked getting dressed up with a sense of high purpose but wasn't sure she believed in God. After Cassie's father died, Betty stayed away from churches except for her wedding to Royal and later the few pre-election Sundays at Baptist-by-the-Sea. In Cassie's view, Betty's staying home from church was one of the last remaining vestiges of the independent woman she'd been in Baltimore, back when she carried jumper cables in her old car and used them three or four times a week.

"I mean, I don't want you to confuse Janet Foy with churches and what they mean to people, and especially not to Royal," Betty was saying.

"Oh, Mama. Royal's a politician, and politicians believe something different every day."

Betty got the sort of calm look on her face that meant she was not. "When we first got married and Royal wanted me to go to church with him, it had nothing to do with politics," she said seriously. "It had to do with saving my soul."

"Oh, Mama!"

Betty ignored her. "I'd say, Royal, I try to be a decent person, I really do. Do you really think I'm going to rot in hell for eternity just because I sleep late on Sundays? And Royal would think about it—he *would,* honey—and then he'd say, I'm sorry, Betty, but I do believe it. And he does."

On the other side of the garden, Janet Foy had joined the group of women around the Reillys. She was laughing and talking. Sucking up to them. That was exactly what Royal would do in public.

"The point is, he has a lot of sincere beliefs. He thinks a nude Azalea Queen is just wrong. He has more principles than you give him credit for."

"You mean principles like grounding me every time I get on his nerves? Like threatening me with Caitlin Academy?" Janet Foy had adjusted the neckline of LaMonica's dress for everyone to see.

"He's more concerned than you think," Betty said. "If you gave him a chance, you'd see he's only doing what he thinks is right—not trying to harm you. If you leave boarding school out of it, what else is there that you really care about? Being grounded isn't so terrible. And don't tell me you care about dating before you're sixteen."

Cassie rolled her eyes, but Betty went on as if she hadn't seen. "Why, for a long time you weren't that interested in boys;

don't say you were. Or maybe interested on a lower level—like when you'd watch that singer George Michael on television."

"George Michael is probably gay," she said, feeling suddenly weary. She didn't listen to George Michael anymore. Her heels were sinking into the ground. She couldn't even lean back against the tree without her hoop bending all out of proportion.

"Well, maybe not George Michael, then, maybe some other rock star. But the point is, what was the purpose of saying you couldn't date when it didn't really matter yet? It wasn't to hurt you—it was more a matter of principle with him. To show he was concerned for your welfare. In a way, it was a kindness."

"A kindess he's planning to extend for another year," Cassie said. She wanted to say that if it weren't for Royal forbidding her this and forbidding her that, maybe she wouldn't have ended up with Brian Ivey on election night on the pull-out bed in Royal's study, half crushed under him with only Black Eve's advice to save her. But she could hardly mention Black Eve, especially now that she doubted her existence. And with Betty giving her these oddball compliments, comparing her to a live oak tree, it seemed wrong even to ask how Royal got off going on television as a spokesman for God and morals and decency, as if he had the direct line. How could he know God didn't approve of women who posed nude? How could he actually *know?*

What she said was, "Mama, I don't know why we're discussing this *now.*"

"Because now that you've changed in so many other ways," Betty said, "I wish you could understand he's a lot more tolerant than you think. There are things he's never even mentioned to you."

"Like what?" She was getting tired of this. In the distance LaMonica and her mother were breaking away from the circle of women. It looked like they were going to leave. Cassie hadn't so much as said hello.

"Like the way you tell people his name is Royal P.A.," Betty said.

"What?" Cassie attention was drawn back to her mother's words.

"The way you call him Royal P.A.," Betty repeated. "See? You thought he wasn't aware of it."

Cassie felt her mouth actually begin to drop open.

"He's known about it for years," Betty said crisply. "And don't think it's so hard for people to figure out what P.A. means, either."

It was impossible to believe Royal had known about P.A. and not mentioned it. Now that she thought of it, it was impossible to believe he hadn't sent her to reform school.

"He thought the P.A. phase was something you just had to work through," Betty said.

Cassie could not utter a word.

LaMonica and Dr. Reilly were moving toward the gate. Cassie could still say hello if she walked fast. Of course, Betty would probably not tell Royal that Cassie and LaMonica seemed to be good friends. There was really no point in rushing over there and fawning over LaMonica if Royal would never know.

Rose Bell came out into the center of the garden and clapped her hands for attention. The Princesses moved toward her in their hooped skirts. They looked more as if they were drifting than walking of their own accord. Cassie felt as if she, too, were drifting, even though her feet hurt.

"Girls," Rose Bell said, "we thought you should be the first to know. The Queen Committee has made its decision—and it's mostly because of concern for you young people that it's turned out this way. The committee has decided to replace Tara Barry with someone of higher moral character."

There was a little clapping, mostly by the mothers rather than the girls. LaMonica and Dr. Reilly were gone. "The new Queen will be announced," Rose Bell said, "as soon as the decision is final."

Betty leaned toward Cassie, amused at Rose Bell's news in a way Royal would not be. "I bet we don't hear an announcement," she whispered, "until they investigate this new Queen up and down." She spoke as if they were still sharing confidences and comparisons to live oak trees.

But Cassie felt ridiculous. She was standing here in a gown she had vowed never to wear, and the black Princess was gone and the Nudist Queen was fired. Probably Royal would gloat about it for a week. Probably he was saving the P.A. issue to use in some horrid and final coup against her. That and Caitlin Academy. Of course. But she couldn't be sure. It was very puzzling.

◆ ◆ ◆

Cassie wasn't certain who started the fight in the cafeteria. Maybe she did it herself. Or maybe it was because of the weather. Even sitting in class, you couldn't ignore the distant smoke that suddenly clouded the sun and blotted out the blue that Friday. The sky looked like mustard watered down and used as finger-paint—thin but bright, with the spring sun behind it.

All Cassie knew, even before the bell rang for lunch, was she felt half-starved and nasty. All her troubles seemed to be rolling around in her stomach, which was making noises loud enough for people to hear. She wanted to quit the festival, but Betty was so pleased with her. She even found herself dieting so her dress would fit better, this in spite of Royal's pointing out his watch-fulness in making sure no porn queen would mar the events for his Southern belle daughter. He'd even needled her about LaMonica.

"They used to have black Princesses back when everyone was big on civil rights," he said, stressing the term, *civil rights.* "But it's been years now. I don't know why they started up again."

"Well, it's only fair," Betty said tactfully.

"Why? The blacks don't belong to the Garden Club. They don't hire the Queen. They don't give a damn about the Azalea Festival except to go to the parade. They don't care about having a Princess. The Nigger Princess was white-inspired, sponsored by some bleeding heart Garden Clubber who uses the Reillys for her family dentist. Correct?"

Betty smiled inscrutably. She didn't deny what Royal had said or confirm it. She didn't volunteer any details. What happened at Garden Club meetings was secret. It was hard for Cassie to picture a member with a bleeding heart. But then, look how all the women had surrounded the Reillys to make them feel welcome. Maybe they weren't just putting up with an annoyance so as not to act ugly. Maybe they had a plan. Cassie was impressed with Betty for refusing to tell Royal. She felt a little smug.

But then the sky turned yellow and there was a muskiness in the air that left everyone high-strung and irritable. Cassie wasn't even especially surprised when Tiffany Galloway approached her in the cafeteria and said, "Well, if it isn't the slut

Princess. I remember when you swore up and down you weren't going to do it. But here you are."

Though she hadn't seen Tiffany for a couple of weeks, Cassie was used to Tiffany calling her a slut. Tiffany and Brian Ivey had been going out again ever since Christmas, and Tiffany blamed Cassie for their brief breakup in the fall. From what Cassie could gather, Brian led Tiffany to believe Cassie had seduced him. He said Cassie had asked him for a ride home from school that first day when he'd pulled his car in front of all the buses. He said Cassie talked him into continuing, trading the ride home for "services rendered." He hinted that, even now, all these months later, Cassie often phoned him. He said exactly what she would expect someone like Brian Ivey to say.

The odd part was, none of it much bothered her. Though Tiffany cut Cassie every time they met in the hall, her insults rarely got through Cassie's mildness. Royal always said you got into trouble when you defended yourself, guilty or not. If you acted like you didn't care, people would assume your innocence, but Cassie wasn't acting. She felt as she had in the fall when Royal's threats of reform school had taught her that sometimes indifference was the best protection. Besides, everybody knew Cassie wasn't a slut.

So she wouldn't have predicted the nastiness that filled her that Friday when the dusky light followed her into the cafeteria, and her stomach rumbled with hunger. Instead of rolling her eyes when Tiffany spoke, or smiling in a secret way at Janet Biggs like she usually did, she said, "Give it a rest, Tiffany."

Tiffany squinted at her. "If you think Brian wants you for yourself, think again," she said. "Some guys feel like they have to have a little trinket—a little ornament—now and then. Like a couple of gold chains. Or an Azalea Princess."

Tiffany's face was so pale and angry that she looked like a character out of an "Addams Family" rerun. "Or maybe a vampire," Cassie said.

"Better than a whore in a hoop skirt."

"I'm not the one who takes off every Thursday to screw my boyfriend."

The next voice was cool and rational and addressed to Tiffany. "I understand you weren't an Azalea Princess yourself," LaMonica Reilly said.

Cassie was stunned. No one ever mentioned Tiffany's absence from the azalea festivities her freshman year, something so terrible and secret that it had acquired the power of myth. Why would LaMonica unleash it? To defend Cassie? They weren't even friends, only student and tutor. Then Cassie realized LaMonica was defending the Azalea Festival and her role in it. This had nothing to do with Cassie.

"I might not have been a Princess," Tiffany said to La-Monica, "but if I had been, I would have been wanted."

"Yeah! Not a white nigger!" said a black girl standing in the crowd that had begun to collect.

"I think you're jealous because you missed your chance," LaMonica said calmly.

"Why?" Tiffany sneered. "Because it's such a privilege to be a princess, even if you're only a token black?"

"Yeah!"

"Tell her, sister," a black girl yelled.

"What kind of a bitch are you?" Cassie found herself yelling at Tiffany.

"Not one who goes after someone else's boyfriend!" Tiffany yelled back.

Cassie didn't know who reached out first. One of the black girls was after LaMonica and one after Tiffany. Tiffany was after Cassie. They were all after each other. When Cassie turned her hands into a claw and scratched someone, it wasn't a gesture she could control. She thought in a dark rush of hate how Tiffany was accusing her of sex with Brian in front of the whole school. How Brian would gloat. How LaMonica was so good in math. So unapproachable at the mother-daughter tea. So much *ahead* of her. When her hands clutched the cool black mass of someone's hair, she wasn't sure if it was LaMonica's or Tiffany's or one of the black girls who had joined the fray. White whore! White nigger! Bitch! She knew she could pull until the hair came out by the roots. It was the first time she'd ever wanted to hurt and keep hurting.

The cafeteria was bright, but she was aware only of a smoky cast over the sun, of hair clutched in her fists, of breath rasping in and out of her lungs. Suddenly she realized the person she was clawing was not Tiffany or LaMonica or any other girl, but some man. Mr. Edge.

Jesus Christ.

It didn't strike her as unfair that Mr. Edge gave them in-school suspension. It struck her as perfectly just. A person who had been suspended for fighting couldn't very well be an Azalea Princess. If the Queen couldn't be photographed naked, then the Princesses surely couldn't brawl in the cafeteria. Cassie would have to resign. Betty wouldn't blame her; she'd know Cassie hadn't started the fight. Betty would be forgiving, even after Cassie's name was in the paper. Royal would look like a fool.

Just as Cassie reached this point in her thoughts, an aide came in and handed a note to the suspension supervisor. They were not to be suspended after all. In view of the Azalea Festival, they were to receive a week's after-school detention. Tiffany, too.

Shit.

Royal and Betty arrived together, a united front, to pick her up.

"They didn't suspend you," Betty said frostily as Cassie climbed into the back seat of the car, "because you're not the sort of student who usually fights. None of you are. You should consider yourself lucky."

Royal drove in silence, staring straight ahead. Cassie could feel his distaste for her radiating out from the back of his neck.

"They gave us detention because we're Azalea Princesses and they didn't want the publicity," she said. "Because Princesses with charges against them might get the same bad press as a Nudist Queen."

"This isn't a time to be flip," Royal said.

"You know what's disgusting?" Cassie asked. "It's disgusting that being an Azalea Princess has nothing to do with you yourself. You could be the type of person who fights in the cafeteria and still be in the festival. You could be black like LaMonica. You could be a tramp like Tiffany. It doesn't really matter. It depends entirely on the politics." She remembered her civics class. "Just like Watergate."

"Maybe not the magnitude of Watergate," Royal said snidely.

"Stop it, both of you," Betty told them. Her voice was high and stiff, not at all the tone she'd used getting Cassie's gown, going to the tea. Sitting there beside Royal—under Royal's power—she had another voice entirely, thin and irritating.

"But morally," Cassie said, "we should really be suspended. From school and the festival both."

She expected Royal to speak, but it was Betty who turned around and said, "I hope that doesn't mean you're quitting. Not after we've rented the dress and gone to the tea and you've made the commitment. Not after the school saved your hide."

Cassie knew that six months ago she would have shouted, "Of course I'm quitting! It's only fair!" She would have told her mother to take the stinking dress to Martin's Cleaners, which Janet Foy trusted so much that it was actually in the contract for you to clean the gown there after the festival. Six months ago, Cassie would have said, go ahead, Mama, take the dress to Martin's and then back to Janet's Ruffled Curtains and let it hang there for some other sucker, not me. But the look on Betty's face had nothing to do with Royal's opinion or the Garden Club or the fired Queen; it had to do with Cassie agreeing to something and then backing out, which would show the kind of mother Betty had been for fifteen years. Cassie felt ready to pop, but she managed not to be ugly.

"I'm not backing out," she said.

Royal gave no hint that he heard. He was watching the road. Betty turned on the radio. The music was ripe like flowers, but it didn't soothe her. Smoke hung thick in the sky. Nothing had changed. Cassie wanted to grab Royal P.A.'s double chin and pull until he screamed.

The next day, Cassie read that Janet's Ruffled Curtains had been gutted by a blaze unrelated to the distant forest fires. Though she knew the Azalea gowns were safe in the closets of the Princesses and insurance would pay for the building and the stock, she felt partially avenged, thinking of Mrs. Foy's loss. The newspaper said the fire was caused by a cigarette left burning near one of the displays, but the way Cassie felt, the wicked energy inside of her might have started it. It might have jumped right out of her, across the drawbridge from Festival Beach, all the way to Janet Foy's store, and burned those curtains to the ground.

TEN

*E*ven before I got to King Neptune's, where I knew Fetzer would be after freestyle practice, I had decided exactly how I was going to unload my day. My anger cooled some as I imagined the scene: Fetzer sitting with Ray Pfeiffer and Bobby Newell, other salesmen from Lowe's, pointing his mug in my direction and saying with exaggerated heartiness, "Jordan's here to make sure I go out to fight those fires in Columbus County tomorrow, now that they're so close and their smoke is blowing our way. He's afraid otherwise they'll call our whole unit to help and take him away from his lady friend." Then he'd notice my slashed brow. "Although I see she got you one over the eye."

"This came from a student," I'd reply casually. "A female." And the looks on their faces would give me enough of my sense of humor to make the week into the best story I could—The Trash, the bombs, the cactus spines, Azalea Princesses brawling in the cafeteria and Bob McRae rescinding suspension so I looked like an idiot in front of whatever percentage of the student body was aware of what had happened at sixth-period lunch. It would come out sounding less like an insult than a joke, and everybody would laugh. Then I would start drinking beer, a lot of beer, and the evening would pass.

But when I got there, Fetzer and Bobby and Ray were already finishing their first pitcher, too mellow to notice my distress. Fetzer claimed since he'd turned forty he couldn't drink more than two beers without getting a hangover, but he must have been on number three or four, considering how fast he was talking, and how loud. He noticed me only enough to point me to a seat.

"I was telling them about Darnell and Fred," he said, naming two of his wrestlers who practiced together, one so black his skin absorbed the light, the other a redhead with a complexion the color of typing paper.

"Fred said the reason Darnell lost at the regionals was because he was psyched out," Fetzer said, pouring the last of the pitcher into his mug. "And Darnell—this bull of a kid whose arms feel like metal—I swear to God, he said, 'If I was psyched out, man, it was because the guy was more lily-white than you are. With a white guy, you never know whether or not he can eat you alive."

The salesmen chuckled. I spotted the waitress and signalled.

"So Fred says, 'Yeah, that'll do it every time. The sight of me usually scares them shitless.'"

More chuckles. The waitress ignored me.

"Then Darnell says, 'You white guys look like pussies, but on the mats, sometimes you're stronger than I think. With a black guy you look at him and you can pretty much tell what to expect.' So Fred says, 'Yeah, you look at him and figure he's been pumping iron and popping steroids since he was seven.'"

"Boy, don't they ever," Bobby said, reaching for the pitcher, finding it empty. He raised his hand and the waitress walked right over.

"The point is," Fetzer said, "if these kids didn't practice together every day, neither one of them would have a clue white kids are psyched out by black ones and vice versa. They sure as hell don't learn it sitting next to each other in World History." He tapped his index finger on the table, making slash marks of wetness for emphasis. "If it weren't for sports, they'd go around with their two different mind-sets the rest of their days."

"So what do you do with the rest of them?" Bobby asked. "Have an initiation ceremony where they all slash their fingers and mix black blood with white?"

The salesmen laughed again, but Fetzer didn't.

"I wish I knew. But I'll tell you what: I won't be surprised if Fred and Darnell are still hanging around together ten years from now."

"Be serious, Fetzer," I said. I was in that school every day and saw the great fierce attachments he was talking about—

loyalties fueled by differences of skin color and toughness and style the way brunettes are drawn to blondes or men to women. I'd never seen a single one survive the mats or the football field or the band, no matter how passionate. And Fetzer knew it: that bonds between unlike teammates were circumscribed to their narrow parameters the way a circle is held inside the pencil line of its own rim, and beyond it, doomed. I wanted to get through his social theories and into my rotten day. I wanted a beer.

"You really think Darnell and Fred are going to be hanging out together ten years from now? Then what besides wrestling are they going to talk about?" I asked. "They're never going to date the same girls. They aren't going to live in the same neighborhood."

"Or join the same clubs or go to the same church," Ray added. "He's right, Fetzer."

"Hell, they hardly even speak the same language," I said. "And ten years from now, they won't remember each other's names."

Maybe it was my tone that made Fetzer turn on me, or maybe the way he hated to lose an argument when he was drinking. "That's just the kind of attitude that keeps it from changing," he said. "What's eating you, anyway?"

The waitress brought the pitcher then, so I told him. The beer tasted rank and warm. The story didn't come out as lightly as I intended. Ray and Bobby nodded in sympathy. Fetzer didn't.

"Jordan, my friend," he said, "they might have given you a pretty title when they made you assistant principal, but it sounds like you're really the school bouncer."

I took another swallow. The beer was having no effect. Fetzer's words stung.

"Better a bouncer than a coach who makes social theory out of two wrestlers with the combined intelligence of a chain link fence," I said. "Better than a coach who recruits black wrestlers for their strength but is too chickenshit to admit it."

"He's pissed because they wouldn't let him suspend his black Princess," he said to the table.

"Or the white one either."

"Very egalitarian," he told me. "This from the man who calls the ghetto kids 'The Trash.'"

"Only a select few who *are* trash."

"One question, Mr. Egalitarian. The girl who had the cactus spines in her hand. Black or white?"

"Huh?"

He fished a bill from his wallet, plunked it on the table. "Ten bucks says she was black."

The headache had returned, the little tightening band of anger. I was cautious. "You mind running that by me one more time?"

"If she was white, you'd have sent her to the hospital. You wouldn't have been worrying about what an ambulance would do to student morale—you'd have worried she might have some kind of allergic reaction and wanted to make sure she had it in the emergency room so her parents wouldn't sue." He was performing now, talking louder, not as drunk as he pretended. "You wouldn't figure this consciously, but it would be in the back of your mind. With a black kid, what the hell, you'll get the pickers out with glue. Take a chance. If she has parents who pay any attention to her, it's probably just a mother that works full time and wouldn't be likely to complain."

"That's ridiculous."

"Which was she? Black or white?" Fetzer was using the same tone he had when he told me I wanted Alona to act like a wife, a tone like the whirring of an arrow before it hits its target. The salesmen were rapt.

"Black," I said.

Fetzer opened his mouth and laughed so hard I could see the gold crown just this side of his wisdom teeth. If our pagers hadn't gone off simultaneously, I swear I would have punched him.

◆　◆　◆

The alarm was at Janet's Ruffled Curtains, a shop that looked like an old house from the front but actually had a one-story warehouse/workroom area behind the showroom, so the building was longer and newer than it seemed from the street. The fire was in the back, leaking a little gray smoke, nothing remarkable. It wasn't to the puffing stage where the smoke turns greenish and seeps out from eaves, windowsills, every available crevice. In fact, it looked manageable. But I was edgy even before we went in.

The captain put Fetzer on the line with Andy Wilson. A welcome choice given the way I felt about Fetzer just then, but it left me without the protection of water. Since the fire was apparently small, the captain sent me and Paul Gibbs behind the linemen to do salvage. The department had been taking a lot of grief for destroying as much property as it saved, so we tried to cover up as much furniture or stock as possible in these situations.

Fetzer went in on his knees, five, seven feet, holding the nozzle, with Andy behind him and me and Gibbs following. No one came inside with a radio. The smoke had drifted farther toward the front than anyone thought. We couldn't see to the fire through the smoke. It was slow going for Fetzer, inching back there. I was still pissed at him, but I remembered Andy Wilson not carrying the weight of the line at that other fire when I'd been on the nozzle myself, and my heartbeat grew loud and uneven. I told myself it was nothing; I was just more wired than usual from my rotten day.

I ducked into a small display area on the right and Gibbs went into one on the left, each area dressed up with ruffled curtains at fake windows and hanging on racks, ruffled wreaths and placemats on pine tables, ruffled bedspreads and pillows, acres of cotton and muslin dimly visible through the smoke.

The display areas were separated by partitions that didn't go all the way up to the ceiling. The smoke was traveling high, banking from the fire in the back along the ceiling toward the front, floating over the partitions and obscuring the upper part of the room. I began stacking everything I could onto a big pine table in the center of the display area, pumping more adrenaline than fear for the moment, hoping a couple of minutes and we'd be out of there. I kept low, moving fast, pulling curtains from racks and placemats from their displays, stacking them all on the table. I was almost ready to spread the salvage canvas when my ears began to sting.

I never wore the fire-protective hood under my helmet that most guys used. I'd read years before that when your ears began to burn, that was the best indicator the fire was getting too hot to handle. Fetzer and I had a running argument about this. He said he'd had his ears blistered a couple of times and now he was all in favor of the hood.

"If I think it's getting too hot, I can take my glove off and hold my hand up for a second. What's the big deal?"

"The big deal is, your ears are more sensitive than your hands," I said.

"That's just the point. Even in the middle of a blaze, you can always put the glove back on, but there's nothing you can do for your ears. What are you, Jordan, a masochist?"

I turned and thought I could make out where he stood, wrestling the nozzle with his hood on and what I judged was probably a quart of beer sloshing around in his stomach. The rising heat would have sobered me up even if I'd had more than three swallows of beer, but Fetzer was at least half sloshed and shouldn't have responded to the fire at all—although guys often did. He and Andy were stooping lower, lower, to get under the heat, but they didn't seem aware of it. Maybe the alcohol had made Fetzer numb. I couldn't believe he'd be so unconscious, even drunk.

My ears were a mass of bee stings. I was a couple of feet farther from the fire than they were, burning up, making myself keep piling curtains and crap onto the table. Why didn't they notice the heat? I flattened myself out much as I could and still move, aware of nothing anymore but my ears. Some days get you to the point of not having any judgment left, some days wear you down that much. I was all ears—no pun—angry at Fetzer for wearing his damned protective hood, and rapidly getting spooked by the heat. I remembered Rich Anderson, who'd been in our unit a couple of years ago. One night he walked out of a fire, scared, and ever since had been known as "Rich Anderson-that-fucking-coward." I was scared and angry and ashamed of being aware of rising heat, dangerous heat, when Fetzer and Andy Wilson didn't seem to have a clue. And as the seconds passed and the situation worsened, I was less angry, less ashamed, and a lot more scared.

I undid the canvas and tried to snap it open. Couldn't, what with keeping so low. The smoke was getting thicker, darker, coming lower into the room. I couldn't see Fetzer anymore, but sensed the water he was aiming at the fire wasn't enough—we needed another hand line, maybe two. It was impossible to tell from where we were if the chief had any inkling what it was like in here, or if he did, whether he'd called for more help from mutual aid.

I felt like I was waiting, you'd have thought for hours but it wasn't hours, it was seconds, with my ears smarting and the smoke getting thicker, and so hot I thought any second every-thing was going to light up. I kept saying to myself, take it easy, Jordan, take it easy, but you don't take it easy when you're waiting like that—your whole world reduces itself to a single thought: *flashover*—when all the gases in the room reach the ignition point and everything goes orange, lights up, and there is no air anymore, only explosion, only fire rolling over you.

With the smoke changing color and the heat so intense, I knew everything was ripe for it. The only rational thought I had was that if I was going to get caught, I wanted to be holding water; I had vowed never to face another fire unarmed. But there I was with a sheet of canvas in my hand while Fetzer could afford to be calm, he had the nozzle, he was in control in the hallway and me a sitting duck in this showroom.

Maybe the next thing never really happened. It mustn't have, at least not the way I saw it.

To my left, a red glow became visible through the smoke, the upper part of a curtain bursting into flames. There was no fire around it, at least not any that I saw, though later I figured there must have been, some tongue of flame above that parti-tion. But at the moment, I could have sworn there was only the curtain I'd seen when I first came in and could only imagine now, with the smoke so thick—ruffled on the edges, tied back with a bow, white and shimmering, and then alight. Spon-taneously. I figured that was the beginning, figured we were at flashpoint, superheated, everything about to ignite at once. In a minute, the whole sea of cloth around me would be burning, and that would be all she wrote.

"You see that?" I yelled to Fetzer, but there was no way he could hear, so far away, no way he could do anything but keep pouring water into the flames and heat, his whole energy focused on holding the line.

When Rich Anderson walked out, Fetzer had said, "Any-body worth a damn isn't thinking about themselves, they're thinking about putting out the fire. The key is to think about what you're doing." And for a nozzleman, it's easy; a nozzleman gets totally involved in the flames, in attacking waves of fire through dense smoke. But I wasn't the nozzleman. And there is a certain point when you can't think of what you're doing anymore, when the room closes in and you're no better than a kid of fourteen caught between two walls of flame. I could no more have snapped open that canvas or covered those curtains than plunge into the fire headfirst, I was that afraid.

Then I was backing out, I wasn't thinking about it, just going. "I'm going to tell the chief it's more involved than we thought," I yelled. "And hotter."

I was low, inching backwards on my knees, turning around, crawling on my belly like a snake. I was telling myself Fetzer would buy what I was saying, I'd buy it myself if someone else was talking, alerting the chief was an act of prudence, not of cowardice. I came out into cool air, free, and the glove of panic slipped off smooth and easy. By the time I ran across the lawn to the captain, another unit had arrived, a ladder truck, there were lines all over the place, and I knew if I'd stayed inside another thirty seconds, it would have cooled off enough for me to do what I was supposed to do, to think about saving a couple of pieces of pine furniture and a hundred yards of ruffles instead of my own tender hide. A sheet of sweat covered me like a sticky layer of shame.

The odd thing was, no one knew, no one cared. Everybody carried on. If the place was mostly gone by the time we finished, still the only victims were an insurance company and a bunch of ruffles. Nothing the world couldn't do without. Afterward, Fetzer didn't seem to have noticed my brief absence. When we finished cleaning up at the fire house, he was ready to get fresh clothes and then continue drinking.

"Come on, Jordan, you must be dry."

But I said no, a shower and a sandwich were all the excitement I could handle. I spoke so smoothly even a guy like Fetzer wouldn't have guessed the self-hatred and disgust that wracked me. I got out of there fast. My thoughts were sour the whole way home. I kept saying to myself, Jordan, you may be a fucking coward, but at least you're smart enough not to get caught.

◆　◆　◆

I still reeked of smoke when I turned onto the dirt road to the cottage, the taste of ashes still thick in my mouth. I didn't expect it, but Alona's car was in the driveway. What would have been welcome four hours before was like a slap, a reminder of pleasure I'd wanted once, deserved once—a long time ago— pleasure offered too late. She'd turned the lights on in the living room, and the shades were open. She was lying on the sofa, her back to me. I thought she was asleep, but when I walked in, I saw she was awake, studying a row of earrings she'd set in a line on the coffee table, probably some of the new stuff she'd made, which she was forever bringing over to show me—new jewelry different and more clever than before, but as frivolous as the ruffles I'd spent my evening failing to save. Compared to the day I'd had, what were earrings?

Her eyes widened when she saw me. She must have been sitting there a long time, maybe napping after all, thrashing around. Her hair, the thing that had first attracted me to her and normally still did, was messy and tangled, an untidy reddish mop. I hadn't seen it like that. Or had I? After four months, I must have. But I hadn't noticed. Alona was big-eyed, taking me in, maybe suspecting what had happened. I was the puddle and she was ready to sop me up with that mop of hair. I remembered there were some things you didn't tell the women.

"Well," I said to her. "If it isn't Alona the Earring."

I saw how she took it: a little curious, ready to be entertained. Even a taunt is neutral the first time you say it, something you can forgive because it's uttered in anger or in jest. It's only after you repeat it enough, in the wrong tone of voice, that it begins to carry weight, like Marta, then Marta the Bitch, until it's written in black letters and branded in your skin, more poisonous than you imagined. I knew all that when I opened my mouth. "Alona the Earring." Such a stupid phrase. But I could no more have stayed my tongue than stayed in a super-heated room to save a bunch of curtains. I was angry with Alona for not being there earlier, at Bob McRae for making me look like a fool, angry at myself for turning coward in heat Fetzer didn't even notice; I was angry at anyone who'd listen to all that and take it in like a mop. So the second time the phrase came from my mouth, it was on purpose, and I watched as she flinched: Alona the Earring.

I told myself it was a joke.

ELEVEN

*B*looming, blooming, everything was blooming, all of it at once, a frenzy of bloom—dogwoods, azaleas, tulips. And the sky! Robin's egg blue. No rain for weeks. Temperatures in the seventies. They said the azaleas would be mostly finished by Azalea Festival, what with the weather so warm, but Alona didn't care. She knew the tourists would come regardless. They'd go to the beach if the garden tours proved disappointing, and then they'd shop—for necklaces, bracelets, earrings, everything she had in stock. She felt triumphant except sometimes when she wondered...when you did something really immoral, what was it you remembered afterward, the pleasure or the sheer sinfulness of it?

Most of the time, she had difficulty feeling remorseful. It seemed impossible that she'd been having an affair for more than four months. An affair! The word sounded evil, but she felt joyful, cheerful—at the very worst, restless—until the day at the beginning of April when the sky filled with smoke and everything began to go wrong.

The change seemed dramatic and sudden, though she realized later she'd simply been too preoccupied to notice the small signs leading up to it. For four months, she'd been busy inventing ways to see Jordan, busy making sure Elliott didn't find out, busy watching her own fingers weave designs into bead and metal faster than they ever had before. Though she was aware she was buying her happiness at Elliott's expense, she hardly even noticed the sarcasm that sometimes crept into his remarks.

"Well, I'm glad you're so bullish about the economy," he said as she stockpiled jewelry, looking at her as if she were a child.

The warm winter had slid into a warmer spring. Even Elliott had to admit there was a run on summer goods over at the mall, at Custom-Fit as much as everywhere else, and not just Easter shoes, either. Alona said if you bought shoes, you'd buy clothes, and if you bought clothes, you'd want jewelry to accessorize. Not everyone would do their shopping in town; plenty of people would go to the stores on the way to the beach.

"I've never seen you so hyper," Elliott said, sounding adult and disapproving. "Probably because they're shutting you down."

It was true. The house where she had her shop was being torn down at the end of the summer. She'd gotten the official notice. And she did want to sell out her stock—she didn't want a thousand boxes to move come fall. But that didn't deter her from making more jewelry. Ever since she'd started seeing Jordan, her fingers had become quick and magical, turning out the best work she'd ever done. She'd leaped from the middle of her career to the very pinnacle in a matter of months. Her customers were buying everything. The shelves would be nearly empty by the time she closed. While Elliott had great regard for profits, he watched Alona's success with a distant smile, as if he disapproved not only of her optimistic impracticality in producing so much when closing stared her in the face but also because he knew, in some unconscious way, that she'd been betraying him all winter. Bad as she felt about it, she couldn't make herself stop.

A fine yellow powder of pollen sifted through the screens of the store, coating the polished glass counter and everything on the work table. Alona's eyes watered, her fingers grew more feverish. In other springs, this feeling had unsettled her, coming as it did on top of a metabolism already speeding along. But now the restlessness seemed to suit her. She didn't mind feeling as if she had jumping beans in her fingers. She only rearranged her display case to show more of what she was producing—not just earrings, but necklaces and bracelets of twisted wire, rings studded with colored glass, pins of straw and rhinestones.

"Fanciful," Elliott said.

"Objects of art," Jordan told her.

Objects of love.

Love? But of course it was love! She loved Jordan, she loved Elliott, she loved her whole life now that Jordan was in it. When he walked with her along the section of the Intracoastal bordering the Joyner place or waded with her in Joyner Creek, it was as if they'd been masters of the estate always, though they both knew the rezoning had gone through. They seemed to have claimed the property the first time they made love there, back on election day.

Jordan had taken her for a walk through the grounds after they left the beach and stopped about a quarter of a mile from his cottage, where suddenly they broke through dense trees and stood on the banks of the Intracoastal, in the bright sheen of water and sky. When he began kissing her seriously, he sat her down on warm pinestraw not ten feet from open land where anyone could see.

"Jordan, not here," she'd protested, sounding unconvincing even to herself.

"Oh yes. Here," he whispered dramatically.

She could hardly keep from laughing. After all, she'd been waiting for this for a month. With the pinestraw sticking into her back and who-knew-who out there beyond the trees watching, she ought to have worried the whole time about being seen—not to mention being unfaithful to her husband. But not at all! The pinestraw might have been a down comforter under her shoulders, she felt so cozy. The light coming through the pines was sweet and golden and so old-looking that it might have traveled centuries to reach her, losing its summery bite on the way until it was just late-afternoon warm, autumn warm, the color of pumpkins and squash. Jordan's arms were thick and muscular, but his touch was soft, and he touched her for a long time. She had the feeling he'd stop if she asked him—stop and never touch her anywhere she didn't want. But it was as if her life had lost all its sparkle, oh, years ago, and hadn't gotten it back until his hands were on her breasts and thighs. So she lay there with the scent of pinestraw and aftershave in her head and was almost perfectly happy.

Not until months later did Alona decide Jordan had chosen that particular spot beneath the pines so she'd think him daring and fearless, and be a little frightened as well as impressed. In November, at the beginning, that didn't occur to her.

When they wandered back to his cottage, still dazed from their boldness and the feel of each other's bodies, Alona sipped the strong honeyed tea Jordan brought her and imagined Elliott ushering the last customers out of Custom-Fit and bringing down the metal cage that separated the store from the rest of the mall. To her horror, she didn't feel guilty, only sorry for the smallness of Elliott's life. Looking at Jordan, and around the quaint, unfamiliar rooms where he lived, she imagined herself the only woman in the world who'd ever tasted such sweetness and such bitterness in the same hot brew.

If she had to pick a moment when Jordan became her love and not just her lover, she would have chosen the day he went out to run three or four miles through the woods for exercise and came back with sweat drenching his shirt, dripping from him like he'd been hosed down. The first thing Alona had thought was how Emma would have laughed to see him like that. It wasn't a detail she would have mentioned to Elliott.

"Emma used to think it was ridiculous, grown men running in the heat with their tongues hanging out," she told Jordan. "I think she was talking about you."

"Probably so."

He came toward her with his arms outstretched, as if to hug her before he took a shower. The sweat beaded on his forehead and ran down his neck. Alona put the sofa between them—the only piece of furniture his living room was large enough to hold.

"She'd say, they can exercise all they want—exercise as if they could outrun old age," Alona said, circling while Jordan followed, "but it won't do them a bit of good. They'll get old anyway—and you will, too—just wait and see."

Jordan laughed. "Old age, here I come," he said.

It was then Alona remembered how when Emma spoke of getting old, Alona always thought no, she wouldn't, and a shiver always ran through her like chills. But with Jordan laughing at her, so healthy-looking with the dampness on his skin and color in his cheeks, she could see that exercise would stave off anything.

"Emma used to say it was unnatural, men putting on little nylon shorts and trudging along the street for a couple of miles," Alona told him, grabbing pillows off the sofa and throwing them in his way as he followed her. "She thought men running was as artificial as the rest of modern life. She'd say, 'Why, modern life is artificial right down to those pretty models on TV.'" She was imitating Emma now. It seemed to her that until that moment, she'd forgotten the sound of Emma's voice. "They don't stare into human faces. That would be too normal and natural. Instead they stare into those TV cameras as if they were lovers."

"Lovers, huh?"

Jordan grinned, throwing the pillows back onto the sofa. She knew he was waiting until she became so absorbed in her story that he could switch directions and catch her. But she'd be too alert, she'd wear him down. Circle until he decided to escape by ducking into the bathroom for his shower. Even as she was thinking this, he lunged straight over the back of the sofa. "Surprise!" Catching her around the waist. Tumbling her to the floor. "Take a whiff," he said, raising his arms. "Is that an artificial smell? Or normal and natural?"

"Jordan, stop!"

He didn't move, he pressed into her. "Natural or artificial?"

"Okay. Natural! Horrible!" But she was laughing; it wasn't horrible at all. Much as he was sweating, the smell of his aftershave overpowered the other. Somehow they ended up in the bedroom, in his bed, and the shower was forgotten.

Afterward, lying beneath the covers, she knew it was time to test him.

"You know, they found Emma by the pilings under the drawbridge," she said. "The police decided she jumped off the bridge. But she was so afraid of bridges, I knew it was impossible."

The inside of her mouth felt gray and lusterless, uttering those things, but she had to get it over with. Jordan's heart beat smooth and steady in his chest, against her skin. She told him about the police report, and how Elliott agreed with it, even now.

"Maybe she did jump off," she whispered, saying what must have been in the back of her mind all along. "Maybe it was true."

"I doubt it," Jordan said. He sat up to face Alona directly. "But even if she did jump—so what? She was dying anyway, wasn't she?"

The way he said that made Emma sound brave, not deranged the way Elliott wanted to think of her. "She never did want to go out of this world X-rayed and chemicalized to death," Alona mused.

"Well, who would?"

After that, Alona knew there wasn't a thing she couldn't tell Jordan. It seemed to her that when someone close to you died, all you could think about at first were the unpleasant details, and until you got over that, you couldn't remember their life in a proper way. Or else you could only remember them filtered through someone else's harsh judgment—like Elliott's. It was such a relief to say whatever she wanted to Jordan that she thought maybe such confessions were what made people fall in love. She began to feel that no detail of her life was sanctioned until Jordan heard about it. Even if she said a thing to a dozen people, it sounded new all over again—as if it had never really happened or been important until Jordan nodded and accepted it with his eyes. She didn't know if that meant she loved him; she only knew her skin began shimmering from underneath from that time on, giving off little hard points of light. She could see it in the mirror and wondered why Elliott never noticed.

Because of Jordan, Alona even loved the winter, which she'd always dreaded. As a child, she'd regarded winter as a misery ruled by darkness, not because of the cold—which wasn't much—but because of the diminished light. Emma had struggled out of bed before dawn to get to the Waterway in time for breakfast, and Alona, feeling too guilty to go back to sleep, watched for morning, which inevitably broke pale and bereft. A little of that feeling stayed with her into adulthood. But Jordan made her welcome the short days, the early dusks when she could be at his cottage while Elliott worked. Jordan's bedroom seemed dark and romantic then, as they hid under thick covers to make love and nap. They drank wine in the tiny living room, built huge blazes in the old stone fireplace, inhaled warmth and wood. Even when Jordan's pager sent him rushing out to a fire—even as distracted as he seemed at those times— even then Alona was happy waiting for him in the cottage, imagining herself living there, cooking meals, making beds. It was the closest she'd ever come to feeling perfectly content.

The only thing that didn't please her about that winter was the way Jordan sometimes answered her questions with no answers at all. After he was summoned to a wreck once, where a car caught fire and nearly exploded, Alona asked, "Aren't you afraid, Jordan?"

He put on a smile she could only describe as inscrutable and replied, "Oh, I am. Every time." As if it were normal to seek out the thing you were most afraid of, instead of avoiding it the way Emma had kept away from bridges. There was no fear on Jordan's face, not even the memory of fear, only a glaze of contentment. He'd been twirling a strand of her hair around his finger as he talked, twisting it so tight he cut off the circulation and left the joint a dead-looking white. He shook it to bring the color back. She didn't know what to make of him.

All that was part of his mystery. Alona didn't really mind. The life they couldn't live together—hers in the store, his at school—they could only talk about. It was just that the things they didn't share were sometimes hard to understand, like his devotion to his friend Fetzer.

"Fetzer's heavyweight, Casper, can't even get down to two seventy-five for a match," Jordan said in January, after a wrestling meet where Central High had had to forfeit the weight. "He'll tell Fetzer he's had only fruit all day and Fetzer will say, 'Then you must have eaten a hell of lot of it,' and give him a printed diet there's no way he can follow."

"That doesn't sound very helpful," Alona ventured then. But they were in bed, fooling around a little, and she couldn't make herself feel indignant.

"Oh, the kid loves him. Last week, Casper was arguing with some other kid, so he brought him over to Fetzer and said, 'Violence is never the answer, right, coach?' You should have seen him, so proud of himself, having Fetzer there to settle it."

"Well, I guess...if Fetzer can be a role model," she said, wanting to like Jordan's friend even though she'd never met him. The truth was, hearing herself say "role model," she reminded herself of Elliott.

"You know what Fetzer told him? He said, 'Well, that's probably a good premise you're working from, Casper. Most of the time, it's better to talk it out. But what if someone's trying to rip you off? Are you going to talk to him, or are you going to resort to some old-fashioned violence?'" Jordan laughed.

"Oh, Jordan. That's mean."

"Casper was too confused to know what to make of it."

"Even worse," Alona said.

But Jordan pulled her close, changing the subject. "Brains aren't everything. It isn't your brains I'm rubbing." And of course by then she'd forgotten what they were talking about. That was how most of their conversations ended.

Maybe that was why she was always so glad to get home to Elliott. She'd never lived on the edge of someone's life before, the way she was doing with Jordan, talking and playing and never knowing where she stood. It was like having wine running in her veins, and she could take just so much of being drunk.

She loved Jordan's solitary woodlands, but she loved her cheery apartment, too, surrounded by lawns and neighbors. She loved the excitement of Jordan's touch and the safety of Elliott's. After work, Elliott changed from tie and jacket into jeans and sweatshirt, all the while telling her how his January clearance was going, folding his good clothes and hanging them up as he spoke, until Alona couldn't help admiring his neatness and orderliness and the straightforward way he talked. At those times, it pleased her that his hair was so crisp and black, and that his thick eyebrows made him look so dignified above the startling blue of his eyes. Sometimes he talked about Sally Battle, who worked in his store, trying to make Alona jealous in a joking way. The innocence of his motives touched her. She didn't even mind the longing expression he often wore as he gazed at her. Considering her own transgressions, she didn't want to hurt him.

All that winter, Elliott didn't once mention her having a baby. It was as if he sensed there were deeper issues to be settled. And Alona didn't once dream the strange upsetting dream about the light shining on her hair. In some ways, as long as she kept Jordan separate, living with Elliott made her life almost normal.

Then, one night after the January clearance, Elliott moved against her in bed, stroking as she knew he would, and in a thick voice said, "I love the way you feel."

Alona was so startled by the strangeness of his speaking just then that she felt her whole body lock up inside itself. In the years she'd known him, Elliott had never before uttered a word while they were making love. Never a word. His touch had spoken for itself—a poetry of taut muscle and warm breath and the sweet aching in her belly, blotting out whatever other concerns they had in the world. It was that silence that had sustained them through their various disagreements over Emma's sanity and their readiness for parenthood. It had even sustained them through Jordan. But hearing Elliott say he loved the way she felt, and then a minute later, "I like your flat stomach," which she knew perfectly well he liked, Alona felt jarred as if from sleep. The moment was…polluted. Usually she never had a single thought beyond the spell of Elliott's hands, but suddenly she couldn't concentrate. She let him finish while her mind filled with a jumble of outside concerns—the malfunctioning glue gun she intended to replace, the details of her expired lease. Jordan.

After that, Elliott didn't speak in bed all the time—only now and then. Once he said, "God, Alona, I can't get enough of you." It was such a bad line she didn't even think they would say such things in a movie. Did he expect her to respond? Was he talking like that because he sensed a gap between them? Sensed the presence of someone like Jordan? Maybe, subconsciously, he'd guessed that Jordan talked in bed. Guessed that Jordan would often kiss her and say, not seriously but only for fun, "Delicious." Or do something X-rated and mutter afterward, "Excellent stuff," to make her laugh. She did laugh, too. Jordan chattered in bed whenever he felt like it, and Alona found it entertaining. So why was it that when Elliott talked to her, it was like breaking a sacrament?

She began to fear that Elliott might do something even more unpredictable. Nothing kinky, just…odd. He might start admiring, say, her feet—the perfect normality of her feet. Before she knew it, he'd be kissing them, chewing on her toes. Ugh! She was appalled at the very thought of it. If she couldn't even count on her own husband…but then, of course, he couldn't count on her.

◆　◆　◆

Alona drifted between them, husband and lover, through the short days of winter into February when the sun grew more golden and every robin on the East Coast stopped in Festival on its travels north. Birds dotted the landscape, pecking for worms through tufts of brown grass. The days were warmer than usual except during the brief cold snaps, which came suddenly and vanished just as quickly, bringing brittle sunshine and cold sandy winds. Little by little, while continuing to extol her virtues in bed, Elliott grew somehow disapproving of her work.

Maybe that was why Alona's fingers began to twist earring wires as if they were no heavier than air. If she could not have Elliott and Jordan on her own terms, at least she would exert control over her jewelry.

But somehow that wasn't enough. She and Jordan couldn't go anywhere together. It would disgrace Elliott. But finally, at the end of wrestling season, in February, she did go to a match at Central High. She didn't think anyone would see her, and if they did, so what? She was not with another man, only in the same gym. She wanted to see Jordan in his regular environment for once. She wanted to get a look at Fetzer Laney, about whom she'd heard so much. What could be the harm? If the match—the last of the season—started at seven like Jordan said, she'd be home and showered before Elliott got in from the mall.

The gym was fuller than she expected. Jordan sat in the front row and winked at her when she came in. She moved across the gym from him, up toward the top of the bleachers. When she spotted Fetzer Laney, she saw he wasn't what she'd imagined. He was older—forty if he was a day—and not at all the short, hairy, powerfully built ex-wrestler Jordan seemed to have described. Rather, Fetzer was of medium height and thin except for his head, which was unnaturally round and globe-like. She didn't understand why he was wearing a baseball cap at a wrestling meet until he lifted it to reveal a big bald spot poking up through sandy hair. He looked like an accountant. Alona wondered if everything Jordan spoke about would turn out, in actuality, to be this different from what she'd imagined.

She wasn't sure which she hated most, watching the wrestling or sitting alone. There were plenty of students and a few parents, but Alona wasn't in either category. She'd never been to a high school wrestling match before and didn't know what was going on. Though Jordan had said it was nothing like professional wrestling, more a finesse sport, to her it looked no better than Hulk Hogan or Andre the Giant on TV, throwing around some other muscle-bound man. If Jordan had been next to her to explain, maybe she would have understood the take-downs and escapes and pins. But sitting alone, she could make no sense of the boys writhing around on the mat in their ridiculous singlets, which looked like the body suits women wore to aerobics, only skimpier. And it seemed to her that, instead of getting aerobically fit, the boys were trying to hurt each other. In football or basketball, getting a basket or scoring a touchdown seemed logical; here, there was only the wrenching of arms and legs, the shoving of heads into the mat, until finally one boy got the other one on his back.

And it was loud. Jordan was certainly right about Fetzer's mouthiness. In his harsh, raspy voice, Fetzer yelled constantly, calling encouragement to the struggling boys—"Shoot the half! Now!"—venting anger at those who didn't do enough. He shouted at the referees. He waved and made objections. Mostly Alona had no idea what Fetzer was shouting about. She could only see that he loved the noise and sweatiness and hurting. And below her, across the gym, Jordan was as flushed as Fetzer. He wore the face she imagined he'd have at a fire, excited about walking into the pure red danger of flames.

When it was over, groups of boys were shouting at each other outside the gym. A bunch of blacks stood by the activity buses, and a dozen whites clustered beside the building. They were yelling, "Yeah, well come on over here, then," and replying, "Don't you wish," louder and louder, until she couldn't hear their words at all but only the noise.

She was caught in a group of students and parents coming out the door. No one did anything, only watched. She wasn't sure if they were hoping for a fight or afraid of one, though she remembered from her own high school days that the shouting mostly came to nothing.

Fetzer emerged from the gym through a different door, looking thin and wiry, still wearing his baseball cap. With a slow step, he walked over to one of the biggest black boys. "You have a problem," he said, "why not come settle it in the gym? We'll let you wrestle little Mikey."

"I'm not gonna do that rassling stuff, man, I'm gonna whip his *ass.*" The black boy was pointing to one of the whites. Alona didn't think it was Mikey.

Fetzer moved closer to the black boy. The noise had died to a grumble. Fetzer looked so overly serious that she could tell he wasn't, really, that underneath he was having the time of his life. "What're you afraid of? Come on. We don't have the mats rolled up yet. It won't take long, just go two minutes with little Mikey. You must outweigh him by...what? Thirty pounds?"

"Shit, man," the black boy said. He started to turn away.

Then Jordan was there among them, not saying a word, just looking at the black group and the white group as if he were putting their individual names in his mind, and then sure enough, saying some of the names out loud as if he were greeting them—"Alvin...Shaunessey...Roy..."—but underneath sounding like he was making a list of people something terrible would happen to. The boys began to turn away.

It was as if power were swelling up in Jordan, as if he were having even more fun than Fetzer, though his expression was grave. People began to move toward their cars. Jordan glowed. Alona thought maybe he loved what he'd just done more than he could love *her*. She felt exactly as she did when he came back from a fire or a bad day at school: that she was outside of it.

The night was chilly. She hurried across the parking lot, losing sight of Jordan. As she moved toward her car, it seemed to her that every other person here had a companion. She wanted to get home. She wanted to walk through her apartment and turn on all the lights. She wanted to see Elliott.

Someone took her arm. Jordan. He'd sought her out. She couldn't believe how the touch of his hand warmed her through her jacket and right down to her skin. It was quarter to nine and Elliott got off in fifteen minutes, but when Jordan said let's have some coffee, there was nothing she could do but accept.

"You probably think it was my job to break that up right off," he said in the restaurant.

"I hadn't considered it." She hadn't; she was still thinking how his face had glowed as he greeted the boys in the crowd and how she'd felt outside of his concern, distant and excluded.

"If you've got a guy like Fetzer in charge, you let him be in charge. You don't take over. Except, of course, to take names." Steam from the coffee misted his face. "We have to be at every athletic event to control the crowds. We get scenes like that all the time. Kids acting like dogs barking at each other across the street. Then you single them out, and they're harmless."

She didn't like the idea of dogs barking at each other across the street. Maybe Jordan was saying that because he was afraid and wanted to cover up.

"The ghetto kids don't like the wrestling because it looks something like street fighting, and they figure they should be able to win," he said sternly. "But they find out they can't make up their own rules. One of The Trash came out once and got his butt beat. Now they razz the wrestlers every chance they get."

The Trash. Always the Trash. "There were some blacks on the wrestling team," she said defensively. *"Mostly* blacks."

"Not street blacks. Not Trash. You have to understand the mentality." He sounded irritable, as if she'd missed some important point. He put his cup down and began running his finger around its rim. "The Trash don't wrestle because that's not their sport. Their sport is intimidation. Travel in groups. Talk tough. Make money any way they can, including drug dealing and extortion."

He looked at her then, but his attention went right through her; she might have been anybody.

"They pride themselves that no one tells them what to do, even family. Hell, half of them don't even know who their legal guardian is. Ask them where they live, it turns out they don't live anywhere, they only *stay.* 'Oh, I stay over at Bishop Gardens.' Temporary. The same way school is temporary, so we don't have any sway over them. The same way life is temporary. If they get caught doing something, they cry discrimination, as if they're being punished for being black and not for being cruds. Nobody tells them different. Every year, one or two of them get shot before they're twenty. And good riddance."

She couldn't believe he'd said "good riddance." He wasn't telling her how he felt, he was lecturing her as if she were some dimwitted student. He looked as bitter as the coffee they were drinking.

"I'd think if anybody could handle them, you could. *You* spent time as a street kid," she said.

"Not the same." He waved a hand in dismissal.

"Oh, Jordan, you do pretty well."

But she didn't know whether it was true. Except for tonight and that day last fall with Cassie Ashby, she'd never seen him in action. Except for what he told her, she didn't know a thing about him. She would have liked to ask a few pointed questions, but she just couldn't, not here. She wanted to be back in his cottage, in bed, where she could make light of this, make everything be all right.

She'd spread her hair over Jordan's chest and say the incident in the parking lot reminded her of color wars when she was a counselor at camp—intense but not very serious. She'd stroke his skin and tell how everyone was assigned to the blue team or the red team, how blues went to activities with other blues and ate with them and sat together on the bus, until they knew all the other blues but hardly any reds. And soon they were shouting at the reds and rooting against them, just like at Central High, except that at school the colors weren't assigned, they were what the students were born with, black or white. Then Jordan would have to laugh, to agree that all this wasn't so serious; it was more like color wars at camp. But Jordan's face was all knotted up in the harsh light of the restaurant, so fierce Alona couldn't say a word. Or maybe it was just that they were in a public place where they had no business being together and Alona felt out of her jurisdiction.

She said lamely, "I guess they all have their problems."

"With most of them, it's less a matter of having a problem than *being* a problem," he replied, not kindly.

Alona stared into the bottom of her cup, at little spiderweb stains of coffee. Apparently Jordan hated his students and loved fires and wrestling and facing off angry crowds, and Alona didn't know the half of it; it was his other life that she was out of entirely. He placed two dollar bills on the table, leaving her dismissed, distanced from him. She felt as needy as Elliott with his heavy-lidded gaze. Instead of standing up to go, she pushed her hair around, hoping her eyes would shine, hoping the shimmer on her skin would remind Jordan he was linked to her, even if only since a balmy fall afternoon on the pinestraw by the waterway.

"No sympathy even for Cassie Ashby?" she asked.

He might have laughed, he might have said, well, Cassie Ashby brought me *you*, but he didn't.

"Cassie Ashby seems to have her own agenda," he said, pushing the money beneath his saucer.

Then he moved his knee to touch hers under the table, deliberately ending the conversation the way he always did, by rubbing or kissing. She felt overperfumed and cheap. She wanted him to talk seriously for once, to tell her what he was trying to prove, being assistant principal and crowd-controller and fire-fighter and whatever else he might be that she had no part of. She wanted to know his secrets with an intensity that reminded her again of Elliott's helplessness, and how much she hated it.

"I'm already late getting home," she said, looking at her watch. She stood, hoping her leaving would soften him. Probably the only sway she had over him was that she had another man in her life. It didn't seem like much.

◆   ◆   ◆

So they came to springtime. The early azaleas bloomed in the middle of March, the tulips flamed and faded, the dogwoods began to show white. Pollen floated so thick in the air she felt she was swimming in it. Elliott was at once passionate and disapproving. Jordan told her stories about things she never observed firsthand. Yet despite her moments of confusion, Alona wanted them both. When her eviction notice came, Jordan teased that she'd be selling jewelry on the street corner, hawking earrings displayed against black velvet, in such vivid detail that she had to laugh. And Elliott sat with her to make a list of her options—relocate store, abandon retail operation, seek innovative marketing methods—until she felt calm and secure. She could not do without either man. She couldn't. And she knew she wouldn't have to because never before had her hair hung so heavy down her back; never before had necklaces and earrings dropped from her fingers as if woven by elves; never before had her jewelry shone so unnaturally luminescent in her window, as if it caught every ray of the rising spring light.

She didn't count on yellow smoke invading the sky one Friday morning, making everything seem strange and dangerous. Artificial, as Emma would say. The air grew crackly-dry. The sun was hidden. All day Alona threaded beads on wire, added feathers and ribbons, felt dissatisfied with everything she did. She longed for the gentle water-haze that often floated up from the Intracoastal, for the wet smell of spring. By dusk, she could work no longer, though Elliott wouldn't be home until late. She went to Jordan's and let herself in with her key. She lined up the latest earrings on his coffee table. Maybe she fell asleep. She wasn't registering everything clearly when he first came in, except his mocking tone of voice: "If it isn't Alona the Earring."

"What's wrong?" she asked. "Did something happen?"

"What do you think could have happened, Alona the Earring? You think if something happened I'd be home this early?"

His face was bleached out in the light of the room. He smelled of soot and smoke. He must have come from something terrible, perhaps an enormous fire where someone had died.

"What is it?" she asked again.

He sat down on the couch, but not next to her. "What is what? Nothing. I had a rotten day. I'm in a lousy mood."

"So I see."

"Alona the Earring, go home."

She was still foggy from sitting so long. Was it possible he was dismissing her? Her face grew warm, probably red.

"Come back tomorrow," he said, leaning back, putting a foot on his knee, removing a shoe. He wasn't looking at her.

She stood, because there was nothing else to do. "Not tomorrow. Tomorrow Elliot and I have to go to an art show." This was true, and also an inspiration. She would speak of Elliott. Be victorious. Mistress of two men.

Jordan pulled off his other shoe. "An art show. Right."

"There's this woman who works for Elliott. Sally Battle. It's a show for local artists. I think it's the first painting she's ever had hung anywhere." She heard the smugness in her voice but didn't care. "Sally's worked for him all this time, so he has to go. So do I."

"I see." Jordan took off his socks. His feet looked unnaturally white. "I can envision just how your life is going to go from now on," he said.

"What do you mean?"

"I mean the art show. I see it as just the beginning."

"The beginning of what?"

"The kind of life you're going to live."

"Jordan, be serious."

"This week it's an art show, next week it's going to be your book club," he said.

"You know I hardly ever read books."

He picked up a pair of the earrings she'd spread on the coffee table, burlap rectangles onto which she'd pasted tiny scarecrows made from toothpicks and fabric. He held them aloft for her inspection. *"Art,"* he said.

"Don't be a jerk." It was Sally who was the artist.

"Pretty soon all you and Elliott will talk about is art and culture. I can see it now." He put the scarecrows down and directed his gaze to the other earrings on the table. "You'll go to museums and look at pictures some shoe clerk painted and act as if they're the great triumph of human endeavor."

"What's your problem, Jordan?" She didn't deserve this. She hadn't done anything except mention Elliott.

"Problem? Jordan Edge with a problem?" He raised his damaged eyebrow. He wasn't going to tell her what was bothering him any more than he had the night of the wrestling match. He'd kiss her and get as close to her as two people could get, but he wouldn't speak his mind because he didn't consider her that important. She knew by the way he was accusing her. Even if they were together for years, she'd never know more about him than she did this minute. Maybe that's what it was to be a mistress—to cling to the outside of someone's life and have the main part of his concern eternally hidden. There was nothing she could do but pick up her purse and bend to sweep the earrings into it from the coffee table, and when she was finished, leave.

As she bent over, with her hair falling around her face, Jordan leaned toward her from where he sat on the sofa. There wasn't a trace of affection in his closeness, just anger radiating out like heat. He smelled of smoke and soured aftershave. His fingers traced the freeform metal circles that dangled from her ears.

"Culture," he said softly, bringing his lips close to her. His tone was sarcastic and his breath was warm. It was like being called a bitch in a cheerful voice.

He let his hand rest on the earring. He might have been ready to kiss her. Then he flicked the earring away so that it thumped against her neck. She stared at him dumbly. He flicked it harder. Her neck stung where the metal hit.

"Goodnight, Alona the Earring," he said.

She felt as if she had been slapped.

The night was muddled and gray from the smoke in the sky. She drove the quarter mile to the end of Jordan's lane before she let herself slow and pull the circular earring off. It sat in her hand like the top of a discarded soup can, not stylish but only big and foolish. She cast it out of the window. If she wept, her face would be red and splotchy for hours. She didn't cry.

At home, Elliott was just getting out of the shower. He smelled of soap, sweet and familiar. When he said to her, "Work late?" she made herself nod. She made herself be normal. She made herself say, "I'm beat."

He was brushing his teeth, grinning at her through bubbles of toothpaste.

"You look good, even beat."

It was a lovely thing to say. But all the same, she did not like seeing the toothpaste, the white grinning foam, on someone else's teeth.

She undressed and got into bed. She felt achy and ill, as if the place where the earring had hit had become infected. Growing up around women, one of the first things she'd noticed about men, aside from their physical qualities, was how they imagined you'd make fun of them if they showed the least bit of weakness. Elliott wasn't that way so much, but most men were. Once she'd had a date who was so curt all evening that she thought he hated her, only to discover he'd been cut from the football team a few hours earlier. He'd have rather died than tell her. Or if men did tell, they'd try to get her to a certain point of helplessness first, so she wouldn't laugh. Maybe that was what Jordan was doing. But it was a way of bullying. She couldn't go on with a person who bullied her, because it would only get worse. Next time he would hit her with an open palm. Then a fist. But the thought of ending it, truly, felt like a hand squeezing at her throat.

She had no memory of Elliott getting into bed, or of falling asleep. Her world was darkness until she saw herself walking toward herself, wearing a summer skirt and sandals, her hair with a crisp just-washed feel and her legs shaved and smoothed with lotion. She didn't seem to be wandering just anywhere, but along the Intracoastal near Jordan's house, where they came out of the woods to make love and look at the water. There was a suffused quality to the sky, the same as the real sky now that the smoke had blown into it. Alona knew she wasn't dreaming. The events were actually happening, to the self that was observing and the self that was walking. An eerie orange light began to shine on her hair. The air was dry and hot. The light grew more intense, not gradually but all at once. She raised her hand to shield herself from the glare, but it was everywhere—in her hair and on her skin, needles pushing into her eyes, touching the bruised spot on her neck with the force of pain.

The sound of her own blood woke her up, thundering through her veins. She sat up with a mouth so dry she might have eaten sand. It took her a minute to register her own bed. And darkness. And Elliott. She moved closer to him, into the warm crook of his body.

Though he slept on, he made room for her, shifting. She settled in. When he touched her, she expected it. She was thinking of the eerie light, of Alona the Earring, of the soup-can lid dangling from her ears. Of Jordan's blow. She knew it was wrong to take comfort in one man and think about another, but she did. When he touched her, his hands were skilled and kind. He didn't utter a word. She let him be Jordan. After a while, he was the only kindness she remembered.

TWELVE

Cassie thought she would just about throw up when she saw Wendy Stallings, the new Azalea Queen, get off the plane that Thursday afternoon. As one of the dozen Azalea Princesses who'd been given the honor of greeting the Queen, Cassie was standing in her hoop-skirted gown at the bottom of the portable staircase wheeled up to the jet from L.A. A sudden wind had sprung up, which made all twelve hoops sway from side to side, as if it weren't embarrassing enough to be standing on a runway to begin with, in an airport ten miles out of town the way big-city airports were, but too small and underbudgeted to rate an indoor ramp from the plane to the terminal building. *Underbudgeted* was Royal's word. Cassie knew that indoor ramps were standard in Baltimore and probably everyplace else in the United States except Festival.

The other arriving passengers, most of whom had probably never heard of the Azalea Festival except on the news when the old Queen was fired, were negotiating the portable stairs in single file, staring at the Princesses as if they feared the plane had landed in a time warp where modern clothes had yet to be invented. Of course, anyone who looked closely could see that no plantation maiden ever wore earrings like Cassie's, which consisted of one silver hoop and one blue enamel one, a papier-mache star to match the enamel, a pearl daisy, and a tiny silver bell. Cassie would be a Princess, but she would also be herself. If that annoyed Royal, so much the better.

She'd even made a special trip to Jewels to buy the earrings, after months of avoiding the place. The amazing thing was how

Alona had come up to her as if no time at all had passed, as if Cassie meant something special to her, and said, "Still want that extra hole pierced in your ear?"

Cassie knew if she said yes, Alona would pierce it then and there, even though she'd once sworn not to. But Cassie wasn't sure she did want the extra hole now. All she wanted was earrings. Alona spent nearly an hour helping her pick them out, showing her all the new designs she'd made. And then—get this!—she'd given Cassie a discount. It was almost like having an ally.

After that, she knew she'd get away with wearing them, too. Yesterday, at the rehearsal for the Queen's coronation ceremony which was to follow this airport reception, Rose Bell from the Teen Committee said, "Do you think those earrings are really appropriate, dear?" Cassie put on such an expression of hurt and puzzlement, and whispered in such a quivering tone, "But they're my very best," that Mrs. Bell had no choice but to nod demurely. Cassie had watched Royal P.A. defuse many a situation with just such an expression and vulnerable-sounding voice.

The wind was getting so strong and eerie and dry that they might have been standing in a sauna where someone was fanning them. The Princesses' hair was blowing every which way, especially Cassie's since she was wearing it down, as she'd done ever since Janet Foy told her to put it in an upsweep. A cameraman from Channel 6 news stood with his minicam slung over his shoulder, recording the disarray of the Princesses and preserving the moment when one of them, Tina Lanham, raised her delicate porcelain hand to extract a big old leaf that had blown into her mouth.

The remaining passengers finished coming down the steps, all except for Queen Wendy Stallings, who had remained on the plane to make a proper entrance. The Azalea Festival officials motioned the Princesses to realign themselves into receiving lines on either side of the stairway. Rose Bell stood at the bottom of the stairs with the mayor of Festival, holding a bouquet of azaleas to present.

When Cassie looked at the doorway of the plane, waiting for the starlet to appear, she noticed that though it was midafternoon, the sky was a perfect bright orange, like the glow of a distant sunset. The color seemed just right for greeting a TV personality.

Then Wendy Stallings came onto the platform. She was wearing a fuschia minidress that clashed with the sky. She began descending the stairs, waving to the crowd at first and then devoting her attention mostly to her feet. These were encased in five-inch heels that wobbled on the rickety metal grid of the stairs. When Wendy reached the bottom, it became obvious she was shorter than anyone expected. Even with the high heels, most of the Princesses dwarfed her. She couldn't be five feet tall. This was not apparent on television. It was not particularly regal.

Also, the Queen didn't look real. As the reception committee moved to greet her, the Princesses noted that her thick glaze of makeup left her looking not only smooth-skinned and evenly featured, which they had expected, but also plastic. The oval frame of her hair had, amazingly, not moved at all during her descent into the wind. And in the odd orange sunlight, the Queen's hair was not at all the soft blonde it looked on her soap opera, "Sundown Days," which Cassie had seen exactly twice when she happened to be home at two in the afternoon. It was brassy yellow all the way through, as if colored uniformly with crayon. Cassie had seen this shade only on harsh Northern women who came down to the beach. Wendy Stallings was young enough to know better, young enough to know that real blonde was more of a cream color, sometimes with streaks of tan and brown but not much yellow, or maybe just a little as an afterthought.

"You think it's real? Or a wig?" LaMonica Reilly whispered, as if she'd read Cassie's thoughts. LaMonica faced the crowd as she spoke, and her lips didn't move any more than a ventriloquist's.

"I can't tell," Cassie ventriloquized back.

This was the first they'd spoken since their fight in the cafeteria. It pleased Cassie that LaMonica had initiated the remark. The details of the fight were still somewhat confused in Cassie's mind, what with five or six participants and a duration of under three minutes, but she did remember that at some point Tiffany had been pulled away from her and LaMonica thrust forward, and that she had dug her fingers into LaMonica's hair and vice versa. Although Cassie's own scalp had felt as if it were being detached from her head, she was sure LaMonica had been the first to give a little yelp and break away. Cassie still didn't know why she and LaMonica had attacked each other—probably by accident in the heat of the fray—but it seemed interesting, now, what cool respect you could command just by pulling hard and long on someone's hair.

When the wind gusted again and Wendy Stallings's hair still refused to respond, Cassie turned her gaze in LaMonica's direction and said without moving her lips, "It's got to be a wig, doesn't it?"

The Queen was smiling as she shook hands with the mayor, but she seemed distracted. She was sniffing as if somebody had forgotten to bathe, which wouldn't be noticeable even if it were true, with the wind so gusty. It took a minute for Cassie to realize Wendy was smelling the smoke, which had been in the air so long now she herself hardly noticed it. And of course the sky was that weird color. Cassie thought orange was an improvement over the yellow haze they'd been having for nearly a week, but Wendy couldn't know that. Wendy had just flown over the fires which were burning up thousands of acres of forest not far to the west. Aerial shots of the conflagration appeared every night on the news. When you flew over the fires in person, they were probably more dramatic than on TV, maybe a little scary. If the starlet had seemed real, Cassie might have felt sorry for her, being whisked away from the film capital of the world to a little North Carolina town hemmed in between a burning forest and the sea, where they couldn't even afford a ramp to get you into the terminal.

Wendy was taking the flowers from Rose Bell, lifting hands tipped with what Cassie always referred to as clip-on claws, those long artificial fingernails that could no more grow from actual human fingers than claws could. The wind was carrying Wendy's voice away as she said how proud she was to be here. Her speech ended up sounding like little gasps, such as would come out of the belly of a pull-string talking doll.

One of the reporters said, "On 'Sundown Days,' you play a typical dumb blonde. Is that the character we're going to see this weekend, or are we going to see the real Wendy Stallings?"

Wendy Stallings revealed perfectly even teeth too white to be the originals and said flirtatiously, "Well, I don't know. It all depends."

Hearing that, Cassie knew the character on the soap opera and Wendy Stallings the celebrity were one and the same. The word that popped into her mind was *sleazy*. It was the word Betty used for people whose behavior she would not otherwise care to describe. Royal had assured everyone that Wendy Stallings' record had been searched *thoroughly* and that there was nothing objectionable in her background. But Cassie would swear the woman was trampier than the original queen, Tara Barry, even if Tara *did* pose for *Playboy*. If it were not for Royal and his ilk, Cassie might be standing here next to Tara, a real star, instead of playing handmaiden to this yellow-haired Barbie doll.

Rose Bell shooed the Princesses after the Queen into the airport lobby, where more reporters waited along with anyone who wanted to see the Azalea Queen up close before the official ceremonies began. The Princesses had been instructed to smile and wave at the onlookers. Most of the crowd were older ladies in skirts and young, heavyset housewives in slacks with small children in tow, mostly daughters.

No one had foreseen that twelve hoop-skirted Princesses would take up such a lot of space in the small lobby, so that the crowd and the entourage would be immediately and confusingly entangled. A little girl in pink jeans attached herself to Cassie's skirt. She pinched at the material, following it up and down with her hand. It was a curious gesture, rather than a menacing or unfriendly one. This was fortunate, because if Cassie had wanted to detach herself from the child, there would have been no room to do so. The girl's mother was nowhere in sight.

"Are you a Princess?" the child finally asked.

"Yes," Cassie replied.

"So *this* is what a Princess looks like."

The girl said it with such resignation that Cassie knew she was thinking that Princesses billowed out several feet in all directions, at least from the waist down. The notion would probably haunt the child all the time she was growing up. It was depressing.

A woman took the little girl by the hand. "She's a Princess," the girl said to the woman.

"Yes, she is."

Hearing this made Cassie conscious of the fact that, in spite of all her protests to the contrary, she actually *was* a Princess.

Even wearing her hair down and accessorizing with distinctly non-antebellum earrings didn't change that. She smiled at the little girl and her mother as they retreated into the crowd, feeling as plastic-faced as Wendy Stallings the Queen.

Rose Bell seemed to have realized the unsuitability of packing a dozen Princesses into a small space with the Queen, the dignitaries, and a crowd of onlookers. She was clapping her hands, trying to shepherd the entourage out of the terminal lobby to the parking lot where vehicles awaited—cars for the reception committee and a Wright County Schools activity bus for the Princesses—to take them to the coronation ceremony at the college. The bus was the final indignity, Cassie thought, but the view that greeted them as they stepped outside the terminal momentarily eased her irritation.

The pure orange sky like a sunset had vanished. Now, only the horizon was orange, and the sky above it was filled with nasty black smoke. Not the dim yellow-gray stuff that had been in the air for days, but black, thick smoke rising in the distance. Cassie supposed this was because the airport was so far west of Festival, and beyond it was mostly pine forest, the same kind that was burning on the evening news. She hadn't thought of it as being just ten miles from town. After a minute she realized the brightness on the horizon was *fire*. It leaped up, an orange-red flap of color. Even as she watched, the flames seemed to grow bigger and higher, to dance and throw themselves at the sky. No wonder Wendy Stallings had seemed distracted. Why, she had flown right over that only a few minutes before.

The drone of a plane filled the air, not a commercial jet but a small purposeful plane flying overhead and off toward the black smoke. The plane began dropping something red—a sort of blustery red cloud—which made the fire stop leaping so high. But it didn't put the flames out. There was commotion among the crowd, a kind of buzzing and excitement like the beat of music. This was turning out a lot better than Cassie expected.

The plane flew out of sight and a helicopter appeared. It hovered over the flames for a moment and then dropped water from a bucket that hung from its belly. The water didn't look like ordinary water, either. It was white and foamy at the edge, stirred up because the helicopter was moving so fast. The water looked more like champagne, a giant vat of foamy, bubbly champagne dropping out of the sky.

"All *right!*" one of the Princesses said.

The other Princesses laughed. All except LaMonica. Cassie couldn't tell if LaMonica thought laughing was uncourtly, or if she thought the "all *right*" was a mocking imitation of a black person, which of course it wasn't. LaMonica didn't even look disapproving so much as *distant,* as if she were the only adult among a group of children. Cassie knew that expression from her geometry tutoring sessions, when sometimes LaMonica would look as if she knew all there was to know and not just math. As if she were Black Eve viewing things from the perspective of all human history. Such an expression could almost be why, when LaMonica's hair presented itself in the cafeteria, there was no choice but to pull it.

The helicopter turned away from the fire and thump-whumped in the direction of the airport, just below the smoke, just above their heads. The forest was burning. The air smelled awful. It was wonderful. It was the nearest Cassie had ever come to participating in a major news event. The nearest any of them had, even LaMonica. All *right.* It really was.

The water from the helicopter made the flames die down more, leaving the sky gray and muddy. The crowd began to break up. The Princesses fidgeted, smoothing their skirts, considering the ways they'd learned to finagle them down the narrow aisle of the activity bus and the strategies they'd devised for sitting. It was surprising how in such a short time you could learn to negotiate places you once thought impossible. Even though the excitement was over, Cassie was so keyed up that she didn't get the least bit carsick on the ride to the auditorium at the college. She didn't feel sick until she learned the identity of her escort.

The function of escorts for the Azalea Princesses was to hold the girls' arms as they walked up onto the stage and to lead them off the stage when the coronation was over. According to Betty, it was mainly a way to get males from good families involved along with the females. All thirty-odd Princesses stood in the dim staging area while Rose Bell flitted about with her clipboard, matching the girls up with boys Cassie mostly recognized from school. Cassie was scheduled to be escorted by Paul West, whose father worked on Royal's campaigns. She couldn't locate Paul in the crowd.

"Oh, Cassie, here you are," she said. "Let's see. You go on with Kyle Carter."

"What happened to Paul?"

"He's sick, dear. Didn't I tell you?"

I do not believe this, Cassie thought. The words blared through her mind so vividly that she imagined she was saying them aloud. Kyle appeared before her from out in the corridor. He didn't look like himself. He was wearing a dark tux with a white shirt and blue tie. Dressier than church clothes or even Royal's funeral suit. More like a wedding suit. Oh, gag. In such subdued tones, Kyle seemed to have grown taller. Or maybe not. Since last fall, Cassie had avoided looking at him on the bus. Whenever he got on, she made sure to stare out the window. Even his hair was brushed back from his forehead and not falling in his eyes. He looked civilized. When he took her arm, she didn't shake it off.

"Surprised?" he asked.

"A little."

All the girls had been paired up now. Rose Bell was pointing them in the direction of the stage, where they would enter couple by couple.

"You looked like you'd faint dead away when you saw me," Kyle said.

Although he looked civilized, he sounded as if he were sneering. They were toward the back of the line waiting to go onstage. Cassie considered telling Rose Bell she wouldn't go on with Kyle, she would have to trade escorts with someone else. That was probably exactly what Kyle wanted—for her to make a scene. Instead, she smiled at Kyle. He seemed taken aback.

"I wouldn't have pictured you as Scarlett O'Hara in a dress like this," he said.

"No," Cassie replied, perfectly polite.

"I mean, considering who you pick for your *friends,* and all."

She didn't say, "Considering who you pick to tell lies about." She said, "You mean Curley? That was a long time ago."

The line was moving forward. Each couple stood briefly in the spotlight, and then each Princess was escorted to a position around the Queen's throne, and the escort left the stage.

"I keep trying to think what it was that you liked about Curley so much," Kyle said as they moved forward once more.

"Only that he let me keep my window open in the bus."

"It must have been more than that."

"Not that I can think of."

"Maybe you have a short memory."

"No." Cassie was surprised how calm she felt. Her mother said there were manners for every situation, it was never necessary to get ugly. "I get carsick, you know. Having the window open helped a lot." Her voice was very mild. Maybe her mother was right. There was nothing to do against certain persons but be completely polite.

The couple in front of them walked onto the stage. "As soon as they turn away from the spotlight, you go," Rose Bell interjected.

"Don't give me that carsick crap," Kyle muttered. He tossed his head as if to flip his hair back, but his hair wasn't in his eyes, it was plastered off his forehead with gel.

"*Now,*" Rose Bell whispered, pushing them forward with the tips of her fingers.

Kyle walked stiffly toward the center of the stage, not at all his loose surfer-self. The announcer intoned their names: "Cassie Ashby, daughter of Royal and Betty Ashby of Festival Beach…" Royal was probably having a good chuckle. Kyle's face was full of some other insulting comment he wasn't getting a chance to say. They turned from the spotlight. He guided her to her place on the stage, giving her the once-over like he used to do on the bus. Cassie smiled as if she were flattered. Kyle dropped her arm as if it were hot.

The coronation ceremony was insipid. LaMonica had been positioned almost exactly in the middle of the group of Princesses, so as not to seem too important or too unimportant. She was like a dot of color in a white landscape, drawing everyone's eye. But she stared ahead and kept smiling as if she didn't mind. Cassie was reminded of the time she'd gone to LaMonica's house for a geometry tutoring session, and LaMonica's sister put a cloth on the table before she set it for dinner, and Cassie realized they were the kind of people who used a tablecloth every night and not just for company and never said hell or damn.

Attention stayed on LaMonica until Wendy Stallings was led out by the president of the Jaycees. The Queen had changed from her minidress into a long, silver, sequined gown. The sequins were not in any way antebellum. The dress did not blend well with those of the hoop-skirted Princesses. The Queen looked as if she ought to be in some other kind of show entirely. Next to the Jaycees' president, who used to play basketball, she seemed unnaturally short. Like a miniature queen for a town that couldn't afford the full-sized version. She looked like exactly the type of discount queen who would reign in a place like Festival, North Carolina.

When the escorts returned after the ceremony, Kyle squeezed Cassie's elbow just at the funnybone.

"I see your hair-pulling partner got Antoine Batson for an escort," he said, nodding toward LaMonica.

Antoine was Central High's quarterback, who'd just received a full scholarship to Carolina. Even if he hadn't been the only black escort, everyone would have known who Antoine was.

"Personally," Kyle whispered, "I would have thought La-Monica was too dark to pull hair with. I thought you were too friendly with the darks to fight with them."

"Did you?" Cassie asked noncommittally.

The muscles in Kyle's face knotted up. He guided her into the corridor outside the auditorium, where the Princesses were being joined by family and friends. People were stopping to congratulate Antoine on his scholarship. Kyle held to Cassie's elbow and joined this group. Having gotten no rise out of Cassie, he seemed to need to bait LaMonica.

"Is the quarterback your reward for trading blows in the cafeteria?" he whispered.

"I guess so," LaMonica said. Her smile didn't waver. Cassie was interested that LaMonica was handling Kyle with the same mildness she herself was using. For the moment, LaMonica did not seem ahead of her, but on the same level.

"Anyone else would have been kicked out of school," Kyle said.

"We were lucky," Cassie told Kyle. To LaMonica, she said, "He's retarded."

"So I see."

Both Princesses kept smiling, smiling. Kyle squeezed so hard that jagged stabs of pain skittered from Cassie's elbow up her arm. Cassie moved away from LaMonica and Antoine into neutral territory. Attached as he was to her elbow, Kyle had no choice but to follow. Cassie dislodged herself from Kyle's grip and slid her hand through his arm, as if they were friends. She didn't move quickly.

"Thank you for escorting me," she said to Kyle when they reached the middle of the room.

For a few seconds, he didn't understand that he was being dismissed. He seemed to think Cassie had taken his arm as a gesture of acceptance. His confusion made her think how Betty said Northerners took Southern manners to be an overture of friendship to them personally when really they were only a pleasant way of dealing with people on the surface, where most dealings were. Cassie intended to keep her dealings with Kyle strictly on the surface. What Betty had not said was that, with someone like Kyle, politeness was a layer of protection.

Kyle still didn't move away. Then Royal waved from where he was making his way down the crowded corridor toward them. When Cassie looked back, Kyle had abruptly disappeared. It was just like him. He got away with a lot because of going to church and being a Carter and being nice-looking if you had a taste for bleach. He was so fair-haired that he was going to get away with a lot all his life. It occurred to her that LaMonica, despite the tablecloths on her table at home, was so dark that she would never get away with anything.

Royal wasn't with Betty but with constituents, as Cassie should have guessed. He'd been just about ever-present since the festivities started, always dragging folks up to her like this. He checked out her earrings with his eyes. Alone, he would have pointed to her ears and said, "What a bevy of designs we have here, Cassie—more gypsy than Princess." But with strangers he wouldn't say a word. He held his hand out toward Cassie as if she were some museum piece, perfect in every way, and beamed toward the couple he was escorting.

"Oh yes, and this is my daughter, Cassie."

The thing was, it was hard to hate him at the exact moment he said that. The folks he introduced were perfectly nice, and if you didn't know he was playing a game, you'd think Cassie and Royal were real family. You'd think he was pleased with her for turning out so well and not congratulating himself for raising a Southern belle. You might remember that he hadn't sent her to reform school or punished her for calling him P.A. and forget altogether that he was a bigoted, manipulative, pain-in-the-ass politician. She shook hands, thinking how her mother always said Cassie's feelings for Royal would mellow. If she weren't careful, she'd be part of his agenda before she knew it. She'd imagine he had a genuine special interest in her and not that he was only counting the votes he might get from Cassie's little piece of glory. She made herself look at Royal's neck where it bunched above his too-tight collar until her own throat began to constrict. But she couldn't think of a single damaging thing to say.

Someone opened the doors at the end of the corridor to provide a little extra ventilation. The air that rushed in smelled of smoke and scorch. Everybody was so used to it they hardly noticed, but after the scene at the airport, Cassie believed in the fire in a way they didn't. With a little luck, it would force the parade to be canceled—deprive Royal of his moment of step-fatherly pride when Cassie rode by on the float. She felt secretly victorious. It wasn't until later that she saw how sometimes, no matter how you fought, things out of your control push you in an unexpected direction. And only when you looked back later did you see it was the right direction—maybe the only direction—all the time.

THIRTEEN

*B*y the time our unit was called out to help with the forest fires on Thursday, I was congratulating myself for having managed to dismantle my life. I had walked out of a fire, lost a woman, put my job in jeopardy. Not bad, in less than a week.

And largely unintentional. I hadn't intended to start a war with Alona over my earring remark any more than I'd meant to turn Mary Beth into Marta and then into Marta the Bitch. But as Fetzer pointed out, the idea of alienating Mary Beth had been in the back of my mind all along. Not so with Alona. By the time she walked out of my cottage, I was already sorry. I figured there was no way to get her back except to apologize, be humble, grovel.

I planned to get it over with immediately—to go to her shop the next day, Saturday, and settle things. I never made it. The air was thick and warm and smoky, making me think of Janet's Ruffled Curtains the night before and Bob McRae's not letting me suspend the fighting Azalea Princesses. I was in no mood to grovel. I imagined Alona would forget my quick tongue and, sometime during the weekend, come to see me. She didn't.

Monday after school, I found myself heading toward her shop numbly, as if some other pair of hands were steering. I pulled into the parking lot and was paralyzed by a vision of myself being rejected there among the bins of ribbons and shells and the display cases of costume jewelry. The store was Alona's turf the way certain hallways were the property not of the freshmen but of The Trash. I turned and drove away.

Tuesday, I was assigned to Central's opening baseball game, which lasted until almost dark. I thought about calling Alona afterward but decided that if Elliott were home, she might see my call as a hostile action. By Wednesday, I'd begun to feel Alona's absence the way I might have felt the ghost of an amputated limb. I left school as soon as the parking lot cleared, no longer worried about groveling or Elliott or anything except making immediate and permanent contact. I pulled into Alona's lot. Her store was closed.

It wasn't even four-thirty. Why post hours on the door if she wasn't going to keep them? Then again, why not? She'd been shutting down early for months to see me. The idea that she'd already found other pressing activities threw me completely. Before I had time to think, I was driving to her apartment. I had not been there before.

Maybe because of the murky sky, the smoke in the air, who knows, maybe because of all that, I had a revelation: if I were going to her house, where I might encounter the jealous husband, protective neighbors, and students who knew me—then maybe this was more serious than I thought. Fetzer had said I resented the husband. He said I wanted Alona for myself. I had put it down to his groping for a topic of conversation those Friday nights at King Neptune's. When I nearly missed the turnoff and found myself making a hard left into a wall of traffic, escaping only because of my quick and heavy foot on the gas, it occurred to me that Fetzer was right. I loved Alona. I resented the husband. I would ask her to leave him. It was often done.

But the simplicity of that thinned as I walked up and down the sidewalks of the garden complex looking for her building, searched out her number, knocked on her door, and finally saw the fresh shock on her face, which went quickly expressionless. I said in a tone that would have sent a truant student into tears, "Well, how was the dose of culture?"

She stood in the doorway as if to block my entrance. "You mean the art show?"

I raised my eyebrows. "Was there something else?"

"What are you doing here, Jordan? Elliott could be here, for all you know."

"Well, is he?"

"No."

I searched her face for amusement but didn't find any. "I only came to inquire about your weekend," I said.

As if she'd been drawn away from the kitchen and a sinkful of dishes, Alona wiped her hands—which were not wet—on her pants. She wore black leggings like the girls at school wore to aerobics class. I hadn't seen her in the tights before, and this, too, made me feel in alien territory.

"Jordan, if there's one thing I cannot stomach, it's a steady diet of sarcasm," she said.

The obvious response would have been an apology. I wanted to apologize. I intended to.

"I wouldn't think a little sarcasm would bother you, Alona the Earring, having to deal with your customers the way you do," I said.

The two sides of my brain were in no way communicating, the words I wanted to say on one side and my actual utterances on the other. There were some things you didn't tell the women, and these, it seemed to me then, included not only how I felt about my retreat from a fire that couldn't have been as hot as I thought it was but also my need to confess my love for this married woman. I couldn't do it. My father would have been proud.

Alona's face reddened.

"I am not 'Alona the Earring,'" she said. "I am Alona the person. I am a married woman who wouldn't like to have to explain some man showing up at her apartment while her husband wasn't home. I am not a person who intends to put her marriage in jeopardy for a pompous snot who wants to make a fool of her. Wait here."

She turned, her hair bouncing, and shut the door, apparently for fear that I would follow her inside otherwise. A moment later, she opened it wide enough to thrust out a hand and a wrist.

"Here's your key," she said, and closed the door again while I stood there mutely.

I went to King Neptune's, not expecting to find anyone I knew on a Wednesday, and for the first time in my life, I got stinking drunk alone. Going home, I bent a fender on a pine tree beside the long dirt road through the woods to my house. It was midnight. I got out to examine the dent by the light of the headlights. The damage was minimal. The smell of smoke in the air was either stronger than before or heightened by the effect of the liquor. I stumbled toward the house, figuring I'd be wiser to retrieve the car in the morning. I vomited twice before I reached my front door. Retching in the darkness, I felt the sting of humiliation heaped on humiliation.

◆   ◆   ◆

The next morning, my alarm didn't wake me. A phone call from Bob McRae's secretary did. I claimed a stomach virus that had kept me too flat to call in, but insisted it had run its course and I'd be in as soon as I could. I was reminded of my old friend Hal Crosby, who'd once advised me to keep my lies as close to the truth as possible.

Outside, the smoky light hit me between the brows. I had a gutache and a headache, and my mouth was full of cotton. I didn't remember coming home the night before. The Beretta wasn't in the driveway. I was confused, then alarmed, then relieved to find it around the first bend of the lane. The sight of the dent and the returning memory of how it had gotten there filled me with impotent anger. Who should I punish but myself? I drove to school feeling already stripped of authority, and just as defiant as one of The Trash called down for an infraction. There seemed to be a weight between my eyes, no wider than the bridge of my nose but dense, black, and enormously heavy. I took this to be the physical component of rejection and humiliation rather than the symptoms of a hangover.

At school, the students had grown accustomed to the smoky sky and no longer regarded it as dangerous, but the changed atmosphere seemed to keep them in a perpetual state of ill-will. An argument started in the boys' bathroom over the price of marijuana—almost unheard-of because such prices were so standard at Central that even a nonuser could quote the cost of a quarter bag—and doubly bewildering because the argument involved a white boy and a black one. In all my years at Central, I'd never known a white student to buy drugs from a black or vice versa. Drug dealings, even more than social interactions, were closed and segregated.

It was that sort of a morning.

Also, it was the first official day of the Azalea Festival. Although the azaleas had finished blooming, except for a few strains of the larger ones, the festival activities were going on as planned. Several Princesses, including the Ashby kid and La-Monica Reilly, had been excused early to greet the newly appointed Queen at the airport. The rest of the students were anticipating the coronation that evening and the parade on Saturday, looking forward to the sheer disruption they'd provide. There seemed to be some underlying agreement that spring, having come and gone early, would be replaced by wilder events.

It was just before lunch when my fire chief, Clem, called to say the blaze to the west now extended almost to the Wright County line, with the result that local units were being called upon for assistance. Our particular unit had been asked to stand by in the staging area with a pumper and a brush truck. The wind was expected to change and push the fire away from us to the northwest, but with sea breezes kicking up unpredictably, it was impossible to know for sure.

The first thing Bob McRae said when I told him was, "Jordan, I wish you wouldn't. You see what the kids are like. Frankly I need you here to help maintain calm."

I realized then how little interest I had in maintaining a calm that might later be credited to the administrative skills of Central High's principal. Hadn't I already worked to maintain calm? Hadn't I broken up fights in the cafeteria and removed cactus stickers to avoid ambulances at the door? Hadn't I given out suspensions that should have been upheld?

"Bob, I appreciate your position," I said, "but I can't say no if they need me."

"Of course you can. You're a volunteer. I need you here at the school."

"In my contract," I said slowly, "there's a clause allowing me to leave whenever there's a fire."

"Then I think we may have to have another look at your contract," he said without emotion.

"By all means, look at it," I told him. "I can think of something else you can do with it, too."

It occurred to me that even if he tried to get me transferred or fired for insubordination, even if he wanted me out, with the bureaucracy what it was, it would take him years. Recognizing this made the pain in the bridge of my nose begin to dissipate. I felt light, free. There was nothing holding me—not Alona, certainly not the job. I was a stranger on the planet. Everything was new except the rush of adrenaline that came with the thought of fighting a fire, especially one I'd been watching for weeks on the evening news. In that sweep of emotion, I forgot the ruffled curtain fiasco, my own cowardice, everything but my excitement. I told the secretaries I'd be back when the fire was over, and I left.

◆　◆　◆

Four hours later, I was sitting in a brush truck in the parking lot of a Zip Mart on King's Highway, a north-south road west of the airport that brings most of the traffic down from the upper part of the state. We'd been sitting there since we arrived. The lot was being used as a holding area for extra equipment that had been sent from all over the region—from departments as far away as Fayetteville. In front of us, when they weren't obscured by smoke, the flames shot above the pines eighty, maybe a hundred feet. They weren't more than a quarter-mile to our west.

The fire front was seven or eight miles long by then, and had been divided into sectors, each with its own chain of command. The team leader for our section was a Forest Service guy from Wilmington who was using a tanker as his headquarters. Periodically he talked on the radio to the central command post up the road and then ordered one or two pieces of equipment to move out to protect houses along the side roads where the fire was expected to pass. The six guys who'd come from our unit—me, Fetzer, Clem, Andy Wilson, and two of the young kids who'd joined in the past couple of months—hadn't budged. We'd come to fight the fire and instead we'd been watching it from the trucks like spectators at a drive-in movie.

There was the constant sound of planes overhead—small yellow spotter planes followed by bombers carrying retardant and then helicopters dropping water on the flames in the distance. Between that and the thick smoky air, I felt like I was in a war zone, unable to fight. In retrospect, my concern that we'd never see any action seems ludicrous, but at the time, it was maddening. For this, I'd given Bob McRae grounds to fire me! I'd gotten in and out of the truck a dozen times, talked to guys from other units, listened to theories about where the wind was going to blow. The biggest fire of our lives was overhead, and our job was to sit until our butts got numb.

Then at three, maybe four o'clock, they called us out. Clem's crew was to take the pumper to protect one of the houses along the road, and Fetzer's crew—me and a kid named Joey—was sent with the brush truck down one of the dirt side roads to cover a frame bungalow that probably shouldn't have stood as long as it already had. Brush trucks are slow and ugly, but they're smaller and easier to maneuver than the big pumpers—and cheaper, in case they get beaten up—so they're sent into any rough terrain. The plan was that we'd keep the brush truck in front of the bungalow until the fire rolled through, and then pour as much water as we could on the house, hoping to keep it wet enough to avoid damage.

King's Highway was clogged with equipment when we pulled out, and so smoky that we needed our headlights to see. Forest Service trailers were hauling tractors from one place to another to plow fire breaks; tankers were supplying water up and down the road to the pumpers. Police were still going door to door in the areas where residences were threatened, telling people to evacuate. Rescue vehicles were parked everywhere. It looked like a military mobilization, what we could see of it. With such poor visibility and so much crawling traffic, when we heard later that a news photographer had been hit by a car while standing in the road to take pictures, we weren't surprised. The driver hadn't seen the guy through the dense smoke, and the photographer was lucky to break only a leg.

Some guys had sat with their equipment in front of houses all day, waiting for the fire to get close enough to require action. The main head—the front part of the fire that burns most intensely—kept shifting directions, slowing down and speeding up. That close to the coast, with offshore breezes competing with prevailing land winds, it was impossible to tell from hour to hour where the blaze might go.

We drove down an old rutted road bordered by pine forest and had barely gotten set up when the smoke got blacker all around us and the wind picked up, the insane wild wind a huge fire brings with it, throwing so much smoke into our faces that we could hardly see. I was no sooner holding the nozzle, ready to pour water up onto the roof of the bungalow if we needed to, with the kid Joey handing hose behind me and Fetzer on the second line, than the roar of the fire was in our ears like a jet landing, sap in the pines heating up so fast the trees were literally exploding in the distance, sounding like gunfire, filling us with raw, unconscious fear.

We were inhaling a lot of smoke, the wind jagged and dry like a spray of hot sand, and it was hard to breathe. You could use your mask for a little while if you thought you were going to be in clear atmosphere pretty soon, but in a fire like that, you knew you'd be running out of air and changing tanks all the time, so you didn't bother.

The kid, Joey, started coughing. He was sixteen, as young as a volunteer firefighter could be in the state of North Carolina—a rookie, scared as much as sick, coughing and then choking until I would have been worried if I hadn't had my hands full holding the line. The fire kept coming at us, way over our heads, pummelling us with wind, and finally Joey leaned over and threw up, which seemed to clear him out. He got up with black snot running from his nose, his face covered with it, but he seemed okay, wiped his face and went back to work. I remember thinking he was a good kid, the kind I never saw in my office at school.

Then we were concentrating on holding our position, not blowing away, buffeted by heat, by wind, the roaring, the smoke. I might have been as scared as Joey except that the hose was in my hand. With water, I was armed, a soldier at war, ready for the enemy.

Our brush truck carried two hundred and fifty gallons of water, only enough for a couple of minutes of spray. I didn't open the nozzle until the last second. I turned it to a wide fog pattern and held the stream of water above us to protect ourselves and the truck and the house. Fetzer did the same. The three of us stood in the roaring hot wind, in the sight of flames leaping up above the trees, safe under our umbrella of water, while the fire crested and broke over us like a wave at the beach.

After that, the blaze moved north. The head of a fire creates its own wind, blowing sparks and embers in front of it, which fan out and start spot fires you have to contain before they grow. We paused to fill the brush truck with more water from a tanker parked along the road. Then, as the Forest Service plowed lines around spot fires to keep them from spreading beyond the cleared ground, we threw water on the flames to stop them entirely.

It was fun for a while, me driving the truck while Fetzer and Joey manned the lines. Fetzer was the nozzleman and Joey held on. I steered the truck around and around through the brush, following the circle of the plowed fire break while Fetzer and Joey sprayed. We weren't as close to the main fire as before, but the air was full of soot and falling debris that looked like black snow, making it hard to breathe; and though the orange glow of the main fire rose in the sky above the trees, the smoke was so dark it looked like night. Then it *was* night, or close to it; we'd lost track of time except to know our arms hurt, our eyes stung. Finally someone on the radio told us to pull back, go get some supper.

It's funny what you remember. I remember that food line in the hall of the Zion Church of God, a long social hall in a church bigger than I expected that far from the center of town. There was a kitchen at the far end, and serving tables set up in the social area. Maybe a dozen women were in the kitchen dishing up food from oversized pots that must have come from some restaurant. There were bags and crates of food everywhere: loaves of bread, bottles of Gatorade, boxes of grits for breakfast. It was as if everyone in Festival and all the outlying communities had donated something, each private citizen and every little grocery store. On the serving table were bowls of what was being prepared in the kitchen and casserole dishes that folks must have brought in, everything from hot macaroni to cold potato salad and brownies.

A lot of men were eating, and as the serving dishes were emptied, women came out from the kitchen and took them away, replacing them with others full and steaming.

One woman was standing in a pass-through between the kitchen and the serving area, a chubby middle-aged woman who must have been working all afternoon and evening, sweat glistening on her face and her hair poking out in short gray wisps. She handed a jug of iced tea to someone who put it onto the table, then set out paper cups and took a pile of dirty dishes back. I was filling my plate, not even hungry so much as tired, but it was as if she and the others who had provided the spread—not just the ones there at that moment, but also everyone who had sent over a grocery bag of food or a casserole—wanted so badly to help and to give something that you would be doing them a disservice not to eat. Even the kid Joey, who said he probably wouldn't be able to get anything down, he was feeling so punk from the smoke—even Joey came away from the serving table with a plateful and seemed revived. It was as if we were, somehow, in that church social hall, completely tended to, mothered and wived.

Looking at that middle-aged woman in the pass-through muscling the iced tea jug across the counter, I was reminded—for no reason I could put a name to—of Alona after the ruffled curtain fire, sitting there like a sponge ready to soak me up. Before, that image had annoyed me; in the Zion Church of God, it struck like a little stab in the gut, a longing like homesickness. I couldn't have said why.

Fires burn lower at night. The humidity rises, the wind dies down. You don't often see a fire burning like this one did through the night, not advancing but holding its own, glowing red on the horizon. After we ate, they sent us to a house that would have been thought safe earlier but now was at the edge of the blaze, which when it swept over us earlier had come within a mile of King's Highway. We turned on a portable radio Fetzer had brought, and listened to one of the incident commanders being interviewed. The hope, he said, was that the highway would serve as enough of a fire break that the fire could be contained and pushed back through the night, before the winds rose again in the morning.

"If it gets on the other side of the highway," he said, "there's nothing but trees and Festival."

The air had grown damp, which was good, but it was also thick and unpalatable since the smoke hung in it without moving. You couldn't forget how nasty it was to breathe. There was a drainage ditch at the edge of the yard. Fetzer told Joey to lie down there, out of the smoke, and try to get some sleep. In a situation like that, the senior man—Fetzer—takes charge of the truck. The kid, being subordinate to him, was supposed to listen, but Joey seemed to feel honor-bound to stay awake with us. We sat on the ground, lower than the worst of the smoke, not talking much. It seemed odd that a week ago I had not only performed an act of cowardice but been angry with Fetzer for not sharing my fear—and in a way, angry at his not noticing my defection. All that seemed distant, small in contrast to the furor that surrounded us. We sat too tired and too tense to sleep, relieved not to have to make conversation.

A couple of times, the wind came up, which we didn't expect in the dead of night. We rose to check the area for spot fires. Most of the night, we waited. I imagined we felt the way soldiers do waiting to go into battle again, fuzzy-headed from the day's fighting, not knowing exactly what awaits them, wanting it and not wanting it at the same time. Joey finally made a mattress out of his turnout coat and went to sleep in the ditch. Fetzer and I stayed with the truck, watching the sky glow orange above the trees. I remember thinking that although this fire had to be a hundred times the size of the Conklin fire twenty years ago, the fact of being fourteen back then had expanded the other in my memory, until the sky, the smoke, the colors seemed identical.

The next day, Friday, we worked our asses off trying to hold the fire where it was, the firefighters protecting property and the Forest Service working in the woods. We got a hot breakfast at the Zion Church of God, and at lunchtime, they sent sandwiches out to the field. By then, most of us were too busy to eat. Despite us, the fire had been inching its way east all day. Close to four o'clock, it crossed King's Highway, the last substantial existing fire break between the blaze and the town of Festival.

Along with Clem's pumper and a couple of other trucks, we were hosing down a cluster of houses in the woods at the time, maybe a hundred yards west of the highway. We could hear the fire roaring and kicking up wind—hear a lot more than we could see—when the Forest Service team leader radioed for everyone west of the highway to pull out—brush trucks, pumpers, tankers, the Forest Service tractors which had been plowing fire lines. No sooner had we done that and parked the brush truck on the road in the murk than the head broke through and the blaze became a beast on both sides of us, sending embers and firebrands across the highway so hot and high and unleashed that we couldn't tell the exact time it crossed, just that there wasn't a damned thing we could do about it. We were about as powerful as ants against that sheer heat and anger. The fire had crowned—started burning in the very tops of the trees—and all at once, trees on both sides of the road were burning, and the air was so hot and dry we couldn't swallow. We'd heard that we hadn't lost a single house up until then, but the houses we'd been hosing a minute before were nearly in the path of the head. I figured that was the end of them, and of a whole lot more.

A couple of Marine Corps P-19s rolled by us, sent down from New River Air Station. A P-19 is an armored vehicle used for plane wrecks, completely enclosed, where a guy sits inside wearing a silver fire-retardant outfit that looks like a spacesuit, and from his perch inside he shoots water out of nozzles. These P-19s—three of them—went past us, past all the vehicles that had been pulled back when the situation got too dangerous, and headed for those houses, directly into the blaze. The last thing we saw was flames rolling up to one of them, and fire flashing over the sides. If the vehicle hadn't been moving it would have lit up; it wasn't far from lighting up as it was. Then it was gone into the smoke out of sight. Each of those P-19s carried a thousand gallons of water and I swear, they went in and came out of those woods three or four times, and saved that whole cluster of houses. I wouldn't have believed it if I hadn't seen it with my own eyes.

There weren't enough police to help evacuate the area once the fire got east of King's Highway. So they sent firefighters to help, mostly those of us with brush trucks because of the narrow dirt roads in that part of the county. I didn't realize how it would wear on my nerves after a while, knocking on doors announcing a general evacuation and not knowing how they were going to react. We ran into an old guy who said, "Hell no, let it burn me up if it wants to, I already lived my threescore and ten," and a mother gathering up three little kids, the woman crying all the time, saying does this mean I'm going to lose my house, and the little kids crying too, seeing her so excited. We had to carry the whole family out on the truck. I could have handled fifty kids at school, two days of listening to the shit they dish out, and never felt drained the way that evacuation left me.

We hosed down more houses. We did mop-up in a little development on the edge of the woods, throwing dirt over the smoldering twigs. We didn't know where Clem had been sent with the pumper. Fetzer was the commander for our one little truck, but the Forest Service guy giving us our instructions—the team leader for our sector—we didn't know from Adam. We had supper in the West Festival fire hall, where everyone seemed exhausted or scared or both. Though there was plenty of food, it was nowhere near as pleasant as the night before in the Zion

Church of God. I thought of the woman with the iced tea jug and thought of Alona. Maybe because I was so tired, I couldn't be sure, but it occurred to me that Alona loved me and that she didn't intend to take me back.

"We're never going to put this thing out, are we?" Joey asked after we'd left the fire hall and been sent to another spot fire, which we'd quickly knocked down. Little smile on his face, but also a pallor of defeat. Joey didn't look as sick as the day before, just pale-white tired. He was one of those kids with a pug nose and curly dark hair who usually look cheerful whether they are or not. If I'd been Fetzer, in charge of our little crew and seeing him like that, I would have sent him home.

"You mean the three of us personally aren't going to put the fire out?" Fetzer asked. "Or with a little help from these other four hundred guys?"

Joey didn't lighten up. "You know what I think is going to put it out?" he said. "The Atlantic Ocean."

We didn't know then the kid was right. I thought he was just scared. Or weary. We were twenty hours past the adrenaline rush, leaning on our shovels, standing in a field full of ash and smolder.

"I'm going to tell you what I tell my wrestlers when they're against someone stronger," Fetzer said. "I tell them they have to gut it out till third period. If they're smart and they're up against a muscle man, right from the beginning they've been making him use his strength, doing moves he has to throw his strength at."

"Are we talking about plowing fire lines? Or wrestling?" Joey asked.

Fetzer picked up a rake and started poking at some ashes. "By third period, you're tired as hell. You feel like you've been out there a week and a half. But the other guy's tireder. Then there comes a point...all of a sudden, you start to feel him go, and as soon as you feel that first sign of weakness, then you have to turn it up a notch and use everything you've got left, and that's how you win. In the meantime, gentlemen, these little hot spots are the weak areas, so man your shovels."

Joey did, we all did. Ten minutes later, the kid looked so weary again I wouldn't have been surprised if he'd passed out, but Fetzer didn't seem to notice. The sky above us was glowing, and so was Fetzer's face.

"In the day and a half since we got here, I bet that fire has moved east ten miles. At this rate, it could end up in downtown Festival."

He sounded as cheerful as if he'd just gotten up from a three-hour nap. I wondered then if maybe he was so good at what he did because he regarded firefighting, like wrestling, as sport.

FOURTEEN

*A*lona didn't see any point in opening her shop Saturday morning, what with everyone in Festival downtown at the Azalea Festival parade. Having accomplished practically nothing all week, she thought it was best to spend the time with Elliott. She felt bad for having dishonored him behind his back all those months with Jordan; she honestly did. Now she was going to make it up to him. They were going to hold hands at the parade together, buy hot dogs, see a lot of people they knew. Elliott was eating Cheerios at the kitchen table, still in his bathrobe, with his hair falling over his forehead. As far as Alona was concerned, he looked sweeter and more innocent than Jordan Edge ever had in his life.

Jordan. To think he'd actually come to the apartment! That he'd actually stood at her doorway and called her Alona the Earring again. As if he could talk to her any way he liked. Hearing those words had been exactly like being slapped. Right then she'd known part of Jordan's attraction was the way he kept her guessing at all the secrets he was keeping from her, when in fact, the main thing he'd been hiding was his vileness. As she dropped his key into his hand Wednesday afternoon and closed the door, she'd thought her mind would be clear of him from that moment on. But he was still a little nasty spot inside her brain. Festering. She told herself it was because only three days had passed since she'd seen him, and only a little over a week since the night he first insulted her.

She hadn't finished a single piece of jewelry since then, not even a braided necklace she'd designed and was more excited about than anything. Much as she worked on it, she couldn't translate it into stone and wire without tearing or breaking some part of it. She was sure her mood wasn't related just to Jordan, but to a whole tangle of things—his meanness and the way the fire had become a permanent feature of the sky and the way the smell of smoke had crept into the air, the kind of smell that, no matter how slight, raised goosebumps on her skin and made the hair on her arms bristle.

Most people were used to it by now, but not Alona. She reacted the way she used to every time she smelled a man's aftershave, except that instead of her blood pumping sweeter inside her, the smoke-smell made her want to run and hide. She'd tried to take refuge in Elliott, whose touch was comforting, but by mid-week the smoke seemed to have invaded even their bedroom, lodging on their sheets and pillows, and on Elliott's skin. She felt so strange that all week she'd been careful to put on the zircon pendant she'd once given to Emma, hoping to call up the peaceful state zircons could impart.

Now, her spirit certainly healing, Alona decided she and Elliott would have a good day at the parade. A new beginning. It tickled her how cute he looked. Even with his hair tangled above the cereal bowl, Elliott didn't seem sloppy or lower-class, only a little less serious than usual. He seemed as if he might raise his eyes from the newspaper and say something frivolous, like a knock-knock joke—something she wouldn't expect. There was something almost innocent about him. In contrast, Jordan was almost thuggy-looking. Jordan knew it, too. That was probably why he was so jealous of Alona going with her own husband to an art show. Jordan might be what the board of education wanted in a vice principal for discipline—someone forceful and mean—but he was certainly not what she wanted in a man.

"Let's get to the parade early," Alona said. "We don't want to have to park two miles away."

When Elliott looked up, Alona was startled all over again at how blue his eyes were. "The parade?" he asked.

"The Azalea Parade. Happens every April. Surely there's an article about it in that paper." She knew he was putting her on.

"Oh honey, I wish I could, but you know I have to work at ten."

Alona could not believe it. "I know no such thing."

"Sally is the only one coming in before noon. We don't have the part-timers till later. I told you."

"You didn't say the first word, Elliott Wand."

"Sure I did. Thursday night."

"You did not."

But she thought maybe he had. He'd been talking about work and she hadn't been listening. It was the same rehash as always. She'd been thinking about the woods around Jordan's house—not about Jordan himself, because she was finished with him, but about how she'd liked all that room to wander in under the trees. She'd been thinking how she'd plant in Elliott's mind the idea that maybe they ought to buy a lot in the woods somewhere and build a little house. She hadn't been sure how to approach that without his bringing up the matter of having a baby. But thinking back to Thursday night, she remembered the words "part-timers…time off…parade."

And because she'd missed them then, she was doubly annoyed now.

"Oh, come on, Elliott," she said, "you're the manager, how much business do you think you'll have with everybody downtown at the festival?"

She thought the least he could do was let Sally mind the store for a couple of hours.

Elliott pushed the hair back from his face so the youngness went right out of him. The way he looked at her, he could have been forty years old.

He said, "See, that just shows the way you're thinking, Alona. Most normal people will be at the parade, but not our clientele." He actually used the word *clientele*. "They can't park a mile away and walk down to the parade route with their orthopedic problems. They're more likely to come out to the mall while it isn't crowded."

He got up to rinse his Cheerios bowl, which he never did unless he wanted to show what a responsible equal-rights husband he was. He put the bowl in the drain, dried his hands, and opened the bread box, ready to make himself a bag lunch to take to work. Then he stopped. Seeing that the loaf was half gone from the package, he said, "I'm going to throw the rest of this away."

"There's nothing wrong with the bread," Alona said, irritated.

"It's old."

"Only a couple of days."

"It won't make a decent sandwich."

Sometimes he'd throw away a brand new loaf on the grounds that it was dated, accusing Alona of buying day-old bread to save money, which she never did. He would leave them without a single slice in the apartment.

"I can't believe you really think bread is supposed to hold together like marshmallows," she said.

"If you pick up a slice and it begins to tear apart, it's old, Alona." He was perfectly serious.

"God, I can't believe you."

But Elliott was walking across the room, dangling the plastic sack from his hand as if the bread might contaminate him before he reached the trash bin.

"Put it back, Elliott. I'm serious. If you won't eat it, maybe someone else will. I was just getting ready to have a piece of toast myself."

"For all you know, it's moldly."

"After *two days?*"

"I read that mold is one of the biggest cancer-causing agents," Elliott said. "It penetrates deeper than you can see."

The plastic sack hung limply from his fist as he spoke, the soft slices bending and becoming misshapen.

"That bread is so full of preservatives you could leave it out in the humidity the whole month of July and the countertop would mold around it and the bread would still be sitting there white and pure as ever," Alona said. "It could sit here until you and I are rotting away in our graves and it wouldn't have a spot of green anywhere."

"That's ridiculous."

"What's ridiculous is you throwing away perfectly good food because you didn't see it come out of the oven."

"The reason I throw it away," Elliott said patronizingly, "is because if there's no bread in the house, you don't have any choice but to buy fresh."

"That's weird, Elliott. It's neurotic.

"Neurotic!"

"As in crazy. As in sick."

"The crazy genes are on your side of the family, remember? My people didn't spend their lives trying to avoid driving over bridges."

"No, they're too busy with their lunatic search for mold."

Elliott held the bread aloft in a maniacal and dramatic way, then lowered it grandly to the table. The individual slices were by now compressed to about half.

"Have your toast," he said. "I'll get a sandwich at the mall."

He marched into the bedroom to dress. Alona didn't care in the least. She still had her day off. She could go to the parade alone. She would see everyone she knew. Maybe Jordan would be there. Jordan. Well, she didn't intend to think about Jordan.

Elliott was clunking around the bedroom. She certainly wasn't going to face him again. She'd walk right out except that she was wearing a see-through nightgown. She went into the bathroom and turned on the shower. Having water on her skin and hair always made her think more clearly.

Elliott had no call to be so pompous. No right to assume she wouldn't keep fresh bread in the house, which in fact she was careful to do. And certainly no right to make comments about her family. It was just like him to assume he was the final authority about everything. The only one capable of judgment. If she'd known in advance about his king complex, she never would have married him. As soon as you got to know a person like Elliott, it was as if a subtle shift of the light took place that showed his very ugliness—like the smoke blowing over the sun. Elliott was not what she had expected at all.

Of course she could say the same thing about Jordan.

Jordan!

That sadist.

At least Elliott was not a sadist.

The water was just perfect. She rubbed shampoo into her hair and then washed it out. She applied a dollop of conditioner. It was true that Elliott was on the good side of sadistic. Pompous, yes. Sadistic, no. She shaved her legs. The water was making her feel a little better. Less angry. Really. The truth was, Elliott hadn't actually begun to make his nasty remarks about Emma until after she was dead. It was unfair to question a dead person's sanity but not as serious as if they were alive. He was never hateful about Alona herself. He would never call her names or knock her earring into her neck, even though she'd been unfaithful to him. Not that Elliott knew about her infidelity. He never would. Never. She rinsed the conditioner out of her hair. Everybody had a few idiosyncrasies. A fresh-bread fetish was not particularly serious. Not in the same category as, say, beating her with a belt. Unlike Jordan, Elliott was not an abuser.

The water grew cooler. She turned it off. The truth was, she and Elliott fought about the stupidest things. The bathroom was warm and steamy. She liked getting out of the shower and not feeling cold. By the time she dried off, she was ready to forgive Elliot. But he was gone. Off to work to bring home a paycheck. Hardly a serious crime. Once her shop was closed, he'd have to support her. Alona got dressed and drove toward the mall.

Traffic was light, what with everyone downtown. She made better time than usual. A good sign. There were a number of good signs, now that she thought of it. Maybe even her sudden inability to make jewelry was for the best—an indication that her life was taking a new shape. She'd never been one of those people with some important mission she had to stick with forever. Making earrings was fun, but it was never something she couldn't drop at a moment's notice—not just to see Jordan (which she would sooner forget), but also, for example, when Elliott's car started smoking in the middle of Live Oak Boulevard and she had to close up to go get him. Elliott never understood how she could post a set of hours on her door and not observe them strictly, but there it was. She was lucky *he* was the one with the mission—to fit unfortunate people with appropriate shoes. Now that Alona thought about it, Elliott's seriousness and her lack of it made them fit together perfectly.

For the briefest moment, it occurred to her that Jordan, too, seemed to have a mission, although she'd never quite deciphered what. That didn't matter now. She focused on how pleased Elliott would be to see her coming to the mall to forgive him. The confusion of the last four months was behind them. Everything was falling into place. Even the dream about the light on her hair, which she'd had the night Jordan kicked her out of his cottage—even that seemed a thing of the past. Permanently.

She didn't know why she was so sure, but she was. Driving so fast on the empty streets, she considered the dream with an objectivity she'd never had before. Of course: the dream was about choices. She always had it when she came to a crossroads, a place where she had to make a decision. If she chose right, the dream didn't come back until she reached the next crossroads. That's why she always felt it was jolting her forward to some destination, though really it wasn't. But now, in some way, a lot had been settled. She had chosen Elliott. For the rest of her life. And now the dream would be gone for good.

The sky was murkier than it had been for days. Or maybe with so much on her mind, she just hadn't noticed it getting worse. She really hadn't seen the news or read the papers this past week, what with all the confusion. The smoke gave her the creeps. The cars at the curb looked as if they'd been coated with grime. It was unnerving. She pulled into a parking space at the mall and made for the heavy glass entryway.

She planned to go right to Custom-Fit, to ignore Sally Battle, and to tell Elliott she was going to the parade but hoped they could meet later. She was going to do that no matter how she had to swallow her pride.

When she got inside, the mall seemed abandoned and unpleasantly dusky—even dimmer and stranger than the smoky filtered light outside. Among the potted plants and tiled floors, she felt like she was walking at the bottom of a terrarium. Her high resolve vanished, soaked up by the murky light. She realized she'd forgotten to wear the zircon.

Custom-Fit was one of the corner stores toward the center of the mall, visible from two directions. It had no display windows, only a center post and entries from either side. The first thing Alona noticed was the rack of sale shoes—the same shoes she'd seen weeks ago, though she knew they were probably different sizes and colors. It was just that all Custom-Fit shoes looked more or less alike.

The store was empty except for Elliott and Sally Battle. Elliott was behind the cash register and Sally was in one of the rows of chairs people sat in to be fitted. The two of them were talking. They weren't flirting like Elliott would have her believe, only trying to look like they had important business to discuss. Alona was surprised at her disappointment when she realized there was nothing going on between them. She felt that somehow she'd come here just to find out. And there they were, with empty expressions on their faces, sort of sad and expectant, with not a single prospect of a sale in sight. It made her feel that if she walked one step closer to Custom-Fit, she'd come out with dark, sensible shoes that felt good on her feet—a nice solid arch and plenty of room in the toe—but not the least bit of style to them whatsoever.

Maybe that was why she couldn't bring herself to move forward. She knew Elliott couldn't see her, what with the bright light in the store and the dim light out in the mall. Regarding him from this distance, so sensible and sad and faithful, all she could think of was something Emma had once said about why Dottie had never married Alona's father. Emma had said, "Because the only pleasure they ever gave each other was making you, Alona, and after that they were a chore to each other, which wouldn't have worked."

Emma didn't say so, but Alona knew Emma believed marriage for any reason other than pleasure would be wrong and artificial. Seeing Elliott from this distance, so bored and boring, Alona agreed completely. Jordan Edge might look and act like a thug, but at least seeing him made her happy.

That was the most disloyal thought she'd ever had. She tried to wipe it out of her head, but it wouldn't go. She got a little dizzy. This unexpected feeling swept away even her fury at Jordan's calling her Alona the Earring and slapping those ridiculous metal circles against her neck. It wasn't as if he'd beat her. Maybe he hadn't even been abusive, just preoccupied. Just…hurt. Coming to her apartment must have been hard, after her walking out on him. The truth was, except in the last week, he'd never once been unkind. All he'd ever done was give her pleasure.

She felt cold and shivery clear through, as if a great truth had lodged inside her. She sat down beside a planter in the center of the mall, not sure she could keep standing.

A customer walked into Custom-Fit from around the other corner. A tall stringbean of a man. Narrow feet. Elliott spoke to the man in what she knew would be a serious, reassuring voice. Alona didn't feel kinder, only a little irritated. When it got to a certain point, there was not a thing a person could do to please you. The more they tried, the more annoyed you got. And the reason was, no matter how worthy the one person was, you couldn't help wanting him to be the other.

It was as if a break had been made without anyone saying a word. She knew it was wrong. She told herself situations like this didn't arise because one person was good and the other evil—although in this case, she probably *was* evil—but because two people were living at cross-purposes. And in this case, the cross purpose was…well, Jordan.

Maybe it wasn't too late.

Alona rose, moving quickly before Elliott sensed her sitting there in the shadows. If she hurried, she might still find Jordan at home before he went to the parade. As she headed out of the mall into the ashy light, she thought it wasn't even that she didn't love Elliott. In a way, she did. It was just that he made her feel like she was living her life in a whisper.

FIFTEEN

On Saturday morning, Cassie wandered into the kitchen in her bathrobe, still hoping for some reprieve. She had visions of Queen Wendy Stallings simpering along the parade route while Royal gloated over his Southern belle daughter.

"I assume they canceled the parade," she said to Betty, hoping her show of confidence would make it true.

"What?"

"All this smoke. You'd think they'd cancel just in case."

"Honey, the smoke's been there all week," Betty said, sounding unnaturally cheerful. "I doubt a little smoke ever hurt anybody."

That was when Royal walked into the kitchen, already wearing his politician's outfit, though nobody in their right mind would get so dressed up for a parade. Even the "important local officials" like Royal, who sat in the reviewing stands instead of along the sidewalks, mostly wore shirtsleeves. But Royal's idea of casual was gray slacks, navy blazer, and a bright red tie that a clothes consultant had said was a power color. Fooling with his collar, pulling the tie against the disgusting flab on his neck, he managed all the same to give Cassie a condescending look.

"Why do you think they'd call off the parade 'just in case'? You have any idea how much money this thing brings in?"

"Well, if it's going to burn the town down..."

"Sweetie, the fire's only traveling a couple of miles a day. You really think it's going to surprise you?"

Sweetie? *Sweetie?*

"Without the Azalea Festival, we'd have to wait for Memorial Day to start the season," he said. "It'd take one *hell* of an emergency to make us do that." He adjusted the tie to his satisfaction by staring at himself in the chrome around the oven.

"He's right, Cassie. All the motels are full," Betty said. "I think the fire is part of the attraction. Coming from the west, you have to drive by it to get here."

Royal put his arm around Betty, probably to reward her for defending him. Normally Cassie would have gagged at the sight of this, but instead the two of them seemed far away—or at least her mother did. Like one of those adults who did only one or two little things all their life, and the longer they did them the less they could do anything else.

Seeing her mother leaning on Royal, it was hard to imagine she'd once had a whole independent life, working and supporting Cassie up there in Baltimore. It was hard to imagine that just a few months ago, trying to talk Cassie into being a Princess, Betty had said, "I just hope you'll take all the opportunities like this you can, Cassie, because you're open to them now even though you think you aren't, and when you get older you won't be. It's as if a window shuts in your brain and after that you can never see anything new with fresh eyes."

"Oh Mama," Cassie had protested.

But Betty had put up her hand to shush her and said, "I wasn't any more anxious to move to Baltimore than you are to be a Princess, but when your father and I flew up there...the way I felt when I saw the Chesapeake Bay from an airplane for the first time...honey, I know I wouldn't feel that way now even if I went to the Taj Mahal or China. It's the kind of thing you only feel when you're young."

And now it was as if Baltimore had never happened. Betty was still Cassie's mother, but less and less, and more a politician's wife who planted things in beach sand because they'd let you into the Garden Club no matter how inhospitable your soil.

"Get dressed now, Cassie," Betty said, not moving from the circle of Royal's arm. "We want to get down there in plenty of time."

Royal squeezed Betty's shoulder before letting go of it, as if they had a private language between them. Cassie didn't even care. Much as she wanted to avoid the parade this morning, it was getting easier to be polite to both of them, the way you were to people you hardly knew.

Betty and Royal dropped her off at the assembly area for bands and floats and went to take their seats in the reviewing stand. Cassie made her way through a tangle of drum majors and baton twirlers and onlookers wanting to see the floats up close. A lot of people were examining the Queen's float with special interest, mostly girls from not-so-prominent families who didn't get a chance to be a Princess.

There was a couple with their arms around each other, the girl's hand in the back pocket of the man's jeans and his in hers, as if they were connected at the hip. Sort of like Royal and Betty, only younger. They were touching the paper flowers, pointing and laughing. But sad, somehow, maybe wishing the girl were in a hoop skirt instead of jeans, getting ready to ride on the float instead of watching. The girl had black hair and the man dark brown, and even from a distance, they looked handsome but mournful—like people who'd missed out on something. Then they turned so Cassie could see them in profile, and she realized with a shock it was Tiffany Galloway and Brian Ivey. She knew at once why they were looking so longingly at the float and exactly what Tiffany had missed.

But even knowing that, there was a little ache inside her for the difference between the way they looked and the way they acted. A little ache at seeing them wrapped up together like that. They weren't aware of her, of course. Never had been, really.

But they were envious. And Cassie couldn't help wanting to rub it in.

She wanted to ascend slowly onto the float, into the position Tiffany had never had a chance to occupy, out of range of Tiffany's fingernails. She wanted to smile and say to Brian, "Too bad you have to tell lies about one person in order to make another person jealous." He'd know exactly what she meant. He'd feel obligated to reply sarcastically, with something like, "Honey, you were never known for your purity," while squeezing Tiffany's shoulder the way Royal had squeezed Betty's. But none of it would make Tiffany an Azalea Princess, now or ever. Cassie would smile until her cheeks ached. "Ordinarily, I don't put a premium on purity—although maybe a little more than Tiffany does," she'd say, "but in this case, I was pure all the same." Then she could turn and take her place among the others, and it would be a victory almost worth being a Princess for.

She didn't do it. She waited until they walked off together, laughing in a coarse, artificial way—more like dogs barking than people showing amusement—as if riding in the Azalea Parade didn't mean a thing to them. She waited until she saw LaMonica Reilly and Geraldine Maynard and some other Princesses getting onto the float, and Brian and Tiffany had disappeared. Some things just weren't possible. Doing them would make you feel completely rancid.

After all the campaigning she'd done for Royal P.A., Cassie thought she'd ridden on everything, including an elephant once when the circus was in town. But though she'd waved to the crowd from convertibles and horse-drawn wagons in other parades, she'd never been on a float. Queen Wendy Stallings got to sit on a throne at the front, which might have been tolerable, but the Princesses were situated around the sides and back, each holding to a little metal post with one hand while waving at the crowd with the other. Until she actually experienced it, Cassie wouldn't have believed standing up like that would exaggerate the float's swaying from side to side—not to mention its tendency to lurch forward as the car pulling it stopped and started every couple of seconds. It had never occurred to Cassie that a float might affect a person's motion sickness.

Immediately in front of them was the Central High Marching Band. It played "Dixie," then marched quietly for a while. Then it repeated the performance. The band was off-key and screechy. They had gone less than two blocks when Cassie's headache started. One always preceded the churning in her stomach, which preceded outright nausea.

At least they were in the open air. As long as she wasn't thinking about moving, maybe she'd be okay. She concentrated on LaMonica, who was immediately across the float from her. She concentrated on picking out people she knew in the crowd. Probably everyone she knew was somewhere along the sidewalk. She waved at Janet Biggs and a couple of others. She focused on finding familiar faces and on taking long gulps of air.

But the air wasn't normal anymore. It was so gray and laced with smoke that it didn't help her headache. Cassie was reminded of the other day at the airport when the sky had changed from orange to black. She looked up to see if there was the glow of fire on the horizon again today, but there wasn't. Royal was probably right: the fire was traveling too slowly to come into Festival by surprise.

All the same, the change was very sudden. The wind had picked up, and it was raining a lot of ash, not the white papery fragments that had been in the air for days, but darker, sootier-looking stuff. She didn't realize how it was sticking to everything until she looked at LaMonica. LaMonica's taffeta gown wasn't peach-colored anymore, but coated with gray. Cassie's own dress didn't look much better. Not that that was bad. She hoped the gowns would get so gray even Martin's Cleaners wouldn't be able to clean them; she hoped they'd be so grimy that Janet Foy would no more be able to rent them next year than she'd be able to do business in her burned-down shop.

The wind was blowing potato chip and candy wrappers around, and waxed paper that had held hot dogs. In the crowd, a woman put a handkerchief over the nose of a baby sitting in a stroller. The air was full of trash. Cassie's stomach began to knot and unknot at the sight of all the food wrappers everywhere. When the band played "Dixie" again, the wind took the sound of the music with it, blowing it away in little puffs. The wind was so distracting that finally the band stopped playing.

Some of the spectators were leaving. They came into the street because the sidewalks were so crowded, and walked in the direction of their cars. The police along the parade route—not very many police because it was usually a friendly and pleasant parade—began ordering people out of the street. No one seemed to listen. A policeman on horseback rode up to the Central High Band leader. He leaned down from his horse to speak. Immediately, the music started again. Probably someone like Royal had decided the bands must continue. You didn't stop a parade that brought tourists into your town just because the wind blew away the music.

Two blocks from the reviewing stand, the parade rounded a corner. Sirens began to wail above the commotion. They weren't the sirens of the fire engines in the parade, but real sirens, going to a fire. When Cassie turned toward the sound, she saw a pillar of smoke rising in the distance. Not from the forest fire but from right here in town. It seemed to be coming from the little park near the courthouse a few blocks away.

The town fire and the forest fire must be related, though Cassie couldn't see how. The air was getting hotter. It made her feel worse. She could no longer distinguish the faces of individual bystanders. The crowd was not a fixed thing anymore, it was a moving blur.

The nausea and the hot air made her sweat all over. Her hand was wet against the metal post. She pulled it away and dried her palm against her dress. She couldn't keep it off the post very long or she'd lose her balance. A bunch of balloons got away from one of the vendors and rose into the sky. She couldn't watch them or she'd throw up.

More people came into the street. The road was as full of spectators as it was of marchers and parade vehicles. The police were helpless. In front of Cassie, Geraldine Maynard stopped waving and clutched the metal post with both hands. Another Princess did the same. The Queen, whose unmoving blonde hair was all the Princesses could see through the mesh of her throne, got up and looked back for help, and then sat down again. The air was growing dusky.

"This is crazy," LaMonica said, almost shouting across the float to Cassie. LaMonica looked scared, but she kept smiling. Cassie decided the embers from the burning forest must have blown into town to light up the courthouse park. If the fire could come this far, it could start burning anywhere. LaMonica must have figured that out. But LaMonica didn't stop smiling or waving.

Cassie was so nauseated she was getting dizzy. The sight of LaMonica carrying on as usual seemed heroic and brave. She remembered the tablecloth on LaMonica's table when they weren't even having company, and the black girls in the cafeteria calling LaMonica a white nigger. She knew why LaMonica couldn't drop her smile or stop waving. It was because, even though the crowd on the sidewalk was dispersing, as long as anyone was watching, they would be watching LaMonica.

But they were not watching Cassie. At least not enough to count. The wind whipped the smoky air, the sirens wailed, and still the band kept playing, the float inched along. It made no sense. One more block and Royal would get his chance to gloat over how he'd raised a Princess, and Betty would smile up at him, catering to him, living her narrow life. It occurred to Cassie that Betty couldn't help having obligations, exactly the way LaMonica did, but Cassie wasn't wife or mother or commissioner or Southern Belle—she wasn't anything, except sick. And there was no reason to throw up in front of the reviewing stand even if it would serve Royal right.

Her hand was too wet to stay on the metal post an instant longer. When the wind gusted again, it was almost like a storm wind, except without clouds scudding across the sky, only ashes and smoke. The wind tore sprigs of azalea blossoms from Wendy Stallings' hand. The float lurched. Cassie was part of the rushing air—falling, maybe leaping. LaMonica screamed, but the sound was carried away. Cassie was flying. The float continued by her, down the street. A bright blur of color swept past. She landed on her feet. A few people cheered and clapped. Most of them were too busy running.

The pillar of smoke near the courthouse was higher and darker than before. Cassie wanted to run, too, but couldn't because of the hoop. Because of her damned old hoop. She pulled the petticoat down from underneath and stepped out of it, right there on the street. This was one hoop Janet Foy would never see again.

Her head cleared then, and she turned to get her bearings. People rushed in every direction. There was no one she recognized. She was forced against the wall of a building. The smoke coated her mouth with fuzz.

She pushed against someone's shoulder, trying to ease herself into the flow of the crowd. With the hoop gone, the dress was bulky and too long, and she was tripping over the hem. She wasn't going anywhere. There was fire in the sky, above the buildings.

Her heart thumped inside her throat. The crowd was shouting. Waving its hands. Turning into a mob.

Somewhere the band was still playing.

Smoke stung her eyes.

She couldn't hear anything except her heartbeat.

Then a voice said to her: "Where you headed, Cassie?"

Though officially she didn't believe in her anymore, she knew Black Eve had saved her. "I'm not sure," she said. "Home, I guess."

"Come on." He put his hand out to hers. It wasn't a matter of holding hands, it was a matter of staying together in the crowd. He was pulling her along. He was taller and stronger and could make his way through.

"Where we going?"

"To my car."

It seemed to her that people made way for them. They were moving as if there were no impediment. There were things they could do together that were impossible to do alone.

She wouldn't have known to turn in the alley. It got them out of the mob. She got a chance to look at him. His hair was different than before. A box haircut, short on the sides but maybe six inches high on the top—and so wavy that it seemed to puff out, giving his head the shape of a muffin. Shaved just behind his left ear, in script writing, was his name, framed in a little rectangle of black hair: "Curley." It was the best haircut she'd ever seen.

They came out of the alley to a narrow street. Not a bad street, not slums. The wind was still wild and smoky, but there was more of it to breathe. His car was an old Chevy.

"You got a space pretty close," she said.

"One of the advantages of downtown living. Come on, I'll drive you home."

"You don't have to," she said.

"It's okay."

"Well...thanks." She wasn't afraid now. Flames shot into the sky a few blocks away, but they didn't seem threatening, only exciting. They were safe in the car.

She hoped Royal and Betty got home before she did. She wanted Royal to see her being delivered by the ex-bus-driver alleged homosexual rapist who'd rescued her from the mob. She wanted Royal to have to thank him. She couldn't hear the band anymore, only sirens and noise. They were moving, driving right out of it. They were in the middle of a major news event. Maybe Betty was right about taking all the opportunities you were offered. Cassie never would have believed it but here she was, an Azalea Princess, and—who would have imagined?—she was having the time of her life.

SIXTEEN

*A*sk me what the most dangerous word is and I'll tell you: hope. When the decision to light a backfire was made Saturday morning, it was met with immediate relief among the men, with talk of containment and control. Some of the Festival volunteer units—not ours—were even released to go back to town, to be available during the Azalea parade. That kind of hope is sometimes the gravest, the most dangerous mistake.

We'd been out at the fire forty-eight hours then, since Thursday, and a lot of the units had been there longer. Fetzer's drawn and whisker-stubbled face looked like a month in the jungle, and reminded me how beat we felt, doing hard physical work and going mostly without sleep—except Joey, who'd stretched out on the ground Friday night and not awakened until sunrise. The kid woke up with his eyes as red and gooey as they'd been the night before. Our throats were caked with soot and our mouths so dry that we could hardly spit until we drank the coffee they brought out to the field.

By then, the landscape was all trees and nameless road, smoke that had become the very smell of air itself, the droning of planes, the blank mechanical taste of exhaustion. The fire was blowing east, snarling and spitting, but not moving fast enough, we'd been told, to endanger the town any time soon. We imagined our battle continuing for another week. So when word came about the backfire, the first thought anyone had was of a quick end to this and then home—to a shower, a bed, sleep.

"Must be third period," Joey said to Fetzer, remembering the wrestling analogy of the day before. "They're cranking up a notch. Maybe the muscle man is weakening."

"If they wanted to light a backfire, son, they should have done it yesterday before it crossed King's Highway," he said, pointing upward to boiling smoke, wild wind in the tops of the trees. "Sometimes the muscle man doesn't weaken. Sometimes all you've got left for third period is an act of desperation."

"He's trying to scare you," I told the kid, seeing that his pallor was beginning to show through his smile. "No reason it might not work, even with that wind."

But the truth was, backburning is as dangerous as hope. The idea is to set the second fire, the backfire, close enough to the main one that it gets sucked toward it and finally into it—but to set it far enough away to let it burn off enough ground first to serve as a fire break. Theoretically, by the time the fires meet, the backfire has reduced everything in the path of the main fire to ashes, leaving it nothing to feed on and nowhere to go but out. If everything is done properly, this works, because there's always wind blowing into the main fire—a draft of cooler air drawn in to replace the hot air constantly rising up. But it's easy to misjudge, to apply science to dry tinder and find out Mother Nature is only amusing herself. And then the second fire sets off in its own direction, leaving you in more trouble than you were before.

In view of this possibility, the Forest Service bulldozed a fifty-foot fire break to the east of the proposed backfire, to direct it toward the main fire two miles west. Two miles. Too much. Skeptical as we were, we never imagined that in the next three hours over two thousand acres would be destroyed, or that the Fire Service's broad plowed lines would end up looking like they'd been drawn with a stick.

We'd been moving slowly east for the past two days—east of the airport into the pine woods north and west of town. By then we were about a mile west of my cottage on the edge of the Joyner estate. It was a good place for a backfire, tactically speaking—wooded and remote, with no houses in any direction. After the area's long history of security guards and No Trespassing signs, people usually avoided it, even the normal run of squatters and bums. Walking through the brush with my drip pot, doing my part to begin the backfire, I wasn't displeased that the Joyner estate developers—with whom I'd had so many dealings and to whom I was about to lose my cottage—were about to have thirty percent of their pretty wooded lots reduced to spikes of charred tree trunk and ash. I recalled the cluster of pines beside the Intracoastal, where I made love to Alona early on, as much for shock value as desire—and in spite of our recent unhappy ending, I was glad that particular location was on the other side of the backfire, well east of us, and wouldn't be destroyed.

The fire got going quickly—too quickly, perhaps. We stood watching it, waiting for further instructions, in air filled with smoke and debris. Less than five minutes later, the team leader from the Forest Service came looking for us. He'd been one of the jokes of the past few days because he was so ugly—not more than five feet three and so skinny he probably bought his clothes from the kids' department. He was balder than Fetzer—a guy with deep acne scars that stopped abruptly at the top of his forehead, giving way to the smooth shiny dome of his scalp. But that morning he was no joke. He got out of his car looking grim as concrete, and said not to Fetzer but to me, "A pilot from one of the spotter planes just called down. He says there's two young people back there on motorcycles, between the head fire and the backfire. Two kids. I heard you live out here somewhere and know the trails."

It wasn't a matter of volunteering. We were in the proper vehicle—a brush truck that could get in and out of the un-burned middle before the two fires met. Fetzer's face lost all trace of exhaustion. It turned, I swear, a perfect cheerful pink. He always loved a chance to be a hero. Joey glanced back and forth at the two of us, red-eyed but expectant. I thought, great, twenty years ago I got stuck between two fires and now they want me to do it again. Fetzer started the ignition and we drove toward the old tanker that was serving as the command post vehicle, where the team leader had motioned us to go.

"Joey should stay behind," I said to Fetzer. "They have rules about what sixteen-year-olds can do."

"Hey, what're you talking about?" Joey said, though he knew as well as we did that volunteers could join at sixteen, but not pull certain dangerous duties until eighteen. I didn't know exactly what was forbidden; neither did Fetzer.

"He's a school administrator, he's hung up on rules," Fetzer said, slowing down the truck as we approached the tanker.

Joey smiled, turning on the charm. "Because of some rule, you'd leave me here to miss the great adventure of my life?"

"Could be the last adventure of your life," I said.

The kid put on his gloves and helmet, trying to look professional. Crusted snot had hardened on his cheek where he'd smeared it earlier. Otherwise he might have been a Boy Scout.

"Joey comes," Fetzer said, pulling rank. "He's part of this crew." I felt as subservient to him that moment as I did to Bob McRae at school, and as resentful. I could hear Fetzer lecturing his wrestlers on the value of pushing themselves, seeing what they could do, testing their limits. It was stupid. A wildfire was not a rational opponent and we would have—what?—ten minutes to get in and out of there? My heart was pounding and I feared for us all.

The team leader gave directions the spotter pilot had given, about where the kids were motorcycling. I knew the trail. It veered off into the trees, not far from the creek bed. I also knew what they didn't—that in the trees, the trail was not wide enough to let a brush truck through.

"Take these," the team leader said, handing us some packets he was carrying—five silvery bundles folded like squares of aluminum foil.

"Christ," Fetzer said. "Don't have much hope for us, do you?"

"Every hope. This is just regulation."

"What are they?" Joey asked. Fetzer put the truck back into gear and we bounced off onto the dirt road that led around the backfire into the woods.

"Fire shelters," I said. "Little pup tents the Forest Service uses to protect you if it overtakes you before you can get out of the area." Unfolded and laid out, the shelters opened into lightweight tents made of a thin coating of aluminum over a layer of fiberglass cloth. The idea was to shield the occupant during the passage of a firestorm.

"The aluminum is supposed to reflect ninety-five percent of the heat," I said. "But not flames. If something happens, you have to find a clearing to lie down in where the flames won't touch you." I didn't tell him the packs were known officially as fire shelters but unofficially as brown-and-serve bags. Despite occasional articles in the trade journals about the devices saving lives, the general feeling was that if you actually had to use a fire shelter, you'd probably be roasted like a turkey under foil.

A spot fire flared up beside the trail we were driving down, momentarily producing smoke so thick we couldn't see the road. We knocked it down the best we could, and when the brisk wind cleared the air a little, we drove on, heading into thicker brush that obscured the road except for a path the width of a motor bike. It seemed illogical that kids could be joyriding back here when surely they could smell the smoke and hear the low roaring of the fire to the west. If it came, it would bring the force of a tornado against us, with our measly two hundred and fifty gallons of water, a couple of rakes and tools, and a supply of brown-and-serve bags.

I didn't tell Fetzer the passable trail would end. I thought the cyclists would surely come out before we got there, materialize any minute through the pines. But we heard no motorcycles, only fire like thunder in the distance and vegetation being crushed beneath our wheels. Then the trail was gone. The brush grew too dense on one side to allow a vehicle through, and the pines came too close on the other, stretching down toward the creek.

"You knew about this?" Fetzer said, stopping the truck, looking back at me. I nodded. I'd been there a hundred times.

"I know where they must have gone," I said, jumping out onto the ground. Dry sooty air hung around Fetzer and Joey as they sat looking at me, in full gear, listening to the fire bearing down on us, realizing they had no choice but to let me go. If not for Joey, I felt sure Fetzer would have come with me, anxious not to miss out. But as commander of the unit he couldn't. Joey was too green to wait behind alone, perhaps to have to drive out, too green to judge when and what to do. I watched disappointment and relief flicker across Joey's face, and saw the pure anguished unhappiness on Fetzer's as he realized that, for him, after all, there might be no third period.

"Here," Fetzer said, recovering himself. He threw down three silvery fire shelters, one for me, one for each of the kids. Just in case.

I couldn't have moved fast anyway in turnout coat, helmet, gloves and boots, but though the fire shelters weighed only three pounds each, carrying them made me feel like I weighed a ton. This was not like going into a burning house and feeling protected, not even like the wild run I'd had at age fourteen through the flaming streets of the Conklin project before the blaze came close and I got scared. I was heavy, responsible, running like sometimes in dreams, in slow motion, on a thin trail of white sand carved out of the pinestraw, listening for motorbikes. Before a minute had passed, the sound of my own heartbeat was as loud as the fire in my ears.

I didn't notice much beyond the fire-howl and the pounding of my heart, except to register once that the wind had risen, and that in the flying ash around me were also embers, more than before. I listened for motorbikes. I gave myself the following pep talk: I would be damned if I'd have two kids on my conscience, I would not get scared and if I did to hell with it, I would remember the brush truck was behind me, waiting for me, it couldn't be far. Then three, four minutes later, maybe less, I heard not motorcycles but mopeds coming toward me on the narrow trail, and saw them ahead and waved my arms.

The boys couldn't have been more than twelve or thirteen— thin and childish-looking, nowhere near the size of my students. Their gangliness startled me, though I'm not sure what else I expected. They were wearing shorts and no helmets, legs and arms long and pale, unprotected. I could see they'd noticed the fire now and thought they might be in trouble. Watching me come toward them in full gear, they slowed down and stopped, a little winded, as disoriented as if they'd met an alien in the forest. The sight of them so young and unarmed made me aware of their stupidity, coming in here; made me angry the way I'd seen mothers angry when their children were in jeopardy and finally found to be safe, so when I spoke I was gruff and unkind.

"Don't you know there's a huge forest fire burning right over there?" I said, not wanting to mention the backfire but pointing in the direction of the main fire and realizing as I spoke that the boys' fear was not of me but of the rising heat and the sound-and-light show suddenly visible before them—a sharp crackling and flames snaking up a pine tree not twenty feet from where we stood, blocking the view beyond. It wasn't the main fire but a spot fire they could outrun easily on mopeds. They didn't know that; they thought it was the whole forest alight, bearing down on them. They froze as if in a game of statues.

I took advantage, thinking what the hell, I wasn't an assistant high school principal for nothing. I pulled off my helmet to give them full view of my maimed eyebrow, and removed the glove that hid the scar on my hand, and pointed to the trail in a grand gesture that gave them a clear view of both injuries, screaming at them as I pointed: "Haul ass." And they did.

I started off after them, running toward the brush truck. By the time the mopeds passed the burning pine we'd noted a moment ago, the spot fire around it had grown, engulfing small trees, gaining strength. A rain of flaming pine needles came down in front of me. The pinestraw on the ground lit up. I tried to run faster but heat weighted the air above me, made it dense, stinging. I crouched and kept moving. A burning tree crashed across the trail. Pieces of branches bounced off my helmet. Spots of fire flared up everywhere. Less than a minute had passed. The flaming woods sounded as if they'd become a runway under a landing jet.

The wind grew wild and dense, a hurricane of hot ash, flying debris. Burning cinders blew into my face; I couldn't move forward; I was in a whirlwind. My eyes stung; I couldn't see. Even if I could reach the brush truck, it would be gone. Fetzer would stay if he could, but he had Joey to consider—and two kids on mopeds who'd have to be driven out if they got that far. I realized then I hadn't given the boys their fire shelters. It was not something Fetzer would have forgotten. I pictured Fetzer driving out, outrunning the fire with three kids in the back of the truck. The air got bad, thick and suffocating. I was alone. Without water. Away from cleared ground.

Knives jabbed inside my lungs. I stopped trying to aim for the brush truck. I let the wind blow me. An instinct. I had no sense of where I was going. I leapt over surface fires, choking on fiery wind. I might have been a leaf, a cinder. Heat, roaring. When the wind knocked me over, I landed face down on a small jagged slope. Two feet below me, in the harsh flickering light, I could make out the flat rocks of the creek bed. I saw the thin trickle of water running across the stones and knew I'd been coming in the right direction all the time.

I unfolded the fire shelter. Pulled it around me. Stretched it into shape—a long low triangle held in place by my outstretched arms and legs. Once I was lying flat in the creek, the wind seemed some way above me; I was under the wind. Then the ground shook and the sound grew deafening and the fire that had been burning for weeks swept across like nothing natural, not a storm or a rocket, but larger yet, mythical, a dragon wailing out fury, licking flame. I never expected to hear or see anything else. Rocks popped and chipped. The light through the nicks in the tent fabric went from red to orange to white. Trees arched across the creek in bright strings of flame.

I concentrated on breathing. My nose was next to the creek bed where the air was purest, but even that low, there was no longer even a trickle of water, only hot sand. I inhaled sand and not air and it stung and could not be endured. The heat rose and quivered. I expected to ignite.

I learned that when things became unendurable you simply leave, because the next moment I was not there at all but away, safe, not at my cottage but in downtown Festival at the Azalea Parade, which I knew must be going on even then. The burning woods receded. At the parade, the sky was clearer than it had been for weeks, so cool and blue that the roaring of the dragon-fire melted and became only the music of marching bands, the bright papier-mâché of floats. There were horses and baton twirlers, Shriners in their little cars, vendors selling balloons along the streets. And Alona. Very clearly in the crowd I saw Alona, not with Elliott but by herself—watching, scanning the crowd. Waiting for me.

SEVENTEEN

*A*lona never did make it to the parade. Or rather, to what was left of the parade once fire broke out in the courthouse park. The sky grew smokier as she drove toward the Joyner estate, but she paid no attention. She was thinking of other things. They said on the radio that the courthouse park fire had spread and that a backfire had been lit to control the blaze still raging west of town. To Alona, the words were only background noise. The only thing on her mind was finding Jordan. Sometimes when you settled on a path, you were too committed to veer off, even to hear what might have made you change course. Sometimes you were too busy to pick up on things you should have known.

She took the dirt road onto the Joyner estate, bumping along packed sand beside the Intracoastal, passing tall pines that swayed in the rising wind. On weekends at this time of year, cars were usually parked by the water, and the beach was dotted with people who had defied the no-trespassing signs to fish or picnic. Today there was no one; the whole world was downtown.

When she reached the turnoff to Jordan's cottage, her gaze traveled just beyond it to the spot where they had made love their first time together, so close to the break in the trees that anyone could have seen them. She had felt perfectly secure, lying there. Now she felt foolish. It was ridiculous, really, his taking her there to impress her. Sort of...a *joke*, wasn't it?

A joke for them to laugh at together? Or for Jordan to tell his cronies? Probably the latter. And now, after being so definite about sending him away, after giving back his key, she was going to give him another foolish moment to tell them about if she drove up to his cottage as if nothing had changed. For all she knew, he'd laugh in her face. He would smirk and say, "What brings you here after all, Alona the Earring?"

She could hardly blame him.

She pulled the car over onto the thin strip of beach and parked to think this through. Getting out, she saw that the water was as gray and choppy as her mood.

But whatever happened, she couldn't go back to the mall.

She didn't will it, but she found herself walking. Past the place where they had made love and up the fork of road to his cottage. It was only a quarter of a mile. If he didn't hear her car, he wouldn't have time to prepare himself. In the brief seconds before he arranged his face to show what he wanted her to see, she'd know how he felt about her. She would know absolutely.

She didn't pay attention to the wind or register the change in the odd translucent light. She was wondering why things always got out of hand when people pursued her. All of her close relationships started that way. She hadn't been able to refuse Elliott when Emma was sick or turn Jordan away when she was still happily married. And now she was doing the pursuing herself.

The wind in the trees was low and malevolent. She tried to walk faster, to reach Jordan and get this over with, but the slick undersides of her flats slowed her down. Shoes not purchased at Custom-Fit. She skidded on the pinestraw. Her toes were caked with sand.

When she came around the bend in sight of the house, she didn't register Jordan's absence at once. She saw there was no car. She felt the silence. And still, for a moment, he might have been there. She might almost have reached her destination.

Then everything became clear to her. Clearly he had gone to the parade without her. Perhaps with someone else.

But no. The air was dead and dry and the tang of smoke was more bitter than at any time these past weeks. It was the air itself—something in the air—that sounded like growling. A fire. Of course. He hadn't gone to the parade, he'd gone to a fire. There were fires all over town.

She would wait. She'd sit in his living room all weekend if necessary, waiting until he returned. There was nothing else to do. She walked up to the front door before she remembered her grand gesture of dropping his key into his palm with her outstretched arm, while standing securely inside her apartment. She was such a fool. He always left the cottage locked because of the people who roamed the woods.

She tried the windows on each side of the front door. Locked. Or painted shut. Maybe both. Then she remembered he liked to sleep with the bedroom window cracked. She could crawl through it if she could reach it. A small, high window. It would surely be open.

Planes passed overhead as she walked around to the back of the cottage. More than one. Maybe an air show as part of the Azalea Festival. Something new. She didn't remember an air show before, but the matter didn't concern her.

The bedroom window was closed.

A sound in the distance. A low roar, steady—not planes anymore, or the growling in the trees. Maybe the ocean. No; you couldn't hear the ocean from here, not with the Intracoastal Waterway and all of Festival Beach in between. The air had changed, had grown more dense and smoky. Eerie. She reached up to test the window, to see if it would budge. The house was all on one floor, but the window was high, a slit. She couldn't get hold of it without standing on something.

A log. Jordan had split a pile of logs in the fall, to use in the fireplace. He'd stacked them beside the house. The pile was gone. Had they burned them all?

The wind was groaning and the air was getting hot. Unnaturally hot for as brisk as the breeze was. The fires must be pretty close. She was getting panicky again—that familiar nervous feeling from smelling smoke, the vestigial caveman fear. She should have brought her car. No matter, if she could get inside, the air would be better.

If not a log to stand on, a rock. Anything to get high enough to open the window. She found herself groping around the yard, unable to see much in front of her. The roaring, oceanlike sound grew louder. As if of a tidal wave. Crashing. As if the wave were breaking. The air felt like it had been blown from a furnace.

Then there was a rain of burning twigs, and a tongue of flame caught in the undergrowth maybe twenty feet from the house. She left the window and ran to the front of the cottage. Fire there, too. Everywhere she looked, a time-lapse film might have been playing in front of her—that fast, the woods were full of fire.

She ran.

Down the driveway, along the road. She could barely see where she was going. Her shoes were slipping, but she thought she was going the right way. The wind was behind her, blowing her toward the car and the water. She would be all right. Coming to a sudden clearing, she found the air better for a second, she gulped it, relaxed. And then the smoke was on her again. The flames to the west were not just in the woods but above them. Huge. Shooting above the trees.

She rounded a curve that gave her a glimpse of the cottage. It was burning—not just burning normally, but in a great flash, all the sides of the building aflame at once, revealing the living room and bedroom—the couch, the bed, every small item of furniture clear in the fierce bright glare. As if the walls had never existed. And then gone. Not burned, but melted. She was still running.

Small fires trailed her on either side of the road and the big one behind her, coming fast. The noise! A thousand sheets being torn apart, cloth ripping, explosions. And the scorching wind, the very air on fire. She slipped on the dry pinestraw. Fell onto her hands. Easier to breathe down by the ground—but hot, hot. She got up and stumbled forward.

Shoes too slippery.

She kicked them off.

A burning ember fell across her toes. Stinging. She bent over, crushing her foot to the sand on the road. Her heart was in her neck, her temples. This was how Jordan felt in fires. Afraid, yes. Another cinder. Running. But slow. Smoke. Coughing. She could not tell how close she was to the water.

A rain of hot pinestraw fell on her blouse. Flame. She batted the spot with her hands, put it out. Heartbeat in her ears. Another line of flame. Beating against it. Her hands covered with blisters. Couldn't breathe.

She ran faster. Wind like a tornado, pushing her. Stinging. The roaring, the roaring. An avalanche of flames. Screaming. Her own?

The light was closer now, all around her.

The light was on her hair.

She knew the water was before her, and her car, just out of the trees. She was almost there. Then she saw it—water just beyond, acres of it, and imagined small transparent fish washing in and scurrying back on the ebb tide, away from the light. She ran, trying to get away from the light. Emma had. Emma had. But it was blinding now, there was no escaping, it was the brightest light she'd ever seen. And even as the fire bit into her scalp, even as the flame danced all about her, even then she was walking toward herself, seeing a different light—and even then, even before she fell, she knew all there was to know about her dream.

◆ ◆ ◆

Cassie was sure they were never going to make it over the drawbridge. Traffic was too heavy, too crazy. There were fire engines everywhere, wind blowing, smoke in the sky. Every car in Festival was heading out of downtown toward the beach. It was the best adventure she'd ever had.

"Here's where bus-driving experience comes in handy," Curley said, cutting around a car, over onto a curb, back onto the street. A horn honked, but Curley pulled in, blended back into the lane. Cassie laughed.

The music on the car radio had stopped, even on Rock 99, and all they could get was news. Motorists were advised to use caution, especially while leaving the parade area. King's Highway and Route 210 were closed to traffic heading north or west out of town. Because of burning debris blowing into town and setting numerous small fires, tourists were advised to avoid heavily wooded areas. The announcers didn't say, but a lot of folks seemed to have figured out that the beach with all that water was the safest place to be. Cassie hadn't seen this much traffic since last Fourth of July.

Jess O'Donovan of Rock 99 was giving a wrap-up of the morning's events. Two young boys had been rescued from a burnoff area after a backfire was lit outside of town. One firefighter was still missing. The backfire, blown by strong opposing winds, had not served its function but instead had joined the main fire, which was quickly heading eastward, ravaging the Joyner estate. Residents were cautioned to avoid the area.

"Seems like the backfire backfired," Curley said.

E L L Y N   B A C H E

"What is a backfire anyway?"

Curley shrugged. "Beats me."

There were horns and shouting.

"Sounds like a wedding," Cassie said.

"Looks like you're dressed for one."

She smiled. Her dress was not Carolina blue anymore, but streaked gray from ashes, grimy from smoke. It would never come clean. And the hoop was lying trampled on a downtown street somewhere, never to be retrieved. The thought made her purely happy.

Traffic inched along, so snarled that they might have been in Baltimore. They might have been in New York! Black smoke curled up from the Joyner place in the distance. The scene made Cassie feel high and restless, the blood in her veins carbonated. She wondered if Royal felt this way after a couple of beers.

She wanted to get going, go fast, *do* something. She could tell Curley felt the same, the way he was drumming the steering wheel with his fingers. The drawbridge was less than a quarter of a mile away but they couldn't see it because of the way the road curved. It would take forever to get there.

More sirens. The traffic stopped. She would die if she sat here another minute. She would jump right out of herself.

"I have an idea," she said. In fact, Cassie didn't have the idea until the words rolled out of her mouth, but as she said them she knew they were brilliant. They were right near Jewels, where she got her earrings. "Park in there," she said, pointing to the lot in front of the store.

Curley gave her a look.

"Come on," she said. "Don't you trust me?"

She knew he had to. He pulled up onto the shoulder and made his way into the lot. When they had parked, they walked toward the bridge, the wind blowing them along and the sky getting darker. It might be dusk except for the glow of the fire above the trees to the north. This fire was closer than it had been at the airport, right there on the Joyner estate. She could even hear it.

Sparks were blowing over them, pieces of burning branches. "Better than fireworks," Cassie said. She hiked up her skirt. Curley took her free hand. Other drivers were beginning to pull their cars over to the shoulder, to walk toward the water. Everything was going fast. She and Curley rounded the curve and in the distance saw the drawbridge snarled to a dead halt. People were standing everywhere, outside their cars, shouting and being ugly because they wanted to move off the bridge, get down by the shore and the water.

The air was hot and thick, smokier all the time.

"Over here," Cassie shouted, because the wind was getting bad, almost like a gale.

A dead tree by the road started burning, ignited by the floating embers. Not the trunk but the upper branches, the flames flapping at the sky. There were pops like firecrackers. Another tree caught fire, then another. People abandoned their cars. They ran, heading for the water, wading into the Intracoastal beside the drawbridge, onto that little bit of beach next to the Waterway Restaurant.

Someone pushed her. She would have fallen except that Curley held her up. They were almost to the bridge, just across from the restaurant. People rushed past, scrambling down the bank as if each one would be the last to fit into the choppy water. Cassie wanted to shout that there was room for everyone, miles of shoreline, not just this little space next to the drawbridge. All they had to do was go around to the other side of the restaurant. Fire shot from the top of a motel roof across the street. The wind was scorching, angry.

"Over there," she yelled to Curley, pointing around the building. "To the dock."

She didn't know if he looked at her askance, she didn't look at his face. She held his hand. It was smooth and dry. She didn't know why she was surprised it wasn't oily, just because he was black. Too many years living with Royal. They got to the dock. She was pointing the way, lifting her skirts, climbing into the boat, carrying out her brilliant idea. The boat was Brian Ivey's. She took the key from the battery case where she knew it would be. She put it in the ignition. She drove off into the churning water, toward the drawbridge, heading for home.

"Your boat?" Curley shouted.

Smoke blew into their faces. The wind gusted so high she could hardly hear. She shook her head no.

Behind them the crowd grew larger and rowdier. A whole long stretch of shoreline was visible as the boat pulled farther away, with hardly a soul on it except between the Waterway restaurant and the drawbridge. As if all those people were trying to keep score with each other, scrambling into that small patch of water until they trampled each other down. Someone was likelier to drown than to get hurt by the flames. Then they were under the drawbridge, adjacent to the Joyner estate, where the real fire was burning. It was huge in the sky, orange and black, kicking up so much wind that she couldn't see behind her at all.

Or in front of her, either.

They were somewhere in the middle of the waterway, that's all she knew. She slowed the boat, but then the bow rose up out of the water in front of her, and she couldn't see a thing. She couldn't tell Curley she really didn't know how to drive a boat, that Royal had never let her. In the thick smoke she had no idea how to navigate. Some other boat might come lurching out of the smoke and cut them in half. It was getting harder to keep the boat going perpendicular over the chop. The waves were hitting them almost broadside. She wasn't even motion-sick, only afraid.

"Here, let me," Curley said, as if he knew exactly what she was thinking. She'd already moved over to make way for him when she remembered hardly any blacks had speedboats around here. Curley probably didn't know how to drive one any better than she did, he was just reacting to how scared she was. But when he took the wheel and began steering, he might have been doing it all his life. Maybe it wasn't so different from driving a bus.

Cassie would never have thought to do what he did. All she'd been able to think of was getting across the waterway to Festival Beach. She'd had them right in the middle of the channel. But Curley steered the boat back toward the Festival side until they could see the edge of the Joyner estate. The fire was right there, leaping out of the trees, but even with the smoke, the line of the shore was visible. The water was all around them; they could jump in if it got too bad. Really, they were safe until the air cleared a little. The smoke was blowing over them, everywhere, they had to stay low. But in the heart-pounding fullness of it, despite the chop and the noise and smoke of the fire, they were all right.

Then from the burning trees on shore a figure emerged. It was the most unexpected thing Cassie had ever seen. A woman. With long hair. And the hair burning, burning, a great cape of light all around her head, so bright it might have been a halo, she might have been an angel.

"Oh God, Curley, look!"

Then the woman fell, the cape of light was gone. What had been hair vanished, her head was a black crust. Cassie could not see more from this distance except that it was a horror, a horror, she had not thought of fire this way. The figure lay on the sand, not moving. The fire was just behind her at the edge of the trees.

Curley turned the wheel and they were going fast, not parallel to the shore but toward it. The wind that a second ago had been blowing over them, toward Festival Beach, now changed entirely, pulling them in, sucking them toward shore. As if some other force had taken over. Cassie didn't think how the wind was always toward the direction of the fire once you got this close; what she thought of was how Black Eve could send you wherever she wanted. Cassie had never gone this fast. Her stomach hurt and she was afraid.

Curley cut the motor. They were not sucked forward anymore. He got out of the boat, waded through the shallows, ran up the shore. The smoke was in their faces hard, not just smoke but soot, ashes, sand so hot it burned where it touched. Cassie couldn't see. She didn't know how Curley could. He was carrying the woman toward her, running across the sand, into the water, placing the woman in the front of the boat. His shirt was black and streaked. Burned! But no. The fabric was whole, the bits of debris from something outside—pieces of the woman's skin.

She didn't want to look. But she did. The woman was lying on her side with her back toward Cassie. Her scalp was swollen, charred—a mass of black, giant and round and nothing like the cape of light it had seemed before, golden hair, an angel of flame. The woman's back and arms were alternately black and pink, where she had been burned and where she had not. Her blouse was gone in back, her hands and feet a mass of blisters. She did not have any shoes.

Cassie couldn't tell if she was breathing. She wanted Curley to help, but Curley had started the boat, was aiming toward open water. The fire was closing in on the shore behind them, blowing toward them from that front line of trees. The smoke was a whirlwind. They hardly seemed to be moving at all.

She was coughing from the smoke. Getting sick now. No! She should reach down, feel for the woman's pulse, do something. But where would she touch, on the charred and anguished skin? Would touching be a kindness? She couldn't take her eyes away.

As the boat rolled in the chop, the woman's head turned slightly, giving Cassie a view of her profile. A long metal earring, bent and misshapen from the heat, was welded to the woman's ear. Embedded into the swollen folds of her neck. Tiny shells which had been part of the earring protruded here and there, stuck to the damaged skin.

She recognized the earring.

When the boat rolled again, Cassie saw the woman's face straight on. It wasn't burned much.

Alona.

Cassie leaned over and threw up.

Curley was wrestling with the boat. He didn't seem to be thinking of the burden in front of them. The water was all commotion. They were smacking the waves, up and down. Not going anywhere. Cassie was dizzy, her stomach heaving, about to be sick again. Then she got to the point where it didn't matter, where being sick was only part of something larger—as if they were all caught in the same bond of suffering. She reached down, put her fingers to Alona's chest. All she felt was silence.

The wind was wild, the sound a roar. Nothing visible outside the boat except smoke and the sliver of beach. She willed the heart to beat. Willed life. If Alona was scarred afterward—surely she'd be scarred—still her living would be a victory. Not a matter of winning or losing the way Royal thought, but a victory in itself, just the doing. They bounced forward over the chop, not on a clear course. Maybe in circles. But still the motion seemed a luxury—the very having of it. *Live,* she thought.

When she looked up, she was too distracted to register the danger in a clear way. The small car parked on the beach behind them was burning, taken over by flames. Curley gave the boat all the power he could. A fountain of light erupted in the sky, and more noise than Cassie thought she could contain inside her head—concussion like an earthquake, on and on, rocking the land and the water, until she felt the ground beneath the waves, tens, hundreds of feet to the bottom; until she felt the very seabed rocking, sending shock waves up through the water and the boat lurching, flying, until she thought they would be catapulted out of it, into the hurricane of wind.

Curley held her, his hand on her neck, pushing her down inside the boat. The fire swept toward them and then over, not touching them, rolling toward Festival Beach, out to sea—all in a few seconds, but it felt like forever, concussion that would ring in her head the rest of her life. Curley's arm was around her, and her head was buried in his shirt, and for a time they stayed like that, clinging to each other, afraid to let go.

When Cassie opened her eyes the landscape did not look like itself. The waves were churning and smoke was so thick over the shoreline that the town of Festival had disappeared, along with the thin, distant strip of Festival Beach they were heading for. Even the drawbridge was gone in the smoke. The water was gray and muddy and full of tiny bugs—thousands of them, charred and dead and floating on the waves. Then she saw that the specks were not bugs but pine needles—a forest of pine needles, in the water, on the boat, everywhere. Even the trees were gone. It was as if time had folded back on itself and she and Curley were the only ones left, back at the start of the world. He held onto her and she to him. She knew how Black Eve had felt, there at the beginning, responsible for everything. Cassie had never really wanted to touch a boy before, even Brian Ivey, but now she did.

When Curley let go of her, he seemed to know exactly what to do. Even with the waves churning and the air so full of smoke, he headed them steadily toward Festival Beach. For a moment Cassie was so calm that there might have been no terror, no incinerated landscape, no hellishly charred body in the bottom of the boat—only a figure wrapped in fire like an angel, an explosion that rocked the bottom of the sea but didn't blow them out of the water. Only the fact of their escape.

Then, in front of her, a gurgle came from Alona's throat. A tiny, final utterance that somehow carried above the motor, above every other sound she'd ever heard. Curley heard it too. Cassie clutched Curley's arm because it was the only comfort she could have. Because the memory of this would bind them, weld them, as surely as that earring was welded into Alona's flesh. She reached down and closed the lashless eyes. It was all she could do. Holding to Curley, Cassie knew all she wanted to about power—of the fire and the stillness in a burned woman's chest; of the relentless aching in her groin, and Royal's kind of power, too—how it came to you in the way of things, more absolute than you imagined.

Curley docked at Royal's pier, and Cassie got out to secure the lines. The boat rocked. Though the body was heavy, they knew it was a shell, delicate and fragile. They lifted it slowly, together, as gently as they could.

◆   ◆   ◆

The parade I'd imagined during the worst of the fire was over then. I was sweating, covered with it. When I lifted the flap of the fire shelter and looked up, the white light was gone. The noise had passed, like the wail of a siren. Above the bank of the creek, everything was black or gray, a forest of ash. Smoke hung so thick in the woods that it was painful to breathe. Ironic. Victims often survived the heat, often died of smoke. That smoke was the greater peril was the first thing we learned in training. I put my head to the ground again, to the creek bed. I felt the air grow cooler.

Sensation came back to me slowly. Mouth gravelly, moisture sucked from my skin, eyes dry and burning. I thought if I blinked the surfaces would stick together. As I watched the smoke grow less dense, thirst grew in my throat, in my mouth, spreading like a rash. By the time I had come back to myself completely, I didn't care if I ever ate again if only I could drink.

Casting the fire shelter aside, I crawled along the creek bed, along the stones, seeking water. My eyes stung so, I could barely see. I removed my gloves and felt between the rocks with my hands, looking for a pool of water. I began to believe the fire had evaporated the creek entirely. I imagined my wounded eyes must be playing tricks on me, telling me the water was gone; I imagined that in my thirst a madness had descended, hallucination. I don't know how long it was before my hand found a little hole, a tiny reservoir protected from the blaze by an outcropping of rock.

I cupped the water in my hands and held it to my mouth. A sort of ecstasy. It was cool against my lips, on my tongue. Then I tried to swallow. The water would not go down. My throat was no longer a passageway, only a tiny slit, large enough to let in air but not liquid. I understood that my throat must be burned, but had no sense of how badly. As yet, it was not painful, only odd and uncomfortable. I registered that calmly. I was not upset or frightened.

It came to me then that if I had been passed over by a wall of flame a hundred feet high and was lying in a creek bed recording sensations in my throat, then there was nothing more the fire could do to me. I had been waiting twenty years to be caught by fire and killed, and now it had happened and I was alive. I cupped my hands in the water again. I didn't try to drink. I used the water to wash my eyes. The world was blurred, hazy, but I was not blind, as I had not been blind when I was fourteen. I crawled out of the creek, breathing shallowly in the smoky air. I began to walk.

The path was gone, so I did not know where I was headed, but I was not concerned. I made my way away from the creek, toward where I thought the brush truck had been. I paused in a clearing surrounded by the stubs of burnt trees. The air was thick and gray. Nothing was green. I must have stood there for a minute or more.

I didn't see the doe come out of the trees. I saw her as she was walking toward me. She did not seem disoriented. She came and stood beside me, as if she wanted human company. Part of her ear was burned away, but I saw no dangerous wounds. I reached out and touched her scorched fur. She didn't move. We stood there for a time, surveying the scene. I could see only dimly. When the deer walked off, I followed in the direction she had shown me.

The atmosphere had cleared a little, but I was having trouble breathing. The numb throbbing in my throat gave way to active pain as the air passed across it. The swelling felt red and raw. I was oddly calm and unafraid.

I thought: no one will believe me about the deer. I'd read about such a thing once, about the strange fellowship of men and animals in times of crisis. Perhaps I could find the book. Even so, no one would believe me—not Fetzer, not even the boy Joey. There was no question in my mind that they had escaped the fire and were on the other side. I imagined that the two fires had met, the backfire and the main fire, and that the crisis was past. I didn't know the backfire had leapt its boundaries and started off in a rage toward the sea. I thought it was over and everyone was safe except for me. I hadn't felt alone since before the firestorm, but I did then. I had stood in a field with a deer

beside me, the two of us surveying the scene, and now I was
alone. And no one would believe it.

Then I thought: Alona would.

I remembered the food at the Zion Church of God, and the
look on Alona's face like a sponge and my homesickness for that
expression. When I went home, it would be to nothing—no
woman, perhaps no job. In retrospect, it seemed what Alona
had wanted was for me to tell her what was in my mind. It
occurred to me there might be hope for us if I did that. This was
a strange sensation. It went against everything I had learned.

I was growing lightheaded, wandering aimlessly now. The
pain in my throat and the dryness in my mouth were sharper
and more intense. I could not see where I was going. I stumbled
and fell to my knees.

I considered again the prospect of confiding in a woman. It
seemed better than nothing. A length of time passed. I thought:
what an ass my father was. What good was any experience, even
cowardice and shame, if it could not be shared?

I could no longer breathe evenly, so I imagined what I
would tell her. About the fire. The creek. The deer. How for
twenty years I had been trying to conquer fire but was afraid.
Afraid of a dragon that could no more be stopped than the Gulf
Stream, the seasons, the Milky Way. I would tell her that when
a force got that big, no man could vanquish it as Fetzer would
have his wrestlers conquer each other; he could only endure,
maybe survive.

She would say: maybe you had a right to be afraid.

I would tell her of my fear as I backed out of that curtain
shop. Everything.

Mouth dry and crusted. No air. Sitting on ash. What was I
doing there? Rescuing two boys. Did they get out? Should have
given them the shelters. A mistake. No—no time to tell them
how the shelters worked. I did what was possible. Told them to
haul ass. That was something.

I was disoriented. My sense of being in the woods diminished, gave way to dizziness and then spinning, to the throbbing in my mouth, my throat. But my thoughts were perfectly
sensible; I was taking stock. The past two days, all my life—what
had I done? Evacuated houses, held the hose on the brush truck
until my arms were sore—and once—couldn't remember when,
stuffed ice into the pants of a dying boy and he had lived. I was

a better vice principal than a fireman. I would tell Alona that. Would tell so as not to reduce my life to what Fetzer's had become: rote work and beerfests and tests of physical courage. If Alona did not flinch, I would ask her to live with me, not hiding in the woods but in some house of our own, in sight of everyone. I put my head to the ground to search for purer air. I could hardly breathe.

Lying under the scorch of trees, on a forest floor of ash, on pine cones that had to burst in the heat to release their seeds and regenerate—lying there in the smoky morning with my mouth dry as paper and my throat swollen closed, in the minute before I lost consciousness, I knew absolutely that Fetzer and Joey were coming to get me. I was free; there was nothing more I could do. So I thought of Alona and what I would tell her...and I imagined how, once I got out of those woods, all the rest of my life would be bliss.

Fiction from August House Publishers

Fielder's Choice
a novel by Rick Norman
"An original and engaging addition to baseball literature."—*Publishers Weekly*
"A debut novel with the charm of a Ring Lardner tale."—*The Kirkus Reviews.*
ISBN 0-87483-172-5, HB, $17.95
ISBN 0-87483-204-7, TPB, $9.95

Homecoming: The Southern Family in Short Fiction
edited by Liz Parkhurst and Rod Lorenzen
"The family secrets and truths revealed in this collection will not only enter-
tain, they will remind you that your family is a fragile, precious thing."
—Southern Living
ISBN 0-87483-112-1, HB, $17.95

Dry Bones
a novel by Hope Norman Coulter
"Beautifully wrought fiction...Coulter packs her novel with genuine people and
their equally real hopes, deceits, and ordinary pursuits." *—Booklist*
ISBN 0-87483-152-0, HB, $17.95

Jujitsu for Christ
a novel by Jack Butler
"Brilliant and telling...sums up the whole strange world of the post-segrega-
tion South, a place simmering with previously undreamed-of possibilities."
—New York Times Book Review
ISBN 0-87483-015-X, HB, $14.95

Civil War Ghosts
John Jakes, Ambrose Bierce, Vance Randolph, Manly Wade Wellman, and
other great American writers remember the war
in which everyone took sides—even the dead.
ISBN 0-87483-173-3, TPB, $9.95

The Errand of the Eye
a novel by Hope Norman Coulter
"Coulter's characters, black and white, are wonderfully real and edgy, com-
pelling and complicated in just the right way to give their story energy."
—The Kirkus Reviews
ISBN 0-87483-056-7, HB, $15.95

Dreaming in Color
stories by Ruth Moose
"Rich with gentle humor...sharp characterizations and a strong evocation of
a gritty, working-class milieu." *—Publishers Weekly*
ISBN 0-87483-078-8, HB, $15.95

August House Publishers,
P.O. Box 3223, Little Rock, Arkansas 72203
1-800-284-8784